Published by Penfold Books
87 Hallgarth Street
Durham DH1 3AS
England

Author's website:
mileshudson.com

ISBN: 978-1-83812-581-3

Acknowledgements:

Many thanks are due to: Kirsten Crombie; Tato Debernadis; Alice Du Vivier; John Ellis; Liz Gray; Jonathan Hudson; Dave Jones; Hannah Jones; Andy McDaid; Nick Castle Designs;

About the Author

Miles Hudson loves words and ideas.

He's a physics teacher, surfer, author, hockey player, inventor, backpacker and idler.

Miles was born in Minneapolis but has lived in Durham in northern England for 30 years.

Penfold and DS Milburn
investigate The Case of

The
Cricketer's
Corpse

M M Hudson

Friday 22nd March

The man's penis appeared to have exploded. It was very clearly the source of the incredible quantity of blood that covered the bed, and even now was dripping into a puddle on the polished floorboards by Milburn's black leather shoes. The six-foot ginger-haired corpse looked to be sleeping peacefully, seemingly unaware that a small scarlet squid had replaced his genitalia. The man was lean and wiry and suffered from an over-abundance of curly copper hair all over his body.

Detective Sergeant Tony Milburn carefully laid the bloody bed sheet down at the foot of the bed and looked over to his boss. Barnes had stepped back a few paces at the revelation of the body's groin. The two crime scene examiners stood beside him, staring. This was a particularly gruesome dead body.

Godolphin Barnes, Milburn's detective inspector boss, was lanky. At six foot and three inches, he would always have looked tall, but his narrow skinny body heightened his appearance further. His dark wavy hair was parted down the middle to form a ridge on top of his head, adding another inch or two. As a consequence of his frame, the navy blue two-piece suit did not fit properly and hung loosely as if adorning a coat hanger.

THE CRICKETER'S CORPSE

His mouth formed a short tight line across his pale face until he spoke. 'Let's go and talk to the friend and let the crime scene examiners get on with it,' he said, adjusting the crotch of his trousers. He told the uniformed officer who had first attended the scene, 'You may as well leave. This definitely looks like one for CID.'

They stepped into the short hallway that led further into the victim's flat. It was a well-appointed abode in a new block about half a mile from Durham City's busy centre. The site had been a lemonade factory until only ten years previously when the owner had decided that there would be more money and less hard work if they sold up to property developers.

All the interior décor was bright and still looked very new. The hall opened up onto a large living area painted in cream with a sky blue carpet. Seated in the middle of a white cotton three-seater sofa, Jim Harris looked distressed.

The dead man's friend had very short dark hair and the shocked paleness of his face highlighted the brown of his eyes. The young man stared fixedly at the floor and appeared catatonic. His face was as white as DI Barnes'. Milburn mused that, whilst Harris would be in a state of shock, the DI's undernourished figure and sickly pallor always gave off an air of impending illness, which was probably why little was made of his frequent sickness absences.

Barnes sat down in an adjacent and matching armchair. DS Milburn hovered just inside the room on the hallway threshold. 'Whew,' Barnes exhaled deeply, looking for some response from Jim. The brown eyes rose slowly to look at the policeman. 'I can't say I've seen anything like that before.' The inspector's opening gambit ached for agreement, but the man said nothing. His eyes were wide and he would be in need of counselling after this morning's discovery. 'I'm Detective Inspector Barnes, and this is Detective Sergeant Milburn. When did you find him?' The DI moved on to a more straightforward interview style.

'I came to pick up Hamish for training. I got here about nine, I suppose. He didn't answer the door, so I shouted and looked through the letterbox. It looks straight into his bedroom so I saw him.' Harris's wide eyes widened further and he inhaled noisily through his nose. 'There was so much blood. I kicked the door open and...' he stuttered slightly and drew another deep breath. 'I don't know much first aid, but I could see he was dead already. So I called you lot.'

Barnes had been making notes in his small book, and looked up to see if Mr Harris was going to add anything. The catatonic state appeared to have returned, so he prompted again, 'Did you touch him? Or anything else in the bedroom?'

'No,' Jim answered slowly, playing over in his mind what he might have done and what he actually did. 'I was so shocked I just stared for ages. And then I ran to the phone in here and called you. And then I just sat here. I haven't moved, even when the constables came in. I don't want to go back in there. I don't want to do anything.' The man sounded close to tears.

'Ok,' said DI Barnes noting these things down too.

'I might have stood in the blood, I think. Will that matter?' Harris looked up urgently into Godolphin's beady grey eyes. He looked across to Milburn and then down to the floor again. All three men then looked at the trail of bloody footprints leading from the hallway to Harris in the middle of the sofa. The telephone was on a small table just inside the lounge, and

3

the dance pattern of red feet, along with the several leading to his current position, were pretty strong testimony to the truth of the young man's story.

'Tony,' one of the scene examiners almost wailed from the bedroom. Milburn retreated and met the man at the bedroom doorway. In his left latex glove was a piece of Clingfilm balled up, and the right glove held a hypodermic syringe with a cover over the needle. 'These were in the bin, along with little else but used condoms and condom wrappers. The evidence gatherer lowered his voice to an almost inaudibly quiet volume. There's a puncture wound in the crook of the elbow.'

Milburn nodded his vaguely greying head. His temples had turned grey at least ten years previous to his current 34 years of age. He could never remember exactly when it had started, but younger than he would have liked. Fortunately, the remainder of his short, straight hair remained a woody brown colour. His girlfriend, Kathy, always said it looked dignified, but this never reassured Milburn who considered that a euphemism for "old".

'Thanks,' he said and walked back to whisper the narcotics evidence in his partner's ear. In doing so, he got a whiff of whatever it was that kept Barnes' black hair looking so slicked and oily. It was not a particularly unpleasant smell, just wrong for a person's hair. If he hadn't considered it ludicrous, Milburn would have reckoned it had hints of gearbox oil.

'Was Hamish a drug user?' Barnes immediately sprang on Harris. The younger man was big and lithe and gave off an aura of reined in physical power. At this question he stiffened. He looked jumpy and nervous, the presence of strength vanished.

'No. Not that I know of. No. Nothing like that. There's no drugs in our team.'

The two detectives exchanged confused glances. 'I'm sorry, Mr Harris,' Barnes confirmed the name, trying to feel his way through this odd new development. 'I don't quite get what you mean?'

Jim looked up, his eyes squinting as if he had now been launched into unfamiliar territory himself. There was a slight head movement as if something he considered unlikely had just clicked into place in his mind. After looking at DS Milburn, he turned back to the boss to reply, 'We're both players for Durham County Cricket Club.'

'Durham *County*?' Milburn interrupted, stressing the difference between the city club and the professional county team based five miles away in Chester-le-Street.

'Yes, I'm not too surprised you haven't heard of me, but Hamish has been first change bowler at DCCC for the last two seasons.'

Tony Milburn pointed up the hallway and interjected, 'That's Hamish Elliott, the cricketer?' He had never seen Elliott play but had read of his mean bowling figures in the newspaper. The Scot had never been a prolific wicket taker, but was so consistently accurate that he could restrict opposition teams' scoring to miserly, sometimes pitifully low, rates.

Harris nodded slightly and just said, 'Yes,' in a dismal voice.

Milburn concurred by simply saying, 'Wow,' in an equally dismal voice.

Looking over his distinctly beak-shaped nose, DI Barnes asked for clarification about Jim Harris collecting his friend

Hamish Elliott for training. During the following carpool explanation, Milburn scoured his brain for memories of the county cricket club's Jim Harris. He had heard of him: not a regular first team player, but more often in the Sunday and Twenty20 Cup teams. He vaguely remembered reading that he tired easily but was good for the shorter matches. Looking at the racehorse strong body on the sofa, Milburn thought it surprising that he had less stamina than other players and, in particular, the much leaner man in the bed in the next room. Milburn made some notes of what he could remember reading of the two players, just in time to hear Barnes offend the man deeply.

'So you and Hamish were teammates. Were you also friends?'

'Oh yes,' Harris sounded positively jubilant at the fact.

'More than friends?'

Milburn stared in disbelief at DI Barnes, but his disbelief was patently less than that of Mr Harris. 'I'm not gay,' he refuted, perhaps a little too strongly. It was one of those protestations where you wonder if in fact you have found out the truth. Godolphin Barnes was a wily detective. He was regularly crass in an unforgivable way, and yet his bizarrely distasteful questions often threw people into unexpected revelations.

However, the man on the sofa proceeded to say with more dignity, 'And Hamish was a real womaniser. Different girl every night.'

'Hmm.' There was a clear indication in Barnes' tone that was not convinced. He was building up a bad-cop persona and DS Milburn expected that his boss would shortly excuse himself to see if the good-cop could come up with any more from the mediocre bowler. 'So, tell me of his *girl*friends. Any in particular that stayed more than one night?'

He didn't speak for a moment, eyeing the detective inspector. 'There really were so many. Um, Kate Something was quite a regular. I don't know her surname. Posh girl from the university. Blonde. Oh, and Aisha. He's been out with Aisha quite a lot recently. She's our coach's daughter – Aisha Pathan. That really caused some bother with Vivender.'

'Vivender Pathan is the club's head coach. Ex-Indian international.' Milburn threw in this information for Godolphin's benefit, knowing that the DI had no knowledge or interest in any sport of any kind.

'Yeah, and he's a really devout Hindu. Tries to stop Aisha going out at all. You know, really strict Indian family thing. And she's 21. It's hard to believe sometimes.'

'I hardly think a drug-taking queer is going to be any threat to his daughter's virginity. Excuse me.' Milburn was almost as dumbfounded as Harris as they watched the inspector get up and exit towards the bedroom. Tony knew that it was now his turn in the spotlight.

'I'm really sorry,' he said shaking his head with an exaggerated blink. The man's an idiot.' This was only half his good-cop character speaking. He sat on the sofa beside the bereaved and shaken young man, and tried to cajole some more intelligence from him. 'So, lots of women, good friend of yours, you two must have had some right old times together. I bet away matches were a riot.' Although it was a statement, Tony's pitch made it obviously a question. Jim's smile brought some of the facial colour back and his body noticeably relaxed. Tony was on a roll. 'You said there were no drugs in the team. I'm sure you get tested a lot and all that, but surely there's bits and pieces. I mean marijuana's not even a banned substance in cricket is it?'

Harris looked the detective straight in the eye and his smile was gone. 'Why are you people so obsessed with drugs? I don't know anything about drugs.'

Milburn cursed himself for jumping in with both feet before having confirmed that the rapport was actually there. He tried to redeem the situation. 'Sorry, it's just that I want to find out why poor Hamish died. Um, perhaps, did he have any enemies; anyone holding a grudge against him?'

'Oh my god, was he stabbed? Is that where all that blood came from? Jesus, I never thought he'd really do it. I thought he was just blowing off steam. Fuck.' Harris remained seated but was writhing like a man possessed by demons. His large hands pawed at his face until one gripped the little hair available, as if to pull it out.

'Woah, woah,' Milburn almost shouted, putting his hand on the scalp-tugging forearm. 'I don't know what killed him. Alright. But it's a suspicious death so I need to find out about all the possibilities.' Harris stilled, although the grip on his dark hair was not released. 'Now, who are you talking about, and what had they threatened?'

'It was Vivender. Last Monday. He had a big argument with Hamish about Aisha. He was saying stuff like she's not allowed out and they weren't to see each other. All what you'd expect from a strict father. Especially one who knows what Hamish is like.'

His hands were still on his head, and they pressed at his temples at the realisation of the present tense. 'Was like.' He paused. 'But Hamish really fancied Aisha. I mean, who wouldn't? She's gorgeous.' Harris's brown eyes looked at Milburn, imploring for man-to-man understanding of this. The policeman gave a blank nod, which claimed to understand. 'But he said – in fact he shouted so the whole team could hear – he said, 'I'll kill any man who touches my daughter'. Hamish just kept on smiling like the cat who got the cream, and insisted that Aisha could do what she liked and that Vivender would just have to get used to it.

'And did Hamish touch Aisha?'

'Well, the way he told it, they'd been shagging for weeks already. I'm not sure. I mean Hamish'll nail anything in a skirt, but Aisha's a bit different, you know.' This time, Harris's tense error didn't register. 'I don't think she'd be so easy to get into bed. I don't think I can say for sure. She definitely was very keen on Hamish though and they have been out together a lot. I had dinner with Vivender last night, but he didn't mention any of it, we just talked about my training.'

'So when did you last see Hamish? Before this morning, I mean.'

'We came back from the club at about nine o' clock. I dropped him off here without coming in.'

'6pm yesterday? And dropped him off outside the apartment block?'

The witness did not answer, because at that point Andrew Gerard breezed in the front door and stopped dead on the threshold. From Tony's sofa seat position, he could just see Gerard along the angle through the lounge doorway. If the pathologist hadn't stopped, he'd have moved beyond Milburn's vision. Durham's principal medical examiner put down his big black case of equipment and pulled out some white gloves and booties. These were put on before he moved off the doormat.

DS Milburn told Harris to stay where he was and went to talk with the 54-year-old doctor. Gerard was creased and tanned in a way that always made people think he must be an actor. His face lit up like a beacon as the two shook hands, and he smiled broadly. They exchanged morning pleasantries, and Tony passed him over to Inspector Barnes in the bedroom. These two men were of similar height, but very contrasting appearances. Gerard's whole presence was warm and cuddly – the antithesis of Barnes' chilling, alien look. As usual, the pathologist's hair was coiffured to perfection and he looked as if he had actually just come from make-up before stepping into the movie of their lives. Even the white hairnet to preserve crime scenes was unable to damage his hairstyling. Gerard moved in a measured, gentle way, carefully taking in the bedroom scene in order to determine where to start.

The bottle green bed sheets were turning the colour of the polished hardwood floor, as the blood soaked further and further, darkening all the time. An aged mahogany armoire matched the floor, but the bedframe, bedside table and chest of drawers – a matching set with the same detailing – were sufficiently different to suggest that a man had been responsible for the furnishing. 'And not a gay man,' Milburn thought to himself with impish humour. He wondered if the clash of furnishings was grating with Andrew Gerard's sense of colour. Always conscious of the institutional prejudices the police service was susceptible to, Tony quickly told himself to rein in the stereotypical musings and concentrate on the job at hand.

The crime scene examiners were pointing things out to Gerard and displaying sealed evidence bags to him. They explained to him that the only known disturbance of the scene was the removal of the upper bed sheet by DS Milburn. Despite it being a cold March morning, there seemed to have been no duvet or bedspread on top of the cotton sheet. Milburn leapt into the conversation to insist that he had been wearing gloves and had been very careful. He continued by mentioning the lack of warm covers. The taller crime scene examiner, with his thick ponytail tied neatly back and squashed into a white hairnet, drew attention to the blue elbow puncture wound whilst also showing the syringe they had found.

'Well, gentlemen,' the Home Office pathologist said after a full minute's fulmination. 'The one thing I can tell you for certain is that I won't be telling you anything before I get him back for the post-mortem.'

'How about time of death?' DI Barnes ignored Gerard's denial of service.

'Godolphin, I said "no comment". Do you have any circumstances to indicate a window for the time of death?'

Milburn jumped in, 'Between 6pm last night and 9am this morning.'

'OK, looking at the body I can agree with that. He died some time in the last 18 hours.' The pathologist gave a wry smile to the two policemen.

'Just one question, then, Andrew.' The detective sergeant was standing beside Gerard just inside the doorway, almost at the foot of the bed. They had both stopped at this location, as any more steps would have been into the lake of almost dried blood. 'He looks like he was sleeping peacefully and passed away because of the loss of blood.'

The older man interrupted, 'I told you: no conjecture. This is bizarre to say the least, and I'm not going to jump to any conclusions.'

'No, no, I know. All I wanted to ask is – wouldn't that be really painful?' Milburn's finger was indicating the several separated strands of tissue that had once formed Hamish Elliott's penis.

'Yes, I should say that it would be. But don't quote me – we need a tox report first.' The man had not obviously been shot or stabbed, so Tony returned to the victim's large teammate to find out if anyone other than the raving Indian father had a grudge against the dead man.

Harris explained that most of Elliott's female conquests had been one-night stands or brief affairs; women impressed with his celebrity status. The one Harris knew only as Kate had been a much longer proposition. He said that there was something slightly wrong with her. He couldn't quite put a name to it, but her eyes held a distance, a blank wildness that had always unnerved him. And that was quite a statement for such a hulking man. Kate had also been prone to mood swings and emotional outbursts and seemed oblivious to the audience. For a girl of obvious breeding, Harris had always thought this lack of the traditional higher-class reticence just too strange. He said Hamish Elliott had agreed: "a little wild" was the phrase Hamish himself had used, but that was the attraction, apparently.

Generally, Kate had been surprisingly acquiescent about Elliott's promiscuity. Harris presumed that she felt she was in a separate league from all the other women. After all, she was the only long-term woman in Hamish's life. That was until he met Aisha. It had been 18 months before her father had even let her attend one on the County's matches, despite her absolute love of cricket. Harris smiled continuously as he explained how she and his bowling rival and friend, Hamish, had hit it off immediately, and how she had contrived to attend training and other club functions so they could meet and talk under circumstances acceptable to her father. The situation had escalated in the New Year to include surreptitious dates and days out. This was a whole new phase, and Harris had often wondered just how serious it might get. Of course, it hadn't stopped the one-night stands, or overnight visits from Kate.

Harris said that Kate's weirdness was sufficient that he tried to avoid her, where possible. However, on the last few occasions that she had been here in Elliott's flat, she had seemed even more extreme in her moods. The time Hamish spent with Aisha was a patent threat to Kate and she vented this loudly and clearly. The demure and well brought-up Kate had launched into racist polemic, and Harris explained to Milburn how even Elliott himself had been perturbed. '"She's gonna have to go",' Jim reported his friend as having confided only three days previously.

'And what did you say to that?' Milburn was teasing as much information out about Elliott's recent movements as he could.

'I said, "I've been telling you that for six months",' Harris answered. 'But Hamish didn't know how to get shot of her. I just said "Tell her straight mate. Tell her it's over and she shouldn't expect to see you again. You can make it all nice and fluffy with 'You're really special' and 'I'm really sorry', but you're gonna have to lay it down the line with this girl. No ifs or buts – you make it very clear, or you'll never be rid of her. Make sure she's got the message".'

Tony asked if his friend had implemented any of this advice. Harris did not know. The dead man was pretty cowardly at that sort of thing. More often, he'd simply avoid speaking to a woman again rather than have the guts to tell her it had all been a casual thing and he wasn't going to see her again. But they had both been in agreement that Kate would be a very difficult one to shrug off so easily. They had concurred that telling her straight was the best way forward, but whether the plan had been acted upon before he had died, only Kate would know.

DI Barnes stalked back into the room and returned to his armchair. DS Milburn got up and went to poke around the kitchen, which opened off the living area. The flat was sufficiently small that he could still easily hear Godolphin's slick, almost slimy, interview technique. Tony felt relieved that his boss was asking for mundane details, such as relatives to be informed. At least he would not have to take over and appease the mortally offended, recently bereaved again.

The kitchen gave away few clues. It was modern and clean but appeared little used; a bachelor's kitchen through and through. Vodka in the freezer and bottles of lager in the main part of the fridge. Some ready meals in microwave oven packaging, fruit, bread and bottled water. The only anomaly was a box of 12 condoms in the fridge. Milburn had seen people keep ground coffee and pharmaceuticals in the refrigerator. He

14

even thought back to the photographic film his father had kept in it, but condoms was a new one.

When Milburn returned to the lounge, Barnes was onto names and positions of teammates and cricket club management. He wandered behind the long white sofa and stood in front of a desk under a large window. The desk contained the paraphernalia of domestic affairs. Paper, trays of bills, some paid, some not yet paid, and a lease agreement for the flat.

More interesting to him though was the view from the window. The third floor flat looked out across Durham City. There was a sharp drop to the long straight section of the River Wear that runs towards the city centre. Across this stretch of water were the University's premier sports fields, including first team cricket, rugby and football pitches. The grass looked damp and lush in the morning sunshine. A slight glare from the roof of the sports pavilion showed that it was wet too. It hadn't rained recently, so detective Milburn concluded that the overnight dew had condensed on the cold building.

Further west still, the river cut left into its large meander that encircled the city's World Heritage peninsula. He could just make out the roof of the police station and then beyond, and even higher than his own vantage point, the Castle and Cathedral rose above all. Looking from the east, the Cathedral seemed to dwarf everything, its twin sunset towers masked by the monstrous grey central tower. With a bustling of buildings between him and it, the ancient church seemed to rise up as a continuation of the very Earth itself. The peninsula rock appeared to have been hewn by a giant sculptor to leave the orthogonal stone lumps that built the city's history. More quietly and less visible, Durham Castle hugged its end of the craggy outcrop, clinging and slithering around the end, as if in awe of the proud dominant Cathedral. Looking at this view he could well understand the staggering rent figure written on the lease agreement he still held in his hand.

Without thinking, Milburn interrupted the DI, 'Did Hamish have any money problems?'

The well-built young man on the sofa turned around, and dark eyes looked up, a little concerned. 'No, I don't think so. His contract would be for about fifty grand. He doesn't have a car, so he only spent on this place and food and drink.'

'And drugs?' Barnes chimed in.

Harris turned back to him, exasperated. 'No. No money for drugs. He was not killed by some drug dealer he owed money to.'

'So you think he was murdered?' The inspector was starting to get on Milburn's nerves now.

Poor Harris was stuck in a no-win situation and Tony felt truly sorry for him. 'No, y-you,' Jim turned back to Milburn behind the sofa for confirmation and assistance. 'You said you didn't know how he died. I was just saying – I was just saying that it's not to do with drugs.'

'So that's you're story, and you're sticking to it?' To a bystander, Barnes would have looked for all the world like he knew Harris was lying, but it was just his way: bluff and deceit, without any compassion.

'Yes, look, can I go now?' Tony felt like asking the same question for himself. The inspector looked up at him and opened his eyes a little, questioning. Milburn just wanted to get them all out of there – his boss's questions were starting that

16

skin-crawling feeling that they so often instigated in Tony. There was no obvious evidence to suggest that this death was foul play, and the man was being badgered about his sexuality and drug-taking, having just found his best friend's corpse. Milburn felt that Barnes had no humanity.

He answered by speaking to the witness. 'You can go Mr Harris, but we'd appreciate it if you can avoid talking to people about this until we've had time to inform his family. Perhaps you'd better go home and forget about training for today.'

'Too right,' he replied.

'Do you want an officer to drive you?'

'I'll be OK on my own.' He still sounded rather bitter, which did not surprise Tony. He himself would have preferred not to have to drive back to the station in the same car as Barnes. Fortunately, it was little more than five minutes, and only that long because of the traffic queuing down the hill towards the city.

'Wooooff,' flames roared into the air, and Penfold and Milburn both leant back away from the sudden heat. Penfold grinned broadly, like a child, and handed the matchbox back to his host without taking his eyes off the flames. The tall, tanned surfer had insisted on showing Tony just "how we light barbecues in New Zealand". This had entailed first thoroughly soaking the charcoal in lighting fluid. Then, standing some six feet away, Penfold had held the matchbox sideways and placed a match, head down, on the striking strip with his index finger holding it vertically in position. Making a big show of taking aim, his other hand had flicked the match out from its pressurised position. Tumbling through the air, a flame had sparked on the match and as it hit the centre of the charcoal mound, the fluid vapours had ignited in an instant wall of flame. Each holding a bottle of lager, they stared at the dancing flames: pagan. Real men. The initial reservoir of volatile fuel withered, and the fire descended to the occasional flicker as the coals slowly took hold; the two cavemen moved closer.

Milburn wanted to talk to Penfold about Hamish Elliott's mysterious death and he turned to engage his friend. Pyromania still had the taller man enthralled, as his steel eyes danced with the wispy flames which appeared briefly among the rapidly whitening grey lumps.

The barbecue stand was set up next to the small shed at one end of Tony's year-old back garden. At the other end, Kathy was discussing some colourful perennials with Andrew Gerard, the moustachioed pathologist, and his partner, Phillip Wright. Kathy was Tony's blonde-haired, cohabiting – in fact joint house owning – girlfriend. She didn't know a great deal about gardening but, after reading the bulb packets, she could talk a good game. Tony caught her blue eyes and she gave him a secret smile to confirm that she was riding on her wits and the meagre kernels of knowledge she had garnered.

Milburn looked back to Penfold's olive-skinned face and messy golden hair. For this early March barbecue soirée, he had come attired in a long-sleeved red sweatshirt, black baggy shorts with big thigh pockets and a pair of rubber sports sandals. Tony had often wondered, but struggled to work out, if Penfold had a better metabolism than most people, or a screw loose. Despite the eight degrees Celsius temperature, he seemed oblivious to the cold. Penfold's vocation was surfing, and he always dressed appropriately to that. Milburn mused that maybe

18

this was why the fire was holding such wonder this evening. Penfold took the tongs that hung from the end of the barbecue and started to pester the charcoal, prodding and shoving, more in play than in any attempt to bring the coals to cooking readiness. Tony smiled over to Kathy in her jeans and brown cashmere jumper. She loved the medical couple, and they always doted on her. She had a sheepish smile on her face as they crowed over the "marvellous job you've done with it. And in only a year – splendid!"

The doorbell rang, and Tony left Penfold to his charcoal menacing and went to ingress some more guests. This gathering was a chance for Tony and Kathy to show off their brand new stone-built house. It had been a little more than they could afford, but with eleven months of further gardening and decorating, they had created a beautiful home. It had been very much a labour of love, both towards the home, but also towards each other. All the problems with PC Diane Meredith were well and truly forgotten. The home had reached the stage where they felt it was complete and ready. Thus Kathy had suggested starting the barbecue season perhaps three months early for north-eastern England. Luckily her instigation had brought a clear day. It may have been chilly and already dark by 6pm but, as long as there was no rain, they could all contend with the tail end of winter.

Tony opened the door to Detective Chief Inspector Hardwick and his wife of some 30 years, Mary. They presented him with a bottle of red wine that was far too good for the status of the event, and Mary cuddled a dessert pie dish to her coat. After depositing both wine and pie on the kitchen table, he led them back through the wide hall and large living room to exit by the French doors that opened on to the rectangular, fenced garden. It was a long journey though, as Harry Hardwick and his wife were both intent on examining every detail of the new home. Hardwick's broad fingers trawled through the thick pile of the royal blue carpet. 'Mmh,' he mumbled, mesmerised by the touch of the carpet.

'Durham-made, that. Hugh Mackay carpets.'

'Ooh, very posh,' Mary cooed, her face surrounded by chestnut curls which had obviously been "done" for the evening.

The carpet had been expensive, and at this comment, Milburn remembered an image of the high-priced bill. Kathy and Tony had re-assured themselves that the quality would make it last, and that by supporting local industry it was a sound purchase. 'Fingers crossed, it'll last a lifetime,' he breezed.

'And I do like your sofas,' she continued to gush. The sofas were a rusty red thick cotton cloth. Kathy's aim had been to contrast the carpet and blend nicely with the chocolate brown of the doors and window frames.

The compliments were starting to pile up, so Tony ushered them out. 'Come on you two, let's go out and Kathy can show you what she's done with the garden.'

They exited onto the dozen paving slabs that made for a small garden terrace, and almost bumped into two of Kathy's workmates. Clearly not all librarians are dowdy old prudes, as these two were dolled up to the nines. They looked to have sorely misjudged the occasion but, in fact, were planning to go on later to one of Durham's nightclubs. The two bachelorettes had entered via the side gate, which led from the driveway and garage.

'Sue, Amelia, hi,' Kathy walked over smiling. She pointed surreptitiously behind them, towards the barbecue area, and quietly confided, 'Those are the guys I was telling you about.'

Unsubtly, Sue and Amelia both turned their heads to look. Kathy took their hands to turn them back, and much more openly introduced them to her boyfriend's top boss and his good lady wife. Tony smiled inwardly, bemused at how the evening's incongruous group might get along.

Behind the gaggle of university librarians, Penfold was waving the tongs at Milburn, indicating the now fully white pile of charcoal and grinning broadly. The gesture told Tony that his work for the evening was about to begin. He nipped back in to the kitchen to collect more beer and the platter of meat that Kathy had marinated. It was a struggle to carry everything, but he finally dumped them all down on the grass beside the red metal legs of the barbecue.

Beers were distributed to Penfold and Mantoro, Penfold's Mexican friend. Probably no more than five feet tall, he had the most enormous hair. Dark and wavy, it was like a Latino attempt at an Afro hairdo. The most phenomenal bushy moustache complemented it wonderfully. The little man wore black jeans and a puffy black ski jacket, which looked oversized on his diminutive frame. Carrying an eternally serious look, one side of his face was pockmarked with a nasty acid scarring. Mantoro seldom spoke and had a murky criminal past. His association with Penfold was unclear to Tony, and Penfold and Mantoro never gave straight answers to questions about it. Friend certainly, assistant often, employee probably not. Milburn had never managed to engineer a situation that was ripe for asking the right questions, and this had persisted for so long that it now seemed awkward to ask.

Kathy dragged Penfold and Mantoro away to be introduced to her single friends. She literally pulled them along, in the guise of hooking onto each one's arm with hers.

'Ah, Tony.' Milburn visibly jumped as DI Barnes appeared from nowhere. He had come in at the side gate and skulked along by the fence to reach the barbecue corner.

'Godolphin,' he responded trying to get his bearings and welcome the difficult man. Tony had not expected him to take up the invitation, and was convinced that he had never given him directions to the house. However, having waxed lyrical about it for over a year, Tony had to concede to himself that a police detective ought to be able to find his own partner's house. Even if that partnership was de facto part-time as a consequence of Barnes' frequent absences. 'Glad you could make it. Can I get you a beer?'

'Ah, well, that's the thing, Tony.' He looked across the lawn to Harry Hardwick. After introducing the two men to the two women, Kathy had excused herself to show the Hardwicks her flowerbeds, to a further chorus of "ooh"s and "aah"s. Barnes' narrow eyes flitted around the garden scene, calculating. 'After running up the stairs to that flat this morning, my back's gone again. It was all I could do to drive over here. I'm afraid I can't stay, but I thought I'd just show my face – say "Thanks anyway".'

Tony frowned: they had positively sauntered up the three flights of stairs at Elliott's apartment building. 'Oh, no, that's awful. The back again, eh? Don't the doctors have any ideas?'

Barnes was still warily observing the whole gathering. 'No. None. It's got them completely stumped. The only thing they all seem to agree on is to rest it.'

'Oh, yeeess.' Milburn's reply was drawn out – another few days off was in the offing for the inspector.

'Yes. So I figured that I'll rest up over the weekend, and hopefully it'll be good enough so I can go on the course on Monday. You'll remember I'm on that Threat Analysis course at County HQ all next week.'

Tony had forgotten, but such indolence was typical of Barnes. 'Bloody hell, Godolphin, you can't just drop me in it with this murder case after one day!'

Barnes scanned Milburn with the same suspicious eyes as he had the rest of the party, and they then flicked past Tony to see if his outburst had attracted attention to them. It hadn't. 'That man wasn't murdered, Tony, calm down.' He had a point. There was no certainty it was murder. 'Look, I've got to go,' he continued.

'It's lucky Harry is here, actually. You can tell him about resting your back tomorrow, and then you won't need to call in the morning.' The younger man's tone was thoroughly sardonic. Working for two was starting to wear his spirits.

He put his hand to the small of his back and winced slightly. 'Ow. Actually, I'd better get home before this is unbearable. Perhaps you could pass on the message for me, Tony. He looks rather engrossed over there.'

Tony wondered if DI Barnes realised how farcical he looked. 'Ooh, the old shrapnel wound again,' he muttered as the narrow man slinked along the fence and out of the gate.

Penfold extricated himself from small talk, and came to play with his fire some more. 'Was that Barnes I just saw insinuating himself into the night?'

'Yes, the bastard's off skiving again for at least a week.'

Penfold picked up a string of Lincolnshire sausages. Flicking open his penknife one-handed, he cut them off, dropping them individually into different parts of Hell. 'That's a bit off, you've just picked up a murder, too, haven't you?'

'Yes. Well, as he was only too quick to point out, it's just a mysterious death at this stage. Gerard's cutting him open in the morning.' Tony poked a sausage with the barbecue fork, doing a mini autopsy of his own, and followed up with, 'The guy's penis had exploded.'

Penfold looked sidelong at his friend. 'What on Earth do you mean?'

'Exploded. Um, you know in a cartoon if Bugs Bunny puts his finger in the end of a rifle just as Yosemite Sam pulls the trigger.'

'Yes,' the answer was elongated, as Penfold was unsure of this sudden diversion.

'It makes the barrel blow up, splitting it into half a dozen long strips which splay outwards.'

Comprehension came to Penfold, and he scowled at the thought. 'How the hell do you do that to a penis? Actually, don't answer, I don't think I want to know.'

They both chuckled. 'That's lucky, 'cause I have absolutely no idea. That's why it's a *mysterious* death you see. Looks like the poor guy bled to death from the wound.'

'Wow.'

'Yeah. Cricketer, you know. Played for Durham County, First Team and everything.' Tony paused in contemplation for a second. 'Actually, I wonder if he's the biggest celebrity corpse I ever had.'

Penfold was fascinated by the nature of the death only – he had little interest in cricket. 'And you don't know how he could have gotten the wound?'

'No clue. There were signs of intravenous drug use, no signs of a struggle, a shitload of blood, and his mate had kicked in the door to find him, so we're not certain if he was properly locked in. Depends on whether his mate panicked – and if he's telling the truth.'

'And how does that stand up? You know, half the time, the one who reports it did it.'

Tony did, of course, know that it was in fact more like two-thirds of cases for which this was true. Penfold's casualness suggested that this was another titbit of knowledge that only Penfold knew. That was absurd, but Penfold often came across as arrogant, and DS Milburn had to keep reminding himself that he was the policeman. He looked into the New Zealander's face. The skin was browned to perfection from so much time sitting on his surfboard, the sunlight constantly drumming off the water surface. Beside each eye, his crow's feet were streaked slightly lighter. Despite having the lithe, strong body of an eighteen-year-old, Penfold's skin was aging faster than the rest of him. On his exposed face at least. Whilst his features looked less than his 30 years, the actual skin itself was lined and crinkled.

Tony's anger at his patronizing comment subsided before he could snap at him. He shuddered though. It might have been cold, but this was unease at his friend's true feelings. Penfold was not mean or crass, so this was merely ill judged, but Tony felt as if there was a pattern developing. He wondered if Penfold considered him stupid, dim-witted, inept. Was he just using Milburn to access police investigations for his own amusement? 'I'll get us some more beers,' Tony excused himself.

In collecting beer bottles and some plates and bread rolls, he did a complete circuit of the house. Having entered by the patio doors at the shed end of the garden, Tony left the kitchen via its external door exiting to the side of the house, and thus entered the garden at the opposite end. He wended his way through all the groups of guests. Kathy and her two girlfriends were squeezed onto the little bench at the very end. It was like a football goal at one end of the lawn, whilst Penfold and Mantoro were defending the barbecue goal as Andrew Gerard and Phillip Wright surged up the flowerbed wing towards them.

The three women cackled like Macbeth's witches. It was the sort of loud, tipsy laugh you might hear from any group of women in Durham's pubs on a Friday night. Tony smiled, cheered by their infectious happiness. Harry Hardwick and his wife looked a little uncomfortable standing near the bench, unsure of how to extricate themselves from conversation that had clearly moved away from their experience or interest. Out of their depth, maybe. Out of their generation, certainly. Harry and Mary joined Tony walking towards the food, as it was nearly all cooked. Relief palpably crossed Mary's face as they tottered off behind their host.

Gerard had been collared by Penfold to talk about Hamish Elliott's corpse. Mantoro stood like a statue, listening without movement. It was one of Mantoro's greatest skills – listening. He had made a career of being an information man. Mostly working for South American drug cartels, his safety had always been ensured by the information he kept secret. 'Quick to listen and slow to speak,' Penfold had once summarized his talents.

However, as usual, Gerard was playing his cards close to his chest. Under his greying hair, the face beamed like a theatre spotlight, almost physically illuminating the group. He jovially parried Penfold's questions in a clever split. Either he repeated the basic visual description, or retreated behind the wall of "no conjecture before post-mortem". Tony thought Penfold had met his match, but Penfold knew how to spot the perfect wave. He could scan the water surface and draw out what each distant ripple would do by the time it reached you. Extrapolation and interconnection of seemingly inconsequential observations were Penfold's forte. So, as he asked tiny questions, like what was the appearance of the man's fingers and if there was any residue in the syringe, Milburn took care to also note the answers. "Gripped like claws – yes that was odd" and "none whatsoever".

Steak in a hamburger roll went to Hardwick, while his short wife insisted on one sausage only, which she bundled off to the kitchen to adorn with salad.

'All sounds very intriguing,' Penfold nodded in Gerard's direction, indicating to the chief inspector that he was referring to the mysterious death.

Gruffly, Hardwick replied, 'Yes, well. We'll probably find it was some deranged girlfriend, took to his dick with a knife.'

27

'You know how I love a mystery. If I can be of any assistance, I'd love to help. I believe Godolphin's off again, isn't he?'

'What?' DCI Hardwick, the head of Durham CID, turned on DS Milburn. He hadn't had a chance, or the inclination, to broach Barnes' absence with their boss and was unprepared. Tony looked back and forth at all the staring faces, like a scared animal.

Penfold interjected to break the increasingly strained silence. 'His back again, isn't it, Milburn?' As he looked at Tony, Penfold flashed his eyes as if suggesting Tony should back up his request to rubberneck the case. Despite Penfold's good record at helping with inscrutable cases, as a civilian, Hardwick was always against involving the New Zealander. It made a mockery of his department to have a surfer swan in and blow a case wide open. Most coppers tended to agree with this view, although Penfold was discreet, and a fine detective. Tony didn't feel he could tackle Harry on getting him involved, and simultaneously explain away DI Barnes' skiving again. And it was Barnes who was on the table, so he went with that. 'Yes, he popped by earlier to say that his back is playing up again, so he's going to rest it over the weekend before that course at Ayckley Heads all next week.'

'Bugger. Bloody hell. Not again.' Harry was a good manager, and did not give away how authentic he considered his inspector's absences. Barnes was always by the book with doctors' notes and courses that nobody could argue would not be valuable to his work, but it would be an unusual month in which he worked more than a dozen days on real detective stuff. 'Don't worry, Tony, I'll get you a partner for this case.'

Penfold's eyes flashed to Tony again, but he grimaced back, indicating he didn't have the wherewithal to propose Penfold at that moment.

Kathy, Sue and Amelia, the triumvirate of librarians, sauntered over to get some food and to break up the testosterone party of the men. 'Enough shop talk,' Kathy instructed, although she had only guessed. She could not hear their conversation over the collection of 80s pop hits she had set blasting from the lounge.

'Yes,' Phillip agreed. 'Something a little more pleasant than dead bodies please.' Phillip was shorter than his partner. Where Andrew Gerard looked like the mature Dick van Dyke, general practitioner Phillip more resembled a stereotypical, bespectacled accountant.

Everybody demurred that the topic should be changed, and it was a convenient moment to adjourn inside. The meat was all cooked, and what had not yet been eaten also adjourned inside on a plate, ready for the first to regain some hunger, or greed. Sue and Amelia stationed themselves at the CD rack and, after a few minutes, turned to the room with a trophy presentation. They had drunk a little more than everyone else and held forward *80's Karakoe Classics*. Sue appealed, 'Who's up for some karaoke then? Come on, Tony, I bet you're a dead good singer.'

'Um, perhaps a bit later,' he managed, startled and a bit scared at the prospect.

'A bit of a sing-song, eh?' Harry was positively rapt at the idea, which surprised everybody and set Mary nagging at his elbow, worried that he had had too much of the whisky. Harry Hardwick's right eye was injured by a horse kick many years ago – before he even joined the police – blinding it. The eye sat dormant, appearing as normal, but did not move from looking straight forward. Over the years, Harry had learnt to use this to great effect to unnerve suspects, and those he had to dress down as the boss. He used it here to ignore his wife, pretending to look at her. However, there was devious method in Chief Inspector Hardwick's apparent madness. He continued, 'Gerard, you can sing; I know you can. What about knocking out a show tune for us?'

Penfold again caught Milburn's eye, but this time in alarm, concerned that Hardwick had indeed had too much to drink and that this comment had perhaps sailed a little too close to the homophobic wind. Tony reassured himself that Harry was making a Dick van Dyke joke, but couldn't figure out anything useful to say to rescue the situation. Fear was in Kathy's face too, as she envisaged their first social event of the summer spiralling down a plughole with the head of the city's CID in a fistfight with its top pathologist.

All was saved by Sue, who did not know Andrew and Phillip were gay. 'Really? Ooh, yes, go on Andrew, I bet you've got a great voice.' She turned her attention to the playlist on the reverse of the CD case. 'What do you reckon? How about Tainted Love?' She was oblivious to the swingeing undercurrent that permeated many in the room.

But her friend, Amelia, joined in cooing, 'No, do Karma Chameleon. I love Karma Chameleon. Here, I'll put it on for you.'

'Ok, hold it right there,' Gerard interrupted as they buzzed about the music system. This was it. Nobody expected things to blow up into a brawl with Hardwick. The cuddly doctors were too old and too professional and too wise for such recourse. But things weren't coming to a head – they had arrived. Milburn anticipated them making their excuses and leaving, with several months of strained relations to come. The over-cautious in the room, namely Penfold, Kathy, Mantoro, Mary Hardwick and Tony were thus stunned when Gerard tweaked his bushy grey moustache with a grin and said, 'Phillip and I have been practising a few songs, but we don't need the backing track thanks. What do you say, Phil, ready to give our first public performance since the Palatine Party?'

'And what a performance that was,' his partner muttered with a faint smile and a re-adjustment of his glasses. 'Oh, what the hell. If you're gonna go down, why not go down singing.'

Phillip was quite innocently referring to a poor performance using a sinking ship metaphor, but the two brash librarians cackled loudly again, nudging each other, and Amelia almost shouted, 'Saucy!'

Phillip looked surprised and confused, but Andrew bustled him over to the now-closed patio doors, as a kind of stage backdrop. They started with an astounding rendition of Ebony and Ivory, and then continued through half a dozen well-known pop classics. Each one was just as good, meriting and receiving a tremendous round of applause, despite the miniature audience. Tony was amazed that what they were doing was even possible. The way their voices complemented and accentuated each other with perfectly harmonised timing showed everyone that they practised a lot.

After 20 minutes, the couple agreed that their voices had had enough. Nobody else dared take on karaoke to follow them, so it was back to background music and idle chat. As the evening wore on, people variously decided it was time to leave. Mary insisted she drive Harry home before he started on a third ice tray to accompany his whiskies. The library duo begged and pleaded with Kathy for her to join them in Zoot, Durham's tiniest nightclub for the very drunk, but she managed to refuse them. With a post-mortem in the morning, Andrew let Phillip cajole him home relatively early too. Thus, Kathy and Mantoro were left listening to Penfold and Tony discussing Hamish Elliott further.

'I'm intrigued by the university connection. A student girlfriend is most interesting. I wonder how they met.' Penfold was musing aloud, reading the label on his beer bottle over and over again.

'It might have been through cricket,' Kathy suggested slowly. She wasn't wholly confident about getting involved in the conversation.

He knew Kathy was a positive mine of facts, so her boyfriend drew her along to see what this was. 'What do you mean?' Milburn asked.

'Well, the county cricket club has close links with the university team.'

'Don't you mean the city club?' Tony asked, thinking that Kathy must be getting mixed up about the various clubs all with the name Durham in their title.

She shot him a withering look. 'No. Listen, the university are by far the best amateur team in the county. They consider themselves a fully professional outfit; and they're generally pretty arrogant about it too. They do a lot of training with the county club, so maybe that's how this dead man got involved with a student.'

'But she's a girl,' Tony said, somewhat lamely.

'There are female cricketers, you know. The uni women's team is coached by Durham County players. And two of them were in the England team that won the World Cup last year.' She turned her fair-skinned face to each of the three men in turn, her blue eyes wide to show that they should be impressed.

Tony was confused. 'We didn't win the World Cup last year.' He was sure Kathy had drunk one (or maybe several) too many of her cans of draught Guinness.

He got the withering look, again, and wondered if she'd been taking lessons from Hardwick in giving the Evil Eye. 'England Ladies did.'

Penfold nodded, and Tony felt rather small and chastened. 'How do you know so much about all this?' he asked, not previously aware that his girlfriend had any knowledge or interest in the leather and willow.

'The uni women cricketers take their studies a lot more seriously than the men, so I see them in the library.' Bucking her head to take a glory swig from her glass sent Kathy's blonde hair flying over her head in a way she often did after a few drinks. Triumphant and proud, it was something of an overblown gesture, as if she were battling for women everywhere against the trio of male chauvinist pigs in front of her: body language hyperbole.

'Really?' Penfold joined in quietly. 'You know what might be quite helpful for Milburn's case would be some background about drug use in first class cricket. Do you think they would talk to you about what people use and what goes on in cricket? I'm afraid I'm very ignorant about the sport and wouldn't know what might enhance performance and what would hinder a player.' Penfold's tone was a deft touch. It wasn't blathering obsequiousness, but really made everyone want to leap on board and help him out in any way possible. And he had very appropriately referred to it as Milburn's case. Naturally, Kathy couldn't help but agree to quiz all-comers the very next day. She didn't work every weekend, but was doing a shift on both Saturday and Sunday that week.

'I don't suppose any of your female cricketers are a posh, blonde one called Kate?' Tony inquired laughing. The joke was lost on everyone else though, as they were not aware that the student girlfriend was called Kate

'Tony,' she said with condescension and a smile, 'every female student at Durham University is a posh blonde called Kate.'

Smiling at Kathy's cynicism, Penfold excused himself and Mantoro for the night. They shook Mantoro's hand on the front door threshold. 'Thanks a lot, Tony,' he bade farewell with his quirky American accent. 'I left you some cashews on the kitchen table.'

'Er, right. Thanks, Mantoro. See you, Penfold.' They both waved as Kathy closed the door on them and, in the kitchen, Tony found a clear plastic bag of unsalted cashew nuts. 'He's a strange man,' Tony tried to say, as Kathy flung her arms around him and sucked at his mouth, more than a little drunk.

Saturday 23rd March

Detective Sergeant Milburn followed Andrew Gerard's bushy grey head through one pathology lab and into the second. They were identically laid out, the only apparent difference being the corpse taking centre stage in the latter. The room was so neat and clean, it looked ready to begin Hamish Elliott's post-mortem. A stainless steel tray on a pivoted arm carried the butchery tools that so effectively gutted and dissected a man's body to examine all its secret nooks and crannies. Milburn paused on the threshold between the two laboratories and played spot-the-difference.

Most importantly, Gerard's chosen workspace had his office attached. The Super Trouper spotlights he still preferred over newer banks of LEDs were raised, ready to burst with light. In the gloom of this basement dead-end, it looked as if flicking their power switch would mimic the moment when Genesis had God saying "Let there be light". The two video cameras were in place on wheeled tripods, gaining a side view and an end view of the erstwhile cricketer.

Cables raining down from the ceiling connected the cameras to power supplies, and to the giant television screens mounted on the wall next to the door to Dick van Dyke's office.

Even in this minutes-to-launch state, the place was immaculate. Gerard's obsessive-compulsive tidiness formed his management style and he expected all of his minions to toe the line and keep the place perfect. Milburn speculated inwardly that it was this precise attention to detail that may have propelled Gerard up the career ladder to his current status as probably the most highly regarded of the three Home Office appointed pathologists in the Northeast. There was no chance of losing vital evidence here.

Milburn's eye also caught the other major difference in the architecture of the two labs: the fire escape. As if in a submarine, a metal ladder affixed to the wall in the deepest corner of this underground world ascended through a hole in the ceiling. Intrigued, he stepped over to look up and, sure enough, there was an exit up to the ground floor, which offered a further route to escape in the event of an inferno when all the metal and glass of these labs went up in flames. Milburn shook his head in bemusement and turned, to be greeted by Gerard, arms folded across his chest.

'You know, I've never noticed that before,' he said, waving his hand in the direction of the ladder. He realised that he was also gesturing towards a large green sign that bellowed *Fire Exit*. Tony corrected himself, 'Or maybe I've just never taken it in before.'

'The whole place is unbelievable. X million pounds to build a brand new state-of-the-art teaching hospital, and pathology gets this.' Gerard in his turn waved a hand to signify his domain, sweeping from the small back office through two labs to the refrigeration room beyond, which also acted as the corridor to access it all.

'What're you complaining about?' Tony jibed. 'This all looks lovely. It's brand new for goodness' sake.' The new hospital had opened about a year previously, and the whole place had an air of lavish newness.

But the pathologist's complaints were serious, and he confirmed, 'The Pathology Suite has no observation room. Can you imagine trying to teach forensic medicine to thirty medical students in here?' There was barely room to swing a leopard at arm's length. Milburn looked around, and mentally estimated room for about eight standing passengers before the place became like a cramped lift.

'My office has enough space for mortuary policy documents and one or two weeks current working files. The rest have to go straight to archive. You've no idea how much time I waste walking to the central records centre because they couldn't be bothered to dig my office another six feet into the mud.' He had become a runaway train. 'And one office? Other than me there are three hospital pathologists and seven technicians. I get the office, and I'm not even paid by the hospital – I just work here!'

Tony tried to interrupt and break the unending chain of architectural mismanagement that was to be inflicted upon him, 'At least when you need a break you've got a quick route to the canteen.' He pointed up the ladder to the aperture in the corner of the ceiling.

'And the bloody fire escape. Who ever heard of such a lunatic thing? You know, I'm certain that was a mistake and they shoved it in when they realised you need two exits to every room. But imagine trying to escape a fire *upwards*, and up that thing.'

Right on cue, as if she had been waiting in the wings for her line, Jan came in with a file for him. Jan was a middle-aged technician in a wheelchair. She had heard Gerard's rant and as she spun her chair round to leave again, she gave Tony a wide-eyed grin. "Picture me escaping up that", the grin said. As Jan continued to exit through PL1 – Pathology Laboratory One – Milburn pointed a dumbfounded finger at her back and stared at his friend in dumbfounded horror at the implications of a fire.

With raised, bushy grey eyebrows and a tight line of a mouth across his face, Andrew nodded in certain agreement. His tone was ruefully cynical. 'You know, there is a clause in the Mortuary Health and Safety Policy, which I am responsible for implementing, despite not being an employee of the NHS, that states that you cannot work in PL2,' he pointed a finger at the ground, 'unless you are physically capable of exiting via the fire escape.'

'Isn't that discriminatory?' Milburn knew that the police station had had to be modified with ramps to comply with anti-discrimination legislation.

'Oh, no. You see, Jan is allowed to work in PL1, just not in here. So, I have to manage the place so she can do all her work in there.'

'But how can that be any different than in here?'

'Well, PL1 has two flat floor exits – out to refrigeration, and into here. So, it's safe for the wheelchair bound.'

Tony was silent. It was bureaucratic logic gone mad but, as a police officer, he was all too familiar with that. From the courts to the rules of evidence to the problems of under-age illegal immigrants, bureaucratic logic gone mad was something he fully understood.

'Look, sorry to go on. Come in to my office, and I'll get started.'

With no viewing gallery, any observers at a post-mortem still had to be accommodated in a manner that would not compromise any trace evidence found. DS Milburn usually paid little attention whilst a PM was in progress. He found the debrief at the end was always more coherent than piecing things together as they went along. He generally used the time to catch up on his email – a euphemism Milburn used for deleting anything more than about 10 days old and still unopened. On this occasion, he ensconced himself in Gerard's office chair, so he could still see through the big window. The pathologist requested that Tony touch nothing and went back into the cutting room to deal with Hamish Elliott.

Two hours later, Gerard returned and Milburn moved to the visitor's chair. After his diatribe against the architects of his underworld, it was surprising that they both fitted into the pathology labs' office. Indeed, with eyes pessimistically refreshed, Tony thought it actually looked larger than he remembered. Gerard sat behind his immaculate desk, the only ruffling presence on it being his manila folder about Hamish Elliott. The detective sat on an uncomfortable, although new, institutional black chair. Gerard's position looked out to towards the labs, whilst the visitor's chair faced in towards the wall-covering bookshelves behind him. He had complained about the lack of filing space, but half the bookcases contained books that did not appear to Tony to have any immediate use. They were all pathology related, but did not look quick reference. Some were technical references, or conference proceedings, but some had more interesting titles, like *The Clue in the Spleen* and *1001 Corpses*.

Gerard had sent the photographs from all angles, including innards and tissue samples, straight to the printer and spread them across the desk.

'Where shall we start?' the pathologist smiled and the bright aura exuded by his face disconcerted Tony that he might be about to break into song again. The words "chim-chiminey, chim-chiminey", from the musical film *Mary Poppins*, lilted their way through his head, but he restrained himself and asked for Elliott's cause of death.

Gerard had two main faces. There was the beaming, cheeky, fading Hollywood star that could wow the old ladies from the Women's Royal Voluntary Service, who ran the hospital snack bar. With that face, people would always watch attentively for him to do a song, or start tap dancing and swinging a cane. The flipside of Andrew Gerard was a sombre, professional expression. Caring and intelligent, his serious face said, "I'm sorry I have to work with death, but I'm sincere and very capable". He gave his work the gravitas it deserved, but only when it was needed.

With his earnest face on, he explained to Milburn that, between midnight and 2am on the 22nd of March, an incredibly effective haemorrhage of the penis had released more than half the blood from Hamish Elliott's body. The detective asked how he could have sustained such an injury. This opened up a Pandora's Box of speculation. Fiddling with his moustache as he spoke, Gerard whizzed through half a dozen similar, but subtly different, injuries he'd seen during his career. It sounded like the "Below the Belt" chapter in *1001 Corpses*. From stabbings and shotgun wounds to self-mutilation Tony moved through queasiness and amazement almost to boredom.

Anecdote number six was of a man whose girlfriend who had bitten his penis almost completely off during some very rough oral sex. This was the closest similar injury Gerard had ever seen or heard of, but he concluded by saying, quite categorically, that Elliott had not been bitten and that the wound had not been caused externally. This was the rub. The various corpse stories were actually something of a cover to guard the fact that Gerard stumped by this case.

Milburn realised the smokescreen and tried to cut through it. 'So how did he end up with that injury?'

'Well, I've never come across a case like this exactly, so I'm theorising.'

'I need hard facts, Andrew. Was it murder, suicide, accident, or natural?'

'That I can't say, but if you let me finish you'll see that it does need investigation.'

'Ok, sorry. Go on.'

He started to collect the photo props into order and passed them one by one to the detective. Firstly, a close-up showed the needle mark in Elliott's left elbow crook. 'The toxicology report of the blood we sent to our lab yesterday confirms several things: a little alcohol, traces of Somnulone, but the killer was Priapra. Your man injected, or was injected with, a very large amount of Priapra.'

'Priapra? Is that the new sex drug?'

'Yes,' he nodded his silver head sombrely, and all his words were spoken without a hint of titillation or smut. 'It's a combination of the active molecular components of Viagra and

41

Ecstasy. But it's a pill. I cannot find any reference to injecting the stuff, and the concentration in this guy's blood would suggest he injected the equivalent of about thirty pills.'

'Um, sorry, I know I'm the policeman, but I've not come across Priapra before. It is illegal, is it?'

'Oh, yes. Remember, it's part Ecstasy.'

'Right, sorry, of course. So could thirty pills kill you?'

'Well, injecting unusual substances is a very easy way to overdose, but it looks like the haemorrhaging beat liver failure to the punch here.'

'How do you mean?'

'In this case, the drug appears to have so over-stimulated him sexually that his body kept on pumping blood into his penis at such a rate that the erectile tissue simply couldn't stand the pressure and split in several places.' Dr Gerard passed over a photo of the man's genitalia which, when cleared of blood, grotesquely resembled a collection of worms crawling over a bed of copper wire off-cuts. His scrotum was barely visible beneath the straggling masses. At the very right hand border of the photo, a yellowish discolouration was just visible, disappearing across Hamish's thigh and out of shot.

'I noticed several big thigh bruises when we found his body.' Milburn pointed at the edge of the photo. Gerard rifled through his pile of photos and pulled one out with a flourish, as if to say, "Was this your card?" The coloured, glossy picture showed the upper left leg only, with four overlapping bruises. They looked like archery target rings, about the size of a fist, with rings of varying shades of brown, green and purple.

'I'm a bit stumped by these too, I'm afraid, Tony. Blunt force bruises – possibly punches. But I just don't know exactly.

They've been inflicted over several days, possibly even weeks, but look a bit uniform in shape and size for fist blows. It's difficult to consistently punch someone with the same force, and you often catch a glancing blow, which produces an odd-shaped bruise. Sorry, I'm no pugilist, that's just my medical experience. A more salacious man than myself might link these bruises with the Priapra and wonder if Mr Elliott was into some unusual sexual practices.

The haze that was fogging Tony's mind about this whole case cleared just enough for a chink of sunlight to shine through. He had seen exactly this kind of bruising before. 'Well, Andrew, chalk up one at least for police detective work: these bruises are cricket injuries,' he beamed triumphantly. 'Hit with a ball during batting practice.'

'Well, I never.' Gerard took the photo back and stared at it, nodding, his lower lip jutting out in acceptance. 'Yes, that works perfectly for these. If only you had been paying more attention during the post-mortem, I could have included that in the voice notes for the coroner. I thought they'd have padding though?'

'Not everyone wears a thigh pad, especially in practice in the nets. I bet there are no such marks below the top of the leg pads? Although he's not likely to be a great batsman, so hitting him so many times is pretty mean going by his colleagues.'

'Somebody got his number – a bit of the old bodyline stuff.' Andrew was smiling at this new departure in his corpse's trail of breadcrumbs. Not quite the radiant beam expectant of song and dance, but it was when tiny nuggets of information led to a great seam of knowledge about the history of the deceased that his work was most fulfilling.

'Well, as you said, I'll discount those. Is there anything else?'

'A man's penis explodes as a result of an intravenous overdose of a drug you normally take orally not enough for you, Sergeant?'

Tony grinned. 'I need something to solve after breakfast!'

Andrew grinned back. Shuffling through the photographs, he pushed them all to one side and picked up the toxicology report. 'Um, a little alcohol and traces of Somnulone.'

'Yeah, what is that?' Milburn had been distracted by the mention of Priapra earlier, and forgotten about the drug he'd never heard of. He had pushed it to one side of his mind on the assumption that it was merely a technical name for some everyday thing, in the way that a medical report might refer to "traces of nicotine".

Gerard proceeded to explain of a breakthrough in performance-enhancing steroids. The story unfolded that the next generation of drugs to increase athletes' muscle build had been so cleverly engineered that the phrase "traces of Somnulone" could mean that he had taken a normal dose. For doping athletes, it was the Holy Grail. The drug did its work and vanished from the system overnight as you slept. In fact, Gerard believed that the only reason it had been picked up at all was that this man had died before his liver could break it down into apparent caffeine waste products. Indeed, it was so effectively dispersed that the Californian university that had discovered it had believed it would be acceptable to international governing bodies and had initially marketed it as a straightforward sports supplement. The International Olympic Committee had not seen things that way, and banned it

44

immediately. In Britain, it was classified as a Class C illegal drug and only available on prescription for some physiotherapeutic uses.

'How exactly does it help build muscles when you're asleep,' Milburn asked, not entirely certain whether being asleep actually made any difference.

'It's rather like those electrical stimulant belts you can buy. "Abs like these in just three days."' Gerard mimicked a crass TV advertisement with a slap of his stomach, and his navy tie flipped about at the impact. He looked a little surprised and held the tie straight again, before looking up with a grin and continuing, 'It knocks you out and makes all your muscles contract and relax over and over again. A high protein meal before bed and the muscles build themselves.'

'A bit like a continuous epileptic fit.'

Gerard laughed. 'Yes, exactly. I'm not sure I would explain it that way, and not quite so violent, but in fact the drug works on the same hormone principles as epilepsy.'

'But surely you can't target any particular muscle group to build up, can you?'

'No, that's its main drawback as a doping agent. Only good for athletes that need overall muscle build. I believe it was developed to bulk up American Footballers and rather took the rugby world by storm before the IOC ban. Anything they ban, all other sports tend to follow suit.'

'Right,' the detective pondered out loud. 'Prescription only, so how would Hamish Elliott get some?'

'Well, check he wasn't prescribed it after an injury. Ask the team doctor. And remember, the prescription may have been a while ago, and he just held on to it till now. But, more likely, the same way you get any black market drug. Maybe from his Priapra dealer? It's mostly manufactured in South Africa and India.'

Milburn looked slightly askew at the bright face and perfect silver hairdo. 'You seem remarkably well informed about it.' He left the statement hanging, having made it interrogative by rising the pitch of his voice at the last words.

'Article in The Lancet only last month, dear boy. Pays to keep up to date.'

Tony shrugged and stood up to leave, but paused once standing. Gerard looked up at him with eyebrows raised to ask "Something else?" He was still smiling in a job-well-done mood, so DS Milburn threw a spanner in the works. 'Ok. Bled to death, but you call it OD on Priapra.'

'Yes.' His affirmative was drawn out as he could tell that Milburn was merely leading up to his real question.

'So, accident, suicide or murder?'

The doctor snorted. 'Unless you lot get some more evidence, I'm going to leave that up to the inquest. In fact, even with more evidence, my job is done. I'll chat to you off the record, but it's over to the inquest now.

'That'll be bloody misadventure then; meaning we haven't got a clue.' Tony shook his head. His voice had been a little loud, and Gerard felt he was being censured for being unhelpful.

'Steady on, Tony. You know I'm not going to send you off with something I've no evidence for.'

Tony simmered down. 'Look, I'm asking for some advice. Based on what you know of these things, what would be your best guess as to where I should go from here?'

'I'm sorry to say that I really don't think that you should limit your thinking at all. You don't inject Priapra normally, so that would mean something unusual was intended. Could be suicide. With no signs of a struggle, it's a bit tricky to inject someone to murder them.'

Milburn interrupted, 'But didn't you say the Salmonole knocks you out?'

'Somnulone.' Gerard paused nodding slowly. 'Indeed. Yes, you're right. Could be murder. Like I said, not as violent as an epileptic fit, so you could probably hold the arm still to apply the needle. The only accidental way I can think of is if he thought it was some other ...'

Once again, Milburn's interruption was louder than necessary in the small office. 'No, no. If Somnulone knocks you out, could he have injected himself at all?'

Gerard's eyebrows furrowed. He looked up at the white ceiling and shifted slightly in his chair and leaned forward. A penholder sat on the desk, in which all the writing implements stood to attention in neat rows like little soldiers on parade. He pulled out a black biro, and this was used as an aid to thought as he clicked the lid against his teeth. Tony was itching in his shoes, willing the pathologist to decide and tell him the answer. After what seemed to Tony like a year, but was, in fact, less than thirty seconds, Gerard put the soldier back on parade and shook his head. 'No ...'

The detective leapt in, 'He couldn't! So it's definitely murder then.'

'Woah. I was going to say: "No," comma, "I can't answer that with the evidence we have".'

Milburn banged his fist down on the desk, but quite calmly stated, 'Fuck!' Gerard held his side of the desk with both hands to calm the earthquake the policeman had caused, and quickly scanned the surface for displaced items. Everything had settled as it had been. 'Sorry. Sorry, I'm just not sure where I'm going to go when I leave here, 'cause I'm not really sure what direction to head in with this case.'

'It's all right, Tony. I know you've got a lot on, what with DI Barnes off again. Look, you've got a good point. The only reason I won't put my name to any suggestion of murder is that one could swallow the Somnulone and then, almost immediately, inject the Priapra, before the Somnulone put one to sleep. Or inject them both together.'

'Yes, I suppose you're right.' Tony felt very weary, though it was just past nine in the morning. It would be simple to follow standard procedure and go and flesh out some background about the dead man, but he had a nagging feeling that he was not going to solve it. If it was murder, the circumstances were sufficiently murky that there was no likelihood the murderer need confess.

He looked at the friendly face and felt better, without knowing why. Gerard was patiently waiting for Milburn to decide whether to leave or not. He could probably have remained undecided in the office all day and Gerard would patiently wait it out with him. However, a spark ignited in Milburn's head, on the merest whiff of kindling. 'But why?'

'Sorry?'

'Why would you? Somnulone puts you to sleep, so why follow it up with an injection of a sex drug? Do you think maybe he thought it could have muscle building effects on his dick?'

Gerard looked quizzical at the idea. 'Well, I suppose you probably could. Somebody not educated in such things might well make that connection. Good thinking.'

'Fuck,' Milburn cursed again, very quietly this time, almost under his breath.

'What?'

'Well, that puts us back to square one. Suicide, murder or very possibly an accident. I think I might as well just tell the coroner "misadventure" myself and go and give out some traffic tickets.'

The pathologist smiled but said nothing. There was nothing he could say. They shook hands, and DS Milburn wandered out past the shrouded, sewn-up body that had once bowled six wickets for three runs to see off Somerset in the Twenty20 cup. He shook his fist at it and muttered, 'I'll give you misad-bloody-venture.' The levity did break his black mood somewhat and he smiled at Jan whose wheelchair was parked in front of a microscope and some slides in PL1.

On his way up the stairs, he pulled out his mobile phone, only to be accosted by a sign with a picture of one with a red line through it. He held it in his hand to walk the hundred yards or so through several double doors to the main exit by Accident & Emergency. Milburn intended to call Harry Hardwick and, after a quick rundown of the results of the post-mortem, insist that he could not work on his own, especially as there seemed to be no leads. Moreover, he'd need a partner to witness anything suspects might say. He felt that he had mustered the necessary courage to suggest Penfold's name.

THE CRICKETER'S CORPSE

As he passed the final stretch of corridor, the outside light beckoned, filled with the microwaves of a million phone calls. In the corner, to the right of the door for the ladies' toilets, he noticed a small refuge with the metal rungs of a ladder rising up to the ground floor. The hole was surrounded by a railing, with a black and yellow chain loosely hung across the gap, warning of the danger of the hole in the ground. A big green sign explained that you were looking at a fire escape. Tony chuckled to himself that a person failing to be warned off by the various protection methods employed would fall to their death very conveniently in the mortuary.

Stepping out of the automatic sliding exit doors, he also noticed the wheelchair ramp, so that when Jan escaped the inferno in PL1 by going into PL2 and then ascending the ladder, she would be able to leave the building easily and without assistance. His mood had lightened significantly through his observations of architectural absurdity. So, leaning on the black police VW Golf, he tapped his phone intending to play hardball with Hardwick. His world crashed down.

Diane Meredith was in training to move from uniformed police to become a detective. She was to be attached to Durham City CID from Monday, and the boss had asked her to come in early, over the weekend, to assist Milburn in DI Barnes' absence. The same PC Meredith who had stalked him and Kathy for three months. The same dark-haired lunatic he had dated for three months prior to that. The same "Crazy Cow", as Kathy had nicknamed her, that DCI Hardwick himself had boxed into a corner and got to finally leave Tony alone.

That had been 11 months previously, but he still didn't feel happy to work with her. All their interactions since

Hadrwick's intervention had been professional, but Milburn knew he would never be able to trust her. And now she was coming to work with the detectives. He toyed with the notion that this had been her scheme all along: get through all the hurdles to join CID and have unfettered access to him. Tony's mind was whirling. What would Kathy say? How would he cope without punching Meredith?

Acting Detective Constable Diane Meredith parked the Golf that had been issued to DS Milburn in the car park at Chester-le-Street's Riverside cricket ground. They had sat in awkward silence throughout the 15-minute journey from Durham City's main police station.

Walking towards the training area, Milburn and Meredith saw four uniformed PCs talking to individuals. They were finding out background information about the deceased bowler, and checking up on alibis for all of the cricketers. One by one, as they concluded their mini interviews, the constables came to the detectives and explained whom they had questioned and what the results had been. The detective sergeant pointed out the coach, Vivender Pathan, to Meredith and suggested that she do the initial contact with him, as he had not yet been spoken to. Tony himself collated all the names and information, and then worked through what they had so far to see if anything jumped out at him.

The players were having a nets practice: there were four lanes, corridors made from string netting, with a batsman at the end of each one defending a free-standing wicket. Any well-struck balls were safely gathered by the netting. The remaining players were split into queues, taking it in turns to bowl down their lane. This system made it easy for Milburn to extract people for a few brief questions, without the need for the training session to be interrupted.

On the question of drugs, the team had been unanimous in their stonewall refusal to admit to the constables that performance-enhancing drugs had any place at Durham County Cricket Club. But, as is always the case with police witnesses, many had thrown up some minor drug references. Was this in order to divert attention away from any serious problems? Give away a small secret to conceal a bigger one. DS Milburn was cautious to remind himself that although this was often the case, it was just as often the situation that the witnesses were telling the truth and there was no bigger secret. "Always assume the worst" was Hardwick's mantra, which, as a fresh-faced new detective, was the first thing Milburn had ever heard in CID. So he agreed with himself to assume somebody used steroids, but not to assume who it was.

The consensus of opinion amongst the cricket team was that Hamish Elliott had been an ordinary, red-blooded young man. He enjoyed lager and women, a good game of cricket, the occasional marijuana joint in the off-season (when he was less likely to get drug tested). Two players had mentioned performance-enhancing drugs for Elliott as a younger man. The story went that it was commonplace for players to build themselves up artificially during youth when there was no chance of drug testing, and then once they moved into serious leagues, they had to make do with what they had built up to that stage. They did also comment that whilst Elliott was a very accurate bowler, he lacked the real fiery pace that would make for an international career, or even for an opening bowler.

Looking through the list of those present at the training session, there were five for whom their alibi was as yet unconfirmed, but only one who claimed not to have any alibi at all. Milburn recognised Pieter Hamilton from the club brochure he had picked up on his way through the reception area, but did not recall any news articles mentioning his name. He did not follow county cricket religiously, but the brochure confirmed that Hamilton had only just joined the club after three years as the star bowler at Durham University's Cricket Club. After being berated by Kathy the night before, Tony had done some research on his phone during the silent drive over. The Internet had informed him that Durham University was one of only six in the country to be sponsored by the MCC as a centre of excellence for cricket.

'Mr Hamilton, could I possibly speak with you?'

'I'm training, man. Can't it wait?' The bowler was in a queue of three to send a ball into the nets, and as his turn came up he proceeded to smash the metal wicket that the practising batsman had been attempting to defend. Milburn watched and took in the man's demeanour and build, along with his blue eyes and blond hair clipped short. The South African walked over to him with a swagger and launched straight in. 'Look, it's a pity when anybody dies, and I don't have an alibi. What can I tell you? I didn't like the guy, but I'm not involved.'

'That's fair enough. I'm trying to build up as much information so we can find out how he died.'

'You don't even know *how* he died? Jeez, what do you guys do over here? Look, I've only really just joined this club. I played here a little last season, but I've been in SA for the winter and only rocked up again ten days ago, isn't it. And as for how Hamish died, I just don't care. Get off my back.'

Milburn paused for a few seconds, eyeing up the tall, muscular Afrikaner. 'Well, I'm sure I can't expect you to be sorry that a hole has opened up in the team's bowling line-up, but I will expect your help in any police investigation.

'I'd have taken his spot on the team within a month anyway – he was useless.'

'Hmm. Well, let me confirm that you say you were at home all of Thursday night?'

'Yes. Look, I told the other copper, I drove home after training at about five, stayed at home all night and came to training here yesterday for a ten o' clock start, isn't it. I ate at home, did some weights, watched some TV, made a few calls, and slept. What else can I tell you?'

Milburn identified "isn't it" as a buffer phrase in the South African accent, with no intended meaning. 'Who did you call?'

'What?'

Tony looked up at the tanned face glaring down at him. 'Who did you call?' A vision of Penfold correcting him 'Whom did you call?' floated through his mind, but he banished it quickly to focus on the unsavoury character of Pieter Hamilton.

'Um, my mum, and a couple of mates.'

'When.'

'What? Look, I don't know exactly, alright?' Pieter had raised his voice, and looked around.

'Just tell me roughly, we'll look it up on your phone records to be precise.'

'Look, I don't know. Maybe 8 or 9, isn't it.'

'OK. You didn't think much of his talent as a cricketer then?'

'No.'

'Did the two of you ever argue about it?'

'He wasn't worth it, man. I'm quite happy to let my 140 kph balls do the talking.' The conversion of this statistic into miles per hour was not something that Milburn could do in his head, but it sounded so outrageously fast that he assumed the South African to be stretching the truth, if not out and out lying. Moreover, the man's aggressive body language told the lie to his claim of peaceful protest. His fists were clenched and he leant forward slightly over Milburn's head.

As Meredith walked towards the two of them, from behind, Pieter Hamilton's blond hair appeared to merge with the top of Milburn's and looked to her just like a vanilla-chocolate ice cream cone. The cricketer's stance was aggressive and Diane stepped very close beside them – they were too close for her to actually get between them. Milburn had his head down making notes on his pad and the coconut smell of her hair startled him. It was a smell he had forgotten, and disarmed him with whirling memories, sufficient to make him take a step sideways.

'Excuse me, Sergeant, have you finished with Mr Hamilton?' He failed to answer, but looked at her glaring. Unsure at this response, she dismissed Pieter with a thank you that he did not deserve. The Acting DC pushed some hair behind her right ear and Tony scowled. Looking at her own notebook, she missed Tony's face of thunder, and proceeded with a debrief of the conversation with the team coach, Vivender Pathan.

He had laid out a very firm party line that his team used no drugs of any description, unless prescribed by the team doctor. With this background, he refused to comment on the suggestion that Hamish Elliott may have died due to a drug overdose. Meredith insisted that she was quite coy and general about the toxicology findings – they were both taking care not to let out any specific details of the death.

Pathan had admitted he was unhappy that his daughter had been spending so much time with Elliott. Whilst he claimed to like the man, he emphasised that he was doing what any decent father would to protect their daughter. When pressed as to what he meant by "doing", he had admitted to the rather vague "controlling his daughter's movements and monitoring whom she spends time with". Meredith told Milburn that at this point she had raised sceptical eyebrows and pointed out that Aisha Pathan was 21. Her father had seemed not to understand the point being made. His response had been 'In order to preserve their chastity, unmarried girls are not allowed to stay away from home.' He had also expressed disappointment that his job required him to travel away from his family for days at a time so that he could not enforce this himself.

'So, did he do it?' DS Milburn tried to cut short Meredith's relaying of information.

'Well, he claims the same alibi as Jim Harris. They ate dinner together and talked in the restaurant from about 7 to 11pm. He last saw Harris as they left the restaurant and went straight home. I haven't got hold of his wife yet to check on the timings.'

'Right, I think we should quiz him some more. I wonder where the daughter was whilst dad was at dinner.' Diane nodded in agreement, and the two of them walked back over to the cricket coach and interrupted him again. He shouted to the team that they should all go for lunch early.

'Mr Pathan, I'm DS Milburn. My colleague has passed on the information you gave her, but I'm wondering if you can help with some other questions I have.'

'Yes, of course, Mr Milburn, please ask.'

'I believe your daughter had been having a relationship with Mr Elliott?' Tony had set the phrasing of this question to deliberately push Vivender's buttons about his daughter's purity, and he consciously noted the similarity with DI Barnes interview approach. Milburn appeased himself with the thought that whilst police interviews often had to use psychological tricks, there was a difference between that and Godolphin's crass offensiveness. In considering these things, Tony completely missed all that the Indian man had been saying, and re-focussed in the middle of a long pause where he should have been speaking.

Acting DC Meredith had her notebook to hand and was annotating the notes she had made previously, but at the stall in the conversation, she looked up at Tony, so that they were both looking at him. Spotting her notebook, the detective used that as a ruse to get himself out of trouble. He pulled his own notebook out of his pocket and opened it at random in the middle. Pulling out his pencil, he poised it above the paper and looked back at Vivender. 'Apologies, Mr Pathan, I'll need to write these things down. Could you repeat that please?'

Pathan sighed a little and said, 'My daughter is not "having a relationship". She was friends with Hamish. They talked at training, sometimes, and had coffee together, sometimes, but nothing else. They did not meet in the evenings and she does not have a boyfriend.'

'Right. So where was Aisha on Thursday night whilst you were eating out with Jim Harris?'

The doting father looked slightly taken aback and furrowed his brow. 'She works most evenings. Sometimes at home, and sometimes at the university. She is doing an Economics degree and is top in her class. But you only get to the top by putting in the hard work. I tell these boys that every day. We train harder than other teams so we can be better than them.'

'Mr Pathan, where was she on Thursday night?'

'I told you, she was working at the university.'

'OK. Where exactly and during what hours?'

'She works in the Economics library, which is in that fancy glass Business School building. She often works late and has her smart card has all-hours access clearance. She came home in a taxi at about one o' clock.'

'One in the morning?'

'Yes, I told you, she often works late. Look, why are you asking about her? I told you, she was not with Hamish.' Vivender Pathan had a pleading look in his eyes.

'Sorry, your 21 year-old daughter arrives home in a taxi at 1am, and claims to have been at the library, and you have no suspicions at all? Isn't that a little naïve?' Milburn did not let up on his line of inquiry.

'I trust my daughter, Detective. The nature of Hindu family relationships is not like those in this country. We are bound by strong family ties, and the honour of the family is strong. Aisha is a good girl, and she does what I tell her.'

'That's very noble, sir, but remember that she has been studying here for a while now and subject to plenty of less honourable influences. We will need to interview her in order to check her alibi.'

The man paused for a couple of seconds. 'Of course,' he said with considerable strength. 'We want nothing more than to help you find the killer. Please visit our home this evening.'

'Thank you. I should emphasise that we are only investigating a suspicious death. We cannot say as yet that Mr Elliott was murdered. And we may need to see Aisha before tonight. Where will she be this afternoon?'

'She will be at home all day, but I would prefer to be there when policemen,' Vivender bowed his head towards Meredith, 'or ladies, visit us.'

'I'm sorry, I can't guarantee any timing. Do you have the address?' This time it was Tony who nodded in Meredith's direction.

She confirmed with a quick 'Yup,' and closed her notebook.

'Thank you for your time, Mr Pathan. If you remember anything else, let us know.' DS Milburn handed over one of his business cards. 'Particularly anything that might have indicated Mr Elliott having sour relations with anyone. Do try and think back through interactions you may have observed over the last couple of months. 'Actually, do you know of any bowler in particular who may have bowled rather viciously in the nets at him recently?'

'Well, that'll be Pieter. But he doesn't get on well with anyone.'

'Pieter Hamilton, eh? I believe he's a newcomer to the club. And a rival with Hamish Elliott for a bowling spot on the team?'

'Pieter's very fast, but that means he's less accurate. Unless he improves a lot, I think it'll be next year at the earliest before he gets a regular place in the first team.'

'And what about now, with Elliott not available for selection?' A moment after the words came out of his mouth, Tony kicked himself inwardly for saying something so thoughtless and vulgar. It had seemed so clever when he was speaking.

Neither Coach Pathan nor ADC Meredith showed any response though, and the coach continued, 'Yes, maybe sooner, but there are a lot of people in our squad. Pieter's good, but there are many good ones. He was a star at the university team, and I don't think he likes being just one of many stars here.'

The detective nodded slowly and looked to his colleague to see if she had anything more to ask. A brief shake of her brown bob set Tony on edge again as he remembered the swing carousel of her hair flying outwards. In the image in his mind, she was laughing loudly and twisting her head back and forth in disbelief at some funny story he had told her. The thing that most concerned him was how beautiful she looked. That was the first thing that had come to his mind now, not the misery that she had caused him and Kathy. That order of thoughts scared Tony. Tripping over his words slightly, still perturbed, Milburn released the coach to his lunch.

'Are you OK, Tony?' She put her hand on his forearm and he recoiled. 'What is it?' She sounded genuinely concerned, as if she could have no insight into what was troubling her former lover.

'I'm going to nip to the toilet,' he replied as calmly as he could manage, turned and almost ran into the building following Pathan. Milburn stood in the gents for ten minutes, gripping the counter with three basins inset, and staring at his feet. Occasionally, he looked up at his own reflection and saw his face drained of colour. She was desperately attractive, and his arm had remembered the touch from times gone by. He had felt his body surge at it before his head, or his heart, could control it and remind his body how damaging and damaged Meredith was. Once he had himself under control, Milburn sent a text message to Penfold. 'Need to get away from the Crazy Cow. OK, to come over? Any advance on the case?'

Penfold replied almost instantaneously with the single letter 'Y'. Tony paced the gents a couple of times, wondering if that referred to his visiting, or Penfold's research on the toxicology report which Milburn had sent him, a copy with the case number, name and dates cut off. He decided that it didn't matter which question was being answered, it still meant he could visit. There was also a text message from Kathy about her discussions with students at the university library. She always signed off her messages to Tony with the letters "xkx", and the sight of this small thing gave him the strength to leave the toilets.

The all-glass frontage of the cricket club's main building allowed him to see Diane milling around at the edge of the car park. As he walked over, steeling himself to just dismiss her, she beckoned him to look at something in the car park. Following her silent gesticulation, he saw the back of Pieter

Hamilton leaning to speak into the open passenger window of a green BMW saloon car. The car was not in a parking space, it looked as if it had just stopped to talk to him. Milburn was about to write it off as one of the South African's teammates on their way out for lunch, when Pieter shifted slightly and he could see long blonde hair in the passenger seat. Nothing else was visible but flowing hair. All the remaining windows were tinted.

'Mr Hamilton,' Tony called over. He stood up and swivelled around. As he did so, the tinted glass went up behind him and the green car drove out of the parking area. Milburn and Meredith walked over to him, straining to catch a glimpse of the vehicle's occupants. She wrote down the registration number and showed it to the DS. 'Who were you talking to?'

'Some friends,' he answered deadpan and with a deadpan look on his face to match.

'Could you tell me their names, please?'

'It doesn't matter.' Hamilton walked over to his red Toyota, opened the boot and threw in the small holdall he was carrying.

'Then you won't mind telling me.'

'I've had enough hassle from you coppers today, find out yourselves.' He got in the car and drove off.

'No seatbelt.' Meredith commented drily.

'Yeah. Let's let him think he's won this round though. You follow up on the number plate, I'm going to do some research on the findings in Elliott's tox report.'

'Off to see Penfold?' She sounded cheerful, friendly, and supportive.

Tony had to get away. 'I'll take the car, you get those two to drop you back at the station. I'll text you the details of some students you need to go and interview.' He pointed to a panda car, 30 yards away, in which the uniformed PC driver was reading a newspaper. And without waiting for a response, he walked the other way towards the black Golf. There was no sound from her, and he didn't turn to look back.

Despite sending Acting DC Meredith back in the panda car, Tony also stopped at the police station to pick up the toxicology report that had come back from the Home Office labs at Wetherby. Whilst Gerard had had the preliminary basics done at the hospital, this was the official report that could be used in evidence, and it went into much more depth. Although he had sent Penfold an anonymised copy of this report, Milburn had not had time to go through it himself. He tried his best to read it on the way to Penfold's Hartlepool home, but after some swerving and lapsed concentration on the road ahead, he gave up and accepted that it would have to wait until he arrived.

Penfold lived in a rambling old Victorian house on a small square beside the beach at Seaton Carew, just south of Hartlepool itself. As Milburn walked up to the front door, the small front garden had a dripping surfboard cast aside on the grass. Tony hadn't even thought about the sea as he'd driven down the beachfront road. He stepped back from the front door to get a view past the Norton Hotel and over to the sea. He still couldn't see the actual breakers as the tide was in and the promenade was about 20 metres above the beach, so it blocked his view of the water's edge. It sounded like there were some waves, but the majority of the sea surface was only rippling slightly - this was not a day Penfold would refer to as "barrelling".

There was a chilly wind, so he quickly stepped back up to the front door, keen to get out of the cold as soon as possible. Although Penfold insisted that Tony need not knock but could just walk in, his sense that an Englishman's home was his castle did not permit him to do so. Tony compromised with knocking, pausing and then opening the door slightly to call in to his host.

'In the kitchen,' Penfold called back. He stepped in and closed the door behind. The doorway was on a hall corner, and Penfold breezed past him, depositing a mug of steaming black coffee in Milburn's hand. Tony looked at it, glad of the warmth, but perturbed that after all these years, Penfold still would not buy milk and make coffee to his guests' liking. It was black or nothing. Nonetheless, as they moved along the hall to Penfold's office, the heat enticed him to try a sip of the tar-like drink. It was boiling hot, so worked well to warm him, but put Tony out of action for concentrating on anything else for a few seconds as he wrestled with the pain in his mouth and throat.

Penfold sat back in his brown leather wingback chair and crossed his legs so that one ankle rested on his knee. His coffee cup was hugged to his chest in the manner of a hot water bottle. Tony sat in the other chair and looked over to his friend. From the still wet hair and the clue in the front garden, detective Milburn assumed that Penfold had just come back in from surfing. The bronzed kiwi was wearing his usual uniform of baggy shorts and long-sleeved T-shirt. The winter chill was apparent in the house, although muted in comparison with the outdoors, but enough to make Penfold's clothing seem inadequate to Tony who still wore his coat and scarf. Surely the cup of coffee could not be enough to beat back the cold?

'Right, we've got the full tox report now. They've confirmed the hospital's finding in Elliott's blood: alcohol, traces of Somnulone, and a lot of Priapra.'

'Yes. I've done some preliminary research about Priapra, and I'm not sure how much we're going to be able to work out for certain. It's not clear what a standard dose would be, or how much is too much, or indeed if there even is a too much.'

'Well, I've seen the exploded penis first hand, and I'd say Elliott had too much.'

'Touché, so to speak. What I'm getting at is that there are no recorded cases of overdose from it. At least not that were attributed to Priapra. Often users will take other things with it: coke, or ketamine or whatever, and the ensuing heart attack is always put down as an overdose of the historically better-known drug. Also, the Priapra is not often there in any significant quantity anyway – it's still quite expensive, as a designer drug. Judging by this,' Penfold pointed at a section in the toxicology report he had resting in his still wet lap, 'this guy appears to have had the equivalent of about 30 pills in his system.'

Milburn leaned forward and pointed to the next section on the same page in the report. 'And look here, he doesn't appear to be a regular user at all. No trace in the two months of hair growth that his shaggy ginger mop represented.'

'Hmm, curiouser and curiouser. Normally when using a drug for the first time, or at least as an infrequent user, a person's going to be a bit careful with the dosage. I suppose he could have been off his face already, and not really aware of the amount he was taking. What else was he on...?' Penfold flicked pages back and forth in the thin folder.

'A little alcohol, but he wouldn't have been drunk. And Somnulone, but I don't think that affects your mind, it's just a sort of steroid. In fact, it puts you to sleep. Although, maybe there's some funny reaction between them that knocks your block off? Or perhaps it was bravado, sort of showing off to his partner that he was going to give her a really good time? I dunno.' Simultaneously with this last phrase, Tony shrugged.

'Well, there is always the Ecstasy aspect to it. Ravers usually say they intend to get "off their tits" so it's quite possible that after one or two of these he didn't know what he was doing. Again, the information out there doesn't really suggest how dosage compares with ordinary Ecstasy.'

'So Priapra is a mix of Ecstasy and Viagra, is that right?'

'Yes and no. It's not just a blend of the two drugs, which then separately work on the body. The active ingredient is actually a combination molecule, with the MDMA active part on one end and Viagra's active part on the other end. Very clever chemistry. And by all accounts very good. Works for women as well as men. Keeps you going for hours and hours, and loving every moment.'

'Until the moment when the pod went pop.' Tony sang a little snippet from a song, although he had no idea where he knew it from. 'Thing is, this is a young man, by all accounts a womaniser – he shouldn't need this drug. And he obviously doesn't use it much, presumably because he doesn't need it. So why take so much this time?'

'Well, there is also the question mark over injecting it. There is no mention of intravenous use that I've found, it is always referred to as being a pill. And that's not something you can easily confuse. "Oops, I put my Priapra in the hypodermic instead of my Somnulone." Not going to happen, as you'd need to crush the pills and dissolve them. Was there any evidence of that kind of activity?'

'Apart from the old syringe in the bin, there was no drug paraphernalia at all. Nor any further stash either. It was as if the drugs fairy had been, and just brought enough to kill him and nothing else. There weren't even any alcohol containers in the rubbish.'

'Really? That does seem odd. I assume you guys checked the wheelie bins?'

'Communal dumpsters, unfortunately, serving 45 flats. The scene examiners took one look and told me to forget it. Now you ask, actually, it wasn't clear whether they were telling me there was no way they could be arsed to sift through everything in the three dumpsters and the recycling bins, or if they meant there was no forensic point in it.'

'Too late now anyway, I'm sure.' Penfold closed up the folder and passed it to Milburn. He pulled the chest of his shirt out and let it fall back, in an action that made it appear as if he was too hot.

Tony passed the folder back explaining that it was Penfold's copy and that he had his own. Given that it was the only thing he had brought with him, Milburn found it a bit odd that Penfold should not realise. In turn, Penfold explained that he guessed as much, but knew what Hardwick would think of him having a copy of the official Home Office Toxicology Report. Tony agreed that a defence lawyer would undoubtedly have a field day with this procedural mismanagement.

Strictly speaking, the police were allowed to consult with anybody about anything, and Penfold's involvement could not prejudice the investigation. However, experience told Milburn that a jury were unlikely to understand the difference, and the CPS were always at pains to emphasise that this kind of consultation was rarely acceptable unless some complex case required input from an expert of some sort. The detective had on at least a couple of previous occasions lost the argument that polymath Penfold was an expert in all matters, and thus was suitably qualified to be consulted in any case. The fact that Penfold did not charge a penny, let alone a ludicrous fee, put paid to any expert credibility. However, he knew the score, and the return of the folder was merely a gesture. Tony left it on a coffee table beside his brown leather chair, and proceeded to further break protocol by debriefing Penfold on all the interview information they had gleaned thus far.

After going over the various people that had been established as players in Hamish Elliott's life, an uncomfortable pause developed in their conversation. Tony realised that Penfold was deliberately minimising his responses. He paused for a moment to work out what his kiwi friend was up to. He thought through the last five minutes of chitchat, and realised that he had been repeating himself. There were only so many times that Penfold needed to be told that Pieter Hamilton was not a nice person.

He continued reviewing what had been said and, after a further moment's pause, it dawned on Tony that he was avoiding leaving. His next step that afternoon would have to be a debrief with Meredith as to what she had found out from the students that Kathy had suggested they interview. The idea juxtaposed Diane and Kathy in a way that made Tony shudder.

Penfold remained silent, allowing his friend to fully work out his thoughts without distraction. In the end, they both just nodded to each other, and Tony stood up. Penfold's departing comment was that he would keep Milburn informed as to what Trident and Mantoro came up with. This threw the detective sergeant, as he had not been expecting them to work on anything. Indeed, Penfold had not mentioned his sister, Trident, in several months. Milburn did not argue or question, but only managed to come out with a confused "OK".

Meredith was waiting for Milburn when he came back. She was noticeably doing very little, having parked herself at an empty desk in the open plan CID office space. She almost leapt up to follow Tony into his office, offering up what she had discovered at the university that lunchtime.

Milburn was highly relieved that Kathy had not been needed as an intermediary to the students she had found for them to talk to. He expected that the order of events would certainly have been different if that had been the case, as he would have had to assign Diane to some other task and interview them himself. However, the women had been happy enough for the police to call on them without any moral support, so here was Meredith making it clear to Milburn that he could not adequately pursue any investigation without her immutable talents.

There were a couple of other detectives at their desks, so Milburn felt that he and Meredith should be able to pursue a professional discussion without any untoward overtones which might cause him to over-react, as long as the office door remained open. That didn't stop him from sweating profusely as she sat opposite him and flicked her notebook back and forth, preparing what to tell him. He leant back, opened his own notebook to take down anything useful and looked at her without speaking.

'Ok, first up, Jamie Glister.' Her speech was bright and bubbly, as if she were telling him the story of a day at the beach. 'First team wicket-keeper for the uni women's cricket team. Not a good word to say about any of the men that coach her. At first I would have said lesbian, but she was so scathing that I actually think they weren't interested in her, and that's riled her. She's quite a large girl, and the story keeps coming back that the cricketers only go for the girls that look like models.' Milburn squirmed inwardly. His first thought was that there was no need for Diane to prattle on with such gossip when there was a murder to be investigated. 'So Jamie couldn't tell me anything first hand about the men in bed, or the drugs they might use, but she was quick to sully them with general talk of professional cricket being filled with doping.'

'Look, did anybody tell us anything that was useful?'

'Right, yes, sorry. Sally Oldbury was next. She is your classic posh student. Long blonde hair, skinny, and something of a batsman apparently. Demure, she is not though. She was very quick to tell of how she had bedded both the County players that coached the university women's team. Not at the same time. Well, actually, she didn't say not, but her stories were about different occasions. It seems she did a lot of flirting with them, asking them to show her how to swing the bat properly, so they had to physically embrace her, and she made sure there was a lot of touching. Sally was really proud of her conquests.'

'So what did she actually tell us?'

'She slept with both Elliott and Hamilton. She said in both cases they were good in bed, although Hamilton was a bit rougher than she had wanted. Certainly, she reckoned that neither of them had taken drugs in her presence, or talked about them. And she also reckoned that neither would have needed anything like Viagra. I did try to be as vague about what I was asking about as possible.'

'Hmm, OK well done. What about the third one? Jill Jones, wasn't it?'

'She prefers to be called Jilly, and is also your classic Durham student. I had to go out to her stables to meet her!' This stereotype was so perfect that both Milburn and Meredith laughed. He was still smiling, picturing another blonde in jodhpurs and a riding hat talking from horseback, as Diane continued, 'She was a bit more difficult to get talking about sex and drugs...'

'What about rock 'n' roll?' Tony interrupted.

Diane smiled, dipped her head slightly, and went on. 'I talked to her for some considerable time about what they did at training and what she and the other players thought of the coaches. It is a consistently held view that the men were always rather arrogant, just showing off really, and not especially interested in actually coaching them to improve their cricket. But, in the end, I managed to get Jilly to talk about her out of hours encounters with Hamish and Pieter, and she also went for a drink with Jim Harris.'

'Really? Do tell.'

'Yes, Jilly tells a most interesting set of stories. Jim was a very nice bloke – she used the word sweet. But just not confident enough. He didn't bowl her over...'

Again, Tony interrupted, 'Oh, very funny.'

Again, Meredith did not directly respond to this, but gave him the head nod and another smile. 'I think it was just that Harris wasn't pushy enough. I think the others made a point of being arrogant and swaggering around, and that pushed Jilly's buttons so she slept with them but not with Harris.'

'I wonder how that made him feel, knowing that he wasn't getting the women that his team-mates seemed to bed with ease.'

'Yes, I got the impression that Jilly went out with every coach that the County Cricket Club sent over. Although we only actually confirmed that she'd slept with Elliott and Hamilton. Anyway, she said the same about their not needing any sex drugs. However, she did say that Elliott had on one occasion talked to her about a new steroid that was untraceable in doping tests, and his being quite excited about how this was going to change sports forever. She didn't know any more about it, and couldn't remember what he had called it.'

'OK. Must be Somnulone, but not much to go on there really.'

'She did say though that he had said he could get it from one of his team-mates.'

'Ooh, now that does change things. She's the first one who has put performance-enhancing drugs as definitely going on in this cricket club. Anything else.'

'Not from them, but I did the PNC check on that car we saw Hamilton talking to in the car park at the Riverside.'

72

'And?'

Meredith proceeded to explain that the BMW belonged to yet another posh blonde-haired student, Kate Withenshaw; and that she had already been to interview her. This was a breakthrough. This was the Kate that Jim Harris had been referring to when DI Barnes and Tony had first interviewed him at Elliott's flat.

She readily admitted to it, and was keen to let it be known that she had slept with Hamish on the evening he died. Miss Withenshaw claimed that she did not often stay the whole night and that this had been the case the previous Thursday. She was a second year English Literature student at the university and not a cricketer. She had met Hamish through Pieter. Her housemate and Pieter were friends and it had been him, Daniel Ramsbotham, who had been driving the BMW that morning in Chester-le-Street.

Milburn was surprised that Meredith had managed to conduct so many interviews in only the time it took him to go to Penfold's and back. She pointed out that Durham is a small city and that two of the student households she had visited had been in adjacent streets.

The detective sergeant suggested that they should go and interview Kate Withenshaw further, as she may well have been the last to see Elliott alive. Meredith pouted at him, and paused long enough so that he looked up into her face. As soon as their eyes met, she continued to explain that she had plenty more yet to tell him. This time it was Tony who smiled, apologetically in this case, and gave the slight head nod.

Mr Ramsbotham had not been at home when Diane interviewed Kate, but she offered him as her alibi, claiming that she had arrived home by 11pm and that they had sat up talking and drinking until three or four in the morning. Diane described Kate as extremely skinny and very fashion conscious, and always a little distracted. However, there was a major difference between her and the others in that Kate claimed to have been Hamish Elliott's girlfriend, rather than a one-night stand. She also claimed that he had used many recreational drugs with her, including Viagra.

At the mention of Viagra, Tony interjected, 'That's not true, the toxicology of his hair shows no drug use in the last two months at least.' His tone was more accusatory than he intended, as if he were talking directly to Kate Withenshaw. Again, Diane pouted at him, and he held up his hand to say sorry.

To accept his apology, the acting DC leant forward a little more over the desk between them. Tony also leant forward, so their heads were only a foot apart. She continued, 'No, and I took care to confirm with her that she did mean Viagra. In fact, I asked her to list all the drugs they had taken together. Just about everything you can imagine was in her answer: Cocaine, Ecstasy, marijuana, LSD, and she said Viagra again by name. Interestingly, she did not mention any intravenous drugs, or Priapra, or any performance enhancers. And I mean *sports* performance enhancers.' They both grinned.

'That is odd. She's admitting to doing drugs with him, but we know he hadn't taken any. So, she's lying, unless he just pretended to take them. And, in particular, she's claiming he took Viagra, but his other partners all said he didn't.'

'Full-time girlfriend should know him better. Maybe he didn't take it often, but she was with him on the occasions he did. She seemed like a nice girl. A bit of an airhead, but she's no killer.'

Milburn said, 'No, the tox report says he never took it at all. Or at least in the last two months. I think we'd better get hold of this Daniel Ramsbotham to check out the alibi and, if he's friends with Hamilton, that's a good excuse to talk to him again too. I wonder if somebody was jealous of Mr Elliott.'

'I'm going with sexual jealousy by Jim Harris. Sounds like such a wet lettuce; no wonder he never got any action.'

'The killer wet lettuce.' They both laughed.

'Honey, I'm home.' Tony often called this to Kathy when he arrived back from work. It was satire that they both found amusing. In a paradoxical way, it was their own little catchphrase. Sometimes, she would put on an apron and give herself a dusting of flour to join in the cliché. It was after nine o' clock that Saturday night, so Kathy just looked up at him from watching the television. She pressed the remote control and turned it off, an action that would not have occurred to Tony had the positions been reversed.

He sat down beside her and pulled his tie off. She gave him a small kiss on the cheek and he lay his head back against the sofa cushion and sighed deeply. An end of the day exhale that said, "I'm ready to lie here all evening until it's time for bed." She gave him a moment and then asked what he had found out from the lady cricketers she had recommended.

When he explained that Diane Meredith had gone to do the interviews, her hand became stiff, like a statue's, in his. He gave it a gentle squeeze of reassurance and told her how useful their information had been. Kathy was stuck with concern at

Meredith's presence though. She had been under the impression that the two would never have to work together again. Tony's explanation that she was standing in for Godolphin Barnes at Hardwick's insistence did not ease Kathy. She was now sitting quite upright staring at him.

Tony maintained the tuckered-out pose he had originally struck, and tried to respond to all her questions as nonchalantly as possible. He kept emphasising the amount of time they had spent working separately. He explained the long discussion with Gerard, along with the trip to Penfold's house, and the way they had interviewed different people throughout their time at the cricket training session. He particularly dwelled on the way he had sent her back to the station in the panda car, so that they did not have to be in the car together. Tony made no mention of the debriefing session he had had with Meredith just before coming home.

Kathy was silent for a few moments, trying to work out how she felt about Tony working with the Crazy Cow again. She decided that Tony knew what she was like now, and so his judgement would just have to be trusted. With that decision, Kathy drew a deep breath and dived in to telling him about the additional information she had wrangled from students that afternoon. 'I asked quite a few other people about what went on with drugs in Durham University. It's amazing what students are happy to blab about.'

Tony smiled at her and said, 'You're a naturally trustworthy person.'

'Yes, well, actually some did decline, probably as even a librarian can be an authority figure in the university, so they maybe didn't want to take any chances. Anyway, it seems that all students are doing just about every drug there is and you can buy just about anything you want.'

'Yes, Meredith seemed to find a similar story with the cricketers she interviewed.'

Kathy looked sideways at Tony who still hadn't moved his head from the fully reclined position he had taken up. 'Ok, I didn't write down anybody's name, so you won't be able to follow any of this up directly – that was part of the deal for them talking to me.'

'Did you do any work today?' He had meant this to sound humorous, but didn't manage to hit the right tone of voice, so in the end it sounded rather schoolmasterly, and again made Kathy pause. 'It's probably best that way anyway – if you had turned up anything, we'd be in all sorts of procedural problems.' The fact that Tony kept his head laid back looking at the ceiling meant that he missed Kathy's scowl.

'Look, do you want this information or not?'

'Yes, of course, sorry.' Tony still did not move his head – he had now closed his eyes – but gave Kathy's hand a squeeze.

'Well, some of the sportspeople had heard of Somnulone. In fact, two of the rugby players stopped the discussion at the mention of it. And one of the male cricketers vehemently denied ever having taken it, but gave me the name of a guy you can buy it from here in Durham.'

Tony sat up and looked at her. Then he stopped for a moment before asking, 'How exactly did anonymous questions, that were supposedly just out of your interest, end up naming names?'

A smile flickered at the edges of Kathy's mouth. 'Well, you know, we were just having a friendly chat about drugs in

Durham and I acted all innocent saying "you know I had no idea they were so easy to get hold of. Where do you get them?" and he just blathered on with names of dealers for all sorts of things. I didn't have time to write them all down, but I did get the one for Somnulone.' She looked down at her notepad, a finger tracing down the lines until it stopped at the steroid. 'Um, a guy called Peter Hamilton, apparently.'

Tony grabbed the notepad to look at the entry himself and simultaneously burst out, 'You're shitting me.' He leant right back again, looked at the ceiling and laughed out loud. 'Diane will never believe this.' He looked back at the list again. 'I don't suppose you're going to tell me that he also deals Priapra round town?'

Kathy was a bit nonplussed by his responses, although she guessed that he must know of Hamilton. 'Well, not from that cricketer, but a couple of people mentioned it – they say it's amazing.' She stroked his hand slowly. 'I don't suppose you can pinch any from the evidence room and we can try it one night?'

Tony was distracted with imaginings of the South African peddling white powder to girls at school gates. He completely missed her answer, and her romantic overtones, and followed up, 'Tell me he deals Priapra as well.'

'Who? Hamilton? No, nobody I spoke to said so, they said some total rah was the man for Priapra.' Kathy stared quizzically at her partner who was still gazing at the ceiling in wonder. 'But then Durham uni is full of total rahs.' Durham University has such a large sub-group of undergraduate students from wealthy backgrounds that they have developed their own group nickname – the rahs. Kathy made the point that, in this town, this would not be an identifying feature of the suspect.

'She will not believe this. You're a star; a superstar.'

The compliment failed to ease Kathy. She could not remember Tony getting so distracted by his work since the Case of the Drunken Fifty Pound Notes. Deciding that he needed a reminder about where his priorities lay, Kathy proposed, 'How about we have an early night and I recharge your batteries a bit.' She slowly stroked his thigh and made such a doe-eyed look that it was utterly clear what she meant. Kathy had a strong libido, but this was unusually forward for her.

Tony looked at her a little bewildered, wondering why she was so often up for sex when he was exhausted with a big case on his mind. Not wanting to look a gift horse in the mouth though, he replied, 'You've talked me into it.' They kissed passionately.

That first kiss on the sofa was the best of it. Once their lips parted, they got up from the sofa and walked up the stairs to their bedroom. Tony began undressing himself, and Kathy did likewise. She thought of interrupting him to keep up the romance and passion, but she was a little embarrassed once he had started himself. They did not speak, and Kathy felt more and more awkward. When she was dressed only in her underwear, she tried as subtly as possible to suck in her tummy and push out her chest. She came over to him with a slight hip sway, but was rebuffed even before she reached him. 'Aren't you going to take these off?' Tony gesticulated his hand up and down, indicating her bra and knickers. He was smiling and she took it to mean that he was keen to cut to the chase. As she finished undressing, he climbed into the bed and lay on his back in the middle.

'I hope you're going on top – I'm pooped!' Again, he was smiling, albeit weakly. She pulled back the duvet and climbed onto the bed at his feet. She moved up over the top of him, and started to kiss his chest. It was a solid chest: not pumped-up pecs from heaven, but a nice firm real man's chest. She had always appreciated that look, and Tony personified it well. Manly, but not body builder perfection that might burst at any moment. Solid and reassuring.

She went to kiss his nipple, but felt Tony's hands grip around her buttocks and heave her up to sitting astride his penis. He barely had enough of an erection for them to begin intercourse, but she felt him push it in as best he could. She put her hands on his chest and began to move a little at a time. His cock became harder and, after a few tentative movements, she was able to get a rhythm going. The sex was mechanical. They both knew each other's movements, and had fucked this way a hundred times before.

She knew that Tony would want her to come, and she knew that she would not. Kathy was not one for faking orgasms, but she wanted Tony to remember how great their relationship was so, as she felt his hands tighten on her hips, she dutifully made the sorts of sounds that would confirm she had been satisfied. Nothing over the top – too much noise would be just as unconvincing as too little. They stopped moving and he still had the inscrutable wan smile that she couldn't quite get a handle on. She lay down beside him and watched his face. Tony closed his eyes and the smile was gone.

Sunday 24th March

Kathy was again working at the university library on Sunday morning and had three callbacks from Saturday for her drugs chats: students who had been willing to help but did not have the time on Saturday afternoon. Tony had been up early, preparing to go straight to the station, but Kathy had sat him down and forced breakfast upon him. She convinced him to go along to the library with her, chiefly in order to keep him away from Meredith.

Whilst the friendly librarian spoke to students about their drugs habits in an office, her boyfriend, the detective, listened from the store cupboard with the door propped open just a couple of inches. Kathy loved the clandestine approach – she told him she almost felt like a spy. And best of all, Tony was shut in a cupboard where the Crazy Cow could never find him. Just as she was thinking through how she would have to go to Hardwick to protest that she shouldn't have to monitor Tony's movements, the first student arrived to talk to her.

Kathy was using her boss's office for the interviews, although it was little more than a desk and two chairs in a small rectangular room. The wall facing the rest of the library was all smoked glass, and Kathy closed the vertical blinds as well to offer more privacy. The door to the small store cupboard was opposite the entrance door, and they had wedged it into place, with a pile of books stacked to look casually left on the floor. They took care to also position the students' chair and Tony's chair so that there was no chance of his being seen.

Daria had big, brown, curly hair with a large, black, knitted hat perched precariously on top. She smiled at Kathy with full lips, and dumped her full bag on the floor beside the chair as she sat down. Her open, green, sackcloth bag had books and files and sheets of paper overflowing from it. It was as if her bag had been to the same wild hairdresser as Daria.

She had little new information to impart. However, she went totally off the deep end when it came to discussing Priapra. It had made such an impact on her that she was completely uninhibited about explaining to Kathy the improvements in her sex life. The day before, Kathy would have felt that this was a useful part of her research, to learn why the students use the drugs that they do. Now though, she was very uncomfortable with betraying the poor young woman's trust. Kathy could just picture Tony chortling behind the door. Daria left and Kathy looked into the cupboard. Tony had his notebook on his knee and said, 'Names, I need dealers' names.'

'Look, I can only go there if the situation is right. If it flows naturally so that it makes sense, I'll ask. But I'm not just gonna jump in with both feet and give the game away. And betray their trust at the same time.' Tony scowled and Kathy went back out to collect the next interviewee.

'OK, John, if you sit there, I'll be writing a few things on my notepad, but like I told you before, your name won't be anywhere on it, and there won't be any way to identify you.

And, in fact, we're not interested in individual answers, I'm just trying to build up an overall picture of drug use within the university. We're looking for patterns that the university authorities could use to improve our support services for students generally.'

'No, worries, my parents know I smoke pot, anyway.'

Kathy was becoming more and more used to the apparent disregard that the students had for the law and their health. She wanted to believe it was just an arrogant upper class thing, but knew that there were many just as damaging behaviours amongst working class people.

She took a long look at the fresh-faced cricketer in front of her, and asked the first question from her list. There were a number of introductory facts to find like age and degree course, before she moved into the question of bodily chemical abuse. The first step was a brief discussion of alcohol consumption. Even the answers to this had astounded her at first, but the story had been so consistent across the twenty or so interviews she had conducted, that John's claims of drinking over 40 alcohol units – the equivalent of four bottles of wine – in a sitting no longer surprised her. In his cupboard, Tony kept looking at his watch. He knew Kathy's modus operandi did require a slow build-up to the important questions, but he was desperate to get to the station and tell Diane that they were going to pick up Hamilton for questioning.

Kathy moved on to the question of drugs in sport.

'Absolutely rife,' John admitted with gusto.

'Sorry, did you say "rife"?'

'Yes, all sorts of performance enhancers, pain killers, illegal steroids.'

Tony was listening intently, Kathy paused slightly, and then asked, 'So, are there any sports in particular? I know you're a cricketer.'

'Hardly. I only play college cricket now. I lasted about three months in the university set-up and they said I wasn't going to make it, so I could make up the numbers or leave. They meant leave, but were trying to sound nice about it.' Durham University has an extensive but relatively low level intra-mural sports system that John had descended to, and Kathy could see disappointment in his eyes. 'I was one of the best in the Devon and Cornwall leagues when I was at school, but this place is a different world. Partly, they're just better than me – you know most of the university team have contracts with the big county clubs – but also there's virtually no policing of the doping in student sport. So, if you're prepared to damage your health you can get those big contracts.'

'Can you name any of the drugs being used?'

'Anything and everything you might imagine: nandrolone, human growth hormone, Somnulone.'

'I don't even know what those are, I take it they make you faster or stronger or something?' Kathy knew more than she let on, but not in any great depth.

'Yeah, they mostly build up your muscles. Like you say, stronger and faster. They tend to mess up your body in other ways though. So there's short term gain but the lifelong damage is crazy.' He sounded like a poster boy for an anti-drugs campaign. Kathy wondered how he reconciled his arguments about steroid abuse with the ludicrous alcohol consumption he had claimed.

'OK, where would I go if I wanted some of one of those, let's say the last one, the s-one?'

'Somnulone?' The young blond man crinkled his nose, looked at the ceiling and continued, 'Well, I only really know about cricket. There's talk that the players that come from Durham County to coach the uni ladies can sort you out. There's a South African guy, don't know his name, but anyone who wanted some would probably just need to go along and watch the ladies training to find the right person. That is just the rumour, mind you, I've never actually bought any.'

'No, of course not. I was really just wondering how easy it might be to source these things here in Durham. Now, I'm also asking about recreational drug use. You OK to talk about that?'

'Yes, although I don't really do drugs, so I may not be any use.'

'That's what we call "a nil result" and is just as useful. If nobody is using drugs then the university can save money to not campaign against them, and focus more on anti-alcohol education.' Kathy cursed herself inwardly for having been unable to resist this dig at her interviewee. However, she immediately spotted a chance to continue in the direction she knew Tony wanted. 'Or put resources into sexual health resources. For example, we're hearing about a new sex drug, at least I think it's new, Priapra.' A flash in John's eyes told Kathy he was familiar with it, but she couldn't tell if it was knowledge or personal experience. 'You ever hear of that one?'

The young man nodded. 'Yeah, I've used that a few times. My girlfriend loves it.'

In his cramped space, Tony tried to shift forward silently in order to hear better. There wasn't much light for him to make notes, so he hoped Kathy would go straight for the kill.

'Yes, everybody who's mentioned it has raved about it. Do lots of people take it?' Kathy knew where she was going and was deliberately building up slowly. Tony, though, felt like tearing his hair out, the suspense killing him.

'Sure. I know some people who won't take it, but it's just Viagra and Ecstasy and both have been scientifically proven to have no long-term effects on the body. So, quite a lot of students are into it.'

Kathy had to shift in her seat slightly in order to distract herself from arguing with him about the scientific evidence surrounding Ecstasy. In the cupboard, Tony knew how this would push her buttons, and tensed slightly in anticipation of what might come next. She maintained her line though. 'OK, so if I wanted to get hold of some of those pills, what do I do?'

'Most colleges, maybe all of them I don't know, will have somebody selling them. At thirty quid each, there's quite a lot of money to be made. And they usually bump up sales by doing two for £50 – a sort of couples deal.'

'And where would those guys get their supply from?'

John frowned slightly, and then shrugged. 'No idea.'

Kathy looked at her watch and made a show of not having realised the time. 'Oh, sorry, John, we'll have to stop there. Thank you ever so much, and remember, all your answers are totally anonymous and confidential.'

'Cool, see you later.' John sauntered out as casually as if he had just been telling her about a movie he had seen.

Tony emerged from the listening closet and gave Kathy a quick kiss. 'Nice one, that's gotta be Hamilton. We'll go and pick him up right now.' Whether he meant "we" as the police in general, or he and Diane specifically, troubled Kathy.

'He was lying.'

'What? Why do you say that?'

'He was convincing himself that the reason he didn't make it in the team was because the rest were cheating. I don't think he really cared what I thought; it was all for his own benefit. He claimed to avoid sports doping because of the health issues but contradicted that with taking pot, alcohol and Priapra. I wouldn't be surprised if none of it were true.'

'Hmm. Priapra is more expensive than he said. At least Penfold reckoned it has a designer price tag. But he couldn't have just picked "South African" out of the air as part of his bullshit, when we've already got Pieter Hamilton as a significant person here.'

Kathy shrugged. 'There were probably kernels of truth in there but, from his evidence, I'd guess that drugs in student sport are present but not "rife". Now, don't forget that you arranged with Penfold to go and see him this morning.'

Tony had forgotten the appointment he had arranged and was more inclined to go and pick up Meredith so they could interview Pieter Hamilton together. However, when he phoned Penfold to postpone, his pal was eager to see him to impart some research findings.

DS Milburn was talking on his mobile as he walked back from the library to his car. He tilted his head back and closed his blue eyes, soaking up the sun. The bright light was reflecting from the grey hair at his temples, which would have perturbed him if there was a mirror to hand. He was about to ask Penfold to just give the details over the phone, when he remembered that the county cricket club had a Sunday afternoon training session. This would probably be an easier time and place to catch up with Hamilton, as he would definitely be in a known location at a fixed time. Tony sent Diane a text message about Hamilton and stated that he would pick her up at 2pm.

Sunday morning in early March was not usually a time for many people to go to the beach in Hartlepool. Milburn was thus surprised that he could not find a parking space within a hundred yards of Penfold's house. The late morning sun was bright and surprisingly warm, but even that could not have brought this many people out.

As Tony walked back along the promenade from the place he had finally parked, a man in a tailcoat peered out from the threshold of the main door to the Norton Hotel. The big ochre-coloured cube of a building sat overlooking the sea, on the northeast corner of the grass square in which Penfold's house hid in the northwest corner. Milburn guessed that the cars must belong to a brave wedding party: it looked like the bride and groom had gambled on a cheaper winter wedding date, and won. Tony was wearing a very smart trouser and blazer combination, with a military-style green and red striped tie. He would not have been at all out of place attending a wedding.

'Milburn!' As Tony was walking the last few yards away from the beach road back towards Penfold's house, a shout came from behind. He swivelled and saw a wet, black, rubber man following him. Whilst Penfold wiped back his dripping mop of blond hair with one hand, the other kept a firm grip on the surfboard under his arm. From the back end of the board, Milburn could see a long blue leash trailing on the ground, as if Penfold had a very skinny tail. He was grinning brightly, a white smile the pinnacle atop the black stretch of wetsuit.

Tony followed his friend into the sandstone block house. The gloomy interior was something of a contrast to the bright sunshine outside, but the temperature changed little as they moved indoors. In the kitchen, Tony sat down at the country-style dining table, just in from the hall door.

Penfold leant against the much darker, oak counter at the other end of the room and peeled the wetsuit from his legs, finally leaving it as a watery rubber puddle. This done, he turned and poured coffee for both of them from a filter machine which must have been set brewing before he went out to the surf. Penfold, bronzed and naked, barring a pair of black swimming trunks, placed both mugs on the table and disappeared through the door at the far end of the kitchen, dripping saltwater continuously.

Milburn perused the drink he had been given. Strong and black, as usual. He barely had to time to begin an internal monologue on the distastefulness of the coffee, and the inconsiderate host Penfold was when it came to coffee, before the man himself re-entered the room wearing boardshorts and a sky blue sweatshirt. The shorts were knee-length and colourful, a rainbow sunburst design exploding up the left leg.

The detective picked up both cups and followed the surfer back along the hallway and into his crowded office. Mantoro was already in the room, working at one of the computer screens. As the other men entered, he minimised the window he had been working on, stood up and moved out of the way towards the end of the rectangular room. He stepped behind Penfold's big armchair and, with his squat stature, this left only his head and shoulders visible. Mantoro had very big hair. The Latin American Afro was now silhouetted against the bright light from the tall window in the end wall.

Penfold positioned himself on the office chair just vacated, and joked with Mantoro about how nice and warm the seat remained. Mantoro nodded and grinned, but said nothing – he had already started munching on some cashew nuts from a saucer in his stubby hand.

'Hi, Penfold,' a woman's voice distracted Tony from his staring at Mantoro's shadowy form. He looked at the workstation. There were two monitors in front of Penfold and the left hand one, which had been blank, now contained an animated manga-style cartoon face of a pretty young woman. The face then continued speaking to Penfold, 'I've found out quite a bit about the chemistry of the two drugs we're interested in.'

Tony frowned in confusion. 'Is this some sort of automated research programme?' he asked.

Penfold looked up at him with a little frown of his own. His face then opened up and he brightly answered, 'Oh, sorry, Milburn, meet Trident.' He waved his hand back and forth between Tony and the monitor. 'Trident, this is Detective Sergeant Tony Milburn. Sorry, I thought you guys had met.'

The animated face grinned and said, 'Just because you tell me all about somebody, that is not the same as meeting them. Remember about human interaction?' Her tone implied that she was referring to some previous conversation, and was also said in a way that only a sister could get away with.

Tony had heard from Penfold of his sister, Trident, the super-hacker, but they had never met. He had seen her in a car with Penfold once, but not been introduced. The view through the car's windscreen had not been great, but from that vague memory he supposed that the cartoon avatar on screen could well look like the passenger in that car. But the image spoke in real time, it was like a perfect cartoon. Tony was astounded that the animation could be produced so quickly, but also knew that the marvels of computing were always far ahead of his imaginings.

'Human interaction,' Penfold spluttered as the coffee mug had just left his lips, although it was clear that he was over-acting. 'Hark at the cartoonized girl who never leaves her house.'

'Brother dearest, I would swear at you, but there are gentlemen present.'

Penfold looked up at Tony, smiling. 'Rest assured you have been spared the filthiest mouth on any kiwi rouseabout.'

Trident's voice went up an octave in mock offence. 'Rousie? Why you little....' The animated face screen now also included a fist being waved at Penfold. 'Wait till I get my hands on you, I'll give you a shearing.' The in-jokes had now lost Milburn but he didn't want to interrupt – it was rare to see Penfold in a somewhat unguarded atmosphere, and Tony wanted to make the most of the chance to learn a little more about his friend's personal life.

'Right, then, my little shed sweeper, tell us what you've found out – Milburn here is investigating a murder which seems to involve both Priapra and Somnulone. Tell us all about them.'

'We don't know it's murder. Could still be accidental or even suicide. At the moment, it's just a suspicious death.'

Penfold continued facing Trident on screen. 'And he still thinks it might not be murder.'

'I can't tell you if it's murder or not, but these two drugs together is no coincidence. They are strongly connected and you are likely to find them cropping up together often.'

The DS interjected, 'Why is that then? They seem to be drugs from such different worlds. Performance enhancement in sports is not often going to have a crossover with nightclub sex drugs. Surely their only real connection is that they're both illegal?'

Tony was standing a little to the side of Penfold, and Trident's image turned to the point where half her face moved off the screen. 'I can't quite see you, Mr Milburn, but the answer is not in their consumption, but more in their production and transportation.'

Tony stepped closer to Penfold's side, and Trident followed so that she was now fully on the monitor again. 'Do call me Tony,' he said. 'What do you mean?' He looked at the seated form, Penfold never called him by anything other than his surname.

'OK, Tony,' she said, testing the sound of the word. 'I think it is simply pure good fortune for the drug smugglers, but these two have a weird chemistry when melted together. At the right temperature, their molecules intertwine to produce a plastic quite like polyurethane. If you then bubble air through this during cooling, it solidifies as a strong, dense foam.'

'Often smuggled as the padding in lifejackets; it's as good as the real thing and doesn't dissolve in water.' Mantoro's voice was deep and gravelly, and his strong American accent always threw Milburn.

Trident chimed back in, 'Yes, and the combined smell is very different from each separate drug, which means you have to train sniffer dogs differently.'

'It's too expensive to sell to life jacket manufacturers, but perfect for smugglers. I heard of one guy on a boat that was scuttled by the US Navy: when they picked him up, he sat in the brig for 14 hours wearing his life jacket, cool as you like, and finally handed it over to his rather dodgy lawyer when they landed in San Diego. Paid all his legal expenses and then some.' Mantoro always had a story for every criminal enterprise.

'When you finally want to get the two drugs back, dissolve in acetone and fractionally distil the mixture and they are easily separated with little more than school laboratory equipment.' Trident concluded her research contribution.

Penfold swivelled and looked up at Milburn. 'So, keep your eyes open for lifejackets and chemistry sets, being used by over-muscled rugby players and priapic clubbers.' Tony smiled and nodded. 'Thanks a lot, Trident, we'll let you get back to collecting those shearings now.'

'Up yours.' With that sign-off, Trident's image disappeared.

'Now for my little bit,' Penfold said facing the standing detective and crossed his legs, holding the mug of coffee to his chest. '

'Your little bit?'

'Yes, you mentioned that Kathy was interviewing some students to help with information about dealers for these drugs.'

'Yeah, I was at the library with her this morning. We found out bits and pieces, mostly just corroborating background info, but Pieter Hamilton's name cropped up often enough to warrant more questioning.'

'Pieter Hamilton?' Mantoro interrupted, with a tone of voice that suggested he knew of Hamilton.

'Yes,' Tony replied struggling to look at the silhouette against the brightness of the window. Mantoro added nothing further.

Penfold continued, 'OK, good enough, but do take care not to confuse student sport with the real thing. A contact of mine was recently President of British Universities and College Sport. He put me in touch with current President. Now both of them told me basically the same story – and I reckon they were being genuine – that student sport, at least at domestic competition level, does not really have any problems with doping. They are signed up to the World Anti-Doping Agency although that only really kicks in for international competitions. Nonetheless, they both reckoned that it wasn't a big issue in any sport here. Zero failed tests to date.'

'That's bullshit,' Milburn retorted. 'I heard a lad this morning tell Kathy that doping in student sport is rife. He actually used the word "rife".'

'No personal axe to grind?'

The detective was astounded. How could Penfold have guessed that they were not totally convinced by the college cricketer's doping claims. He stuttered slightly, 'Um, possibly, but he wasn't the only one to mention Pieter.' Milburn was sufficiently off kilter from Penfold's question, that he glossed over the fact that the student had not mentioned Hamilton by name. 'Meredith and I are going to go and check him out now. I'm convinced he's the dealer.'

'Good to have leads, but don't close your mind though.'

Tony exploded, 'I know how to do my bloody job.'

Penfold put up his hands, palms facing his pal. 'Woah, Milburn, of course you do, I'm not suggesting otherwise. But we all need friendly reminders from time to time.'

'Some more than others, in your book,' Milburn answered.

'Not at all. Look, forget it. Tell me how things are going with Meredith.'

Tony's brain was already in a whirl, being angry. This question was so unexpected that he stopped thinking and just blurted out an answer. 'Great, actually. I'd forgotten how good she is at police work.' Penfold eyed Milburn. In his smart blazer and tie, he looked all set to go to an afternoon service at church. But Penfold could see confusion behind his eyes.

'Hmm. Well, I was going to ask if I could come along with you when you interview Hamilton? You're going to do it at the cricket ground aren't you?'

'I'm sorry, you know what a stickler Hardwick is for procedure. He'd go off it if he knew.'

'Right, well I'll tell you my ulterior motive then. I'm sure Kathy will be anxious about you working with Meredith again. I wanted to come along, observe you and Meredith working together, so that I could call her later and tell her not to worry.'

'What would Diane be worried about?'

95

Penfold cocked his head a few degrees to one side, and calmly said, 'I meant I would call Kathy to reassure *her*.' He paused for a moment. 'I'm sure it would make things easier for you at home; just trying to help.' Tony considered this, and before he concluded anything, Penfold continued, 'I believe the cricket training sessions are open to the public aren't they? So Hardwick would not be able to complain.' Milburn nodded with a glum look, and without speaking waved for Penfold to follow him as he walked out towards the front door.

Penfold didn't get out of Milburn's Golf when they pulled into the police station's rear car park in Durham City. The DS stopped at the terrace built for unloading prisoners and left the car running. He walked briskly into the custody suite door, and vanished from view. He and Acting DC Diane Meredith returned a few minutes later, both smiling but not speaking. As she was now working for CID, Meredith wore a dark trouser suit. The white blouse was very tightly fitted, and with a couple of buttons undone, she displayed an incredible cleavage. It was the sort of figure that women would pay plastic surgeons heavily for. Penfold mused to himself that the suit's charcoal colour was a poor choice given the chocolate brown colour of her hair. As the two exited the door, the smiles disappeared and they got into the car in silence, Meredith forced, by Penfold's presence, to sit in the back.

On the journey to Chester-le-Street, there was no talking for several minutes. When he broke the conversational seal, Penfold's New Zealand accent was stronger than usual. 'How are you getting on, standing in for old Bludger Barnes?'

He hadn't turned to look at Diane, and she tipped her dark brown bob to the side to see what she possibly could of his face; it was blank. After a moment, she looked Tony in the eyes in the rear-view mirror and replied, 'I'm loving it. Can't wait to join CID properly. I actually feel like I'm doing something useful, rather than just shovelling shit from one place to another.'

'Milburn certainly seems to think you're doing a good job, so far.' As he said this, Penfold looked slightly sideways at Tony's grey left temple. Tony shifted slightly in his seat, but did not look back at Penfold, or in the mirror.

Meredith paused, gave a swish of the perfect hair, and smiled. 'I suppose that'll be because I'm enjoying the work.' She paused again. 'Why are you coming with us?'

'Well, you may be doing a good job, but I know Milburn here is always only ever half pai.' Penfold turned again, his wavy blond hair rubbing the fabric roof of the little German car. His sergeant friend's face crinkled in a grin.

But his constable retorted, 'What do you mean?'

'Oh, sorry, it's a Maori expression meaning "not good enough".'

'I know that. But Tony's an exceptional detective, so what are you talking about?' Penfold's expression remained expressionless.

DS Milburn, effectively the boss in the car, shifted in his seat again and blurted out, 'He's joking.' Their friendship was familiar to Meredith – she already knew this.

'Or am I?' Penfold's tone was so ironic that he was obviously concurring with Tony.

She continued with a harsh voice, 'Well you should be, I've never known such a good poliss,' and added sarcastically, 'Oh, sorry, that's English slang for a policeman.'

'I think you'll find it's only *north-east* English slang,' the tall man replied sharply almost before Meredith had finished. Again, the DS shifted his body in the seat, but still did not speak. Anybody watching would have thought Milburn had something uncomfortable in his pants.

There was silence in the car for a further few minutes. As they turned into the car park in front of the Riverside cricket ground, Penfold looked at Milburn and asked, 'How are we going to do this, then?'

Before he could answer, ADC Meredith jumped in. 'The police will interview suspects, and members of the public can watch the cricket training. Preferably from the car.'

Penfold did not move his gaze from Tony, who switched off the ignition, pulled on the handbrake, and looked back at the surfer. His face was fearful. He did not turn all the way to look at Diane. She leant forward in the gap between the front seats and instructed, 'Tell him, Tony.'

'Like I said at your house, you will have to simply observe,' Tony croaked.

Penfold resisted the urge to say, 'simply to observe,' and instead pushed both lips forward, then turned to get out of the car. They all walked into the open gate that led to the nets practice area. Vivender Pathan was instantly recognisable, standing aside the four lines of bowlers waiting their turn. Penfold stopped and allowed the two police officers to walk together over to Coach Pathan. Several bowlers watched them approach and this caught the coach's eye. He turned and stepped forward to intercept them away from his players.

The detective sergeant held both hands up with palms facing Pathan. 'We only need to speak to Mr Hamilton, is he here?'

The Indian pointed into the new brick building adjacent to the training area. 'He's just finished his batting session, he'll be in the changing rooms.'

At that moment, Pieter opened the door and exited the building, carrying an old pair of leg pads over his arm. He saw the police presence, but ignored it and walked to the end of the small changing block and out of sight around the back. Having waited at the gate threshold, Penfold had a better angle to see around the building and watched the South African drop the battered pads into a dumpster. Everything at the Riverside was new, and even the dumpster looked clean and fresh in its bright blue plastic.

Milburn and Meredith set off walking after Hamilton, but it was only a few seconds before he was walking back again, so they intercepted him and the three continued back inside the building. Penfold quietly retrieved the discarded leg pads and took them back to Milburn's car. They were well marked with red patches where fast cricket balls had obviously struck. They seemed a bit thin and weak in the face of what he could see being bowled in the nets. "Old age enfeebles us all," he reflected to himself, pressing on one of the red circles.

Inside, the detective and the acting detective were trying to ask Pieter some probing questions without giving away that they didn't have much in the way of actual evidence regarding him. The cricketer was seated on a bench in the changing room, with a chaos of bags and clothing scattered all around the room. There were no other people and the two police officers stood.

When presented with the fact that his name had been put forward by several witnesses, in connection with the sale of performance-enhancing drugs, he shook his blond head and said, 'Not any more.' This was a revelation that was unexpected. Milburn had thought he would stick to flat denials. Hamilton followed up by explaining that he was censured at university for dealing Somnulone. He further explained most of what Milburn already knew as to how it acts as a sleeping muscle builder with virtually no trace remaining during waking hours, thus making it very difficult for the doping tests to catch it. He said he could have kicked himself for getting caught selling it, as that's the only way one could get caught.

Meredith was incredulous that the university authorities did effectively nothing. No report to the police, and they allowed Hamilton to continue playing. He beamed broadly with the claim that they could not let their star bowler go. He had had to show appropriate remorse to the right people, and insist that it would never happen again, and it was all quietly brushed under the carpet.

He rubbed a hand through his short-cropped blond hair, and continued with an explanation of how the risks just weren't worth it as a professional. No carpets to get swept under, and he had the career salary to think of. Indeed, the salary was good enough that there was no longer a financial imperative to make money illicitly. Milburn had been making notes throughout, and at this point showed his notes to Diane. At the bottom, underneath the note that Hamilton was no longer dealing, he had written 'SMALL TRUTH TO HIDE BIG LIE?' She looked in his eyes and nodded slowly.

DS Milburn turned back to Hamilton, and pointed out that these drugs inquiries had come out of investigations into Hamish Elliott's death. Hamilton looked at the beige non-slip-tiled floor and grated a sentence in Afrikaans. It sounded like he was cursing, but Milburn cautioned himself inwardly that Afrikaans always sounded like cursing.

The interviewee looked up at each of his interrogators and re-iterated the position. He was insistent that he had not been involved, and had no knowledge of the murder, although he freely admitted he did not have an alibi. Neither detective spoke when Pieter finished, a classic interview trick. The silence causes social discomfort, and the suspect feels the need to fill that void with further speech, often giving something away.

Hamilton did break the silence. He told them to interview Aisha Pathan. Although she might be a charming, pretty slip of a thing, Pieter claimed that she was both heartbroken and jealous, and had been known to fly into a rage. DS Milburn thanked Hamilton for the suggestion, and pointed out that they were still not investigating a murder, Elliott's death was officially only "suspicious". He realised that they still had not managed to catch up with Aisha, and that he and Meredith should do so straight away. Telling her so in front of Hamilton was Tony's way to make Hamilton believe that they were convinced by his stories.

Returning outside to the training session, Milburn found Penfold being given a practical batting lesson by Vivender Pathan. Penfold had a box strapped on over his shorts, and his leg pads looked like they had been put on by a child –

inexpertly. For the first time since they had known each other, Tony thought the surfer looked unsure of things. Not out of his depth exactly, but not the confidence-oozing natural.

The Durham County players were continuing with their practice, paying little attention to Penfold and their head coach. The bowling and batting coaches were buzzing around the nets, watching and commenting on each ball bowled. Pathan was lobbing very slow balls up for Penfold, who was managing to miss everything.

Milburn smiled and stood still to watch. Meredith stood beside him with her arms folded. Finally, Penfold hit a ball, and it went very hard towards the crowd of players. Good fortune put the ball into the side of one of the practice net areas, stopping it there and leaving the cowering cricketers to straighten up and pretend they had not been in the least bit concerned for their safety.

A fast moving hard ball is an occupational hazard in the sport. Being wary of it is not really much cause for a dented ego, but competitive young men are always vying to be the alpha male. More than a couple had stolen glances at the pretty female detective and her plunging neckline. Chests were puffed out all round, and the practising batsmen were swinging much more wildly than they normally would.

The next ball to Penfold had a bit more spin on it, and as it passed more quickly, the bat only made it down to the vertical by the time the ball was pinging against the metal stumps behind him. Penfold looked up with a sheepish grin, thanked Pathan and started to remove all the padding. Something made Milburn feel uncomfortable. Beside him, Diane was smiling broadly, revelling in Penfold's undoing, but Tony knew that this was not the source of his niggling feeling.

He scanned all the people around the training area. The half dozen public spectators sat idly in the adjacent grandstand, looking over the side rail to the nets area, bemused at Pathan and Penfold. The players and the other coaches continued as before, now paying no attention to the New Zealander's first cricket lesson.

And then he saw it. In the third net along, a very young player Tony did not recognise was congratulated by the batting coach for seemingly missing the ball as it went past. The boy had swung his bat forward into the side of his leg pad and maintained that steady position as the ball went past. A quite classical defensive cricket stroke well executed. It was exactly the position Penfold had finished up in when his wicket was taken. Tony realised that Penfold's whole lesson had been a ruse.

As they walked back towards the car, Milburn asked, 'So, what was that all about?'

'I was trying to get a bit of an insight into Pathan, see what sort of a man he was.'

Meredith looked back and forth between the two men and commented, 'Getting taken to the cleaners more like.'

Penfold shook his head slightly. 'I'd reckon that an Indian international cricketer ought to be able to bowl me out, even if he was a wicket-keeper.'

'How do you know he was a wicket-keeper?' she questioned immediately.

'We had a bit of a chat whilst you two were inside.'

'But why the pretence at knowing nothing about cricket?' Milburn asked his friend, at which Acting DC Meredith stopped dead in her tracks.

'If I'd known about cricket, I wouldn't have been given a lesson, and so it allowed me to get more out of him – he's not your killer.'

After a couple more paces, the two men stopped as well and looked back at Diane who had folded her arms again and was pouting slightly. The brown bob of hair framed her face perfectly, and her figure was proportioned in a way that made men want to hold it. Penfold and Milburn both took in how beautiful she was. The phrase "black widow" went through Penfold's mind, whilst Tony harked back to Kathy's nom de guerre for her: "Crazy Cow". At this point though, she was more concerned with the apparent slight that she had not been told Penfold was acting. It was more of a concern to her than his claim that Pathan was innocent.

Tony decided it best not to give her the attention, and looked back to Penfold. 'How do you know? And in any case, we still can't say it's murder.'

'Well then, he didn't murder your guy who wasn't murdered.'

The shorter man smiled and said, 'Alright, tell me.'

'Well, quite apart from his dinner date alibi with Jim Harris, which will obviously need verifying, he's a devout Hindu. It would contradict his approach to life.'

Meredith stepped into the space between them. 'Well, that'll stand up in court – he's not the type your honour.'

'I didn't say he wasn't the type, I said *he's* not your man.'

'And why should it be a man?'

Penfold rolled his eyes to the sky and walked around the black police Golf.

The sergeant stood at the driver's door for a moment, looking at the handle and then looked up again. 'Actually, she's right, whilst we're here we should check his alibi with his wife – they only live across the road here. If I remember correctly, he claimed he got home about 11pm after dropping Harris off.'

Penfold added, 'He said that Aisha is at home now, so you could speak to her too.'

'And when were you going to share that titbit of information with us?' She did not wait for him to answer but turned to walk over to the houses across from the cricket ground. Tony joined her and Penfold climbed into the car.

The Pathan's house was newly built, as part of the same development that built the cricket ground itself. It was a large executive home, fit for an ex-International cricketer and his family, neat and well appointed.

Aisha opened the door, and Milburn had to make a conscious effort to stop his jaw dropping. She was truly stunning. He could sense Meredith bristling and went through the introductions. Aisha was petite, with long dark hair, which shone in the light. Her hair was the colour of black coffee, her skin was tea with milk. She wore black jeans and a red silky shirt, buttoned up to its round collar.

Aisha was a model of politeness and invited them into a front room, which was maintained purely for hosting important guests. The room was painted as many new build houses in a simple cream colour. It reminded Tony of his own new house. The bay window looked out onto a quiet road, which led into the housing estate directly from a mini roundabout, across which Tony could see his car and Penfold bent over fiddling with something in the open hatchback. Sumptuous, thick, red and gold curtains were held back from the window with golden ropes. It looked like a mini theatre stage. The rest of the room was furnished following the red and gold theme, and the two police officers sat on one of the two sofas that were upholstered in a blood red fabric. Aisha sat on the other facing them.

'I'm sorry, my father is not at home – he's at a training session at the club.'

'Yes, we spoke to him a few minutes ago. We need to confirm his movements on Thursday night. Just a formality, you understand.'

'I'm sorry, I was at the university till very late that night, and my mother is out crashing the car again in Sainsbury's car park.' Tony did a double-take at this. The last thing he had expected from a demure daughter was sarcasm about her parents.

ADC Meredith jumped in. 'That's OK, we need to talk to you as well. Can anyone confirm your alibi for that night?' Milburn stared at his colleague. The word "alibi" was sufficiently accusatory that it would put both innocent and guilty on the defensive in equal measure. It was avoided where possible. Diane was giving Aisha a hard stare, but it seemed to pass her by entirely.

'Um, well no, sorry. I was in the Economics department library until about 1am and then came home. When my mother comes back, you can check with her about that, but I was alone at the department, so I can't prove anything, I'm afraid.'

Milburn tried to soften things up a little, with his knowledge of Kathy's workplace. 'Surely your campus card will be recorded entering and leaving the library?'

'No, sorry, it's the department's own small library. It's reference only and works on an honour system. Good students can get their own key for it. There'll be no record I was there. I don't think they have CCTV.'

'And you're a good student are you?' Meredith's tone was unforgiving.

Aisha gently pushed her hair back, so that she could look straight at the policewoman and say, 'I have my own key.'

'Doesn't sound very scholarly,' Diane emphasised the word "scholarly", 'having to work till the small hours, failed to plan your time properly? Or had other things been taking up all your time?'

The younger woman's face remained in control and passive at all times. 'Constable…'

'Detective Constable.' Meredith interrupted.

Tony found her manner unnecessarily badgering, even rude. He weighed in here to try and keep her in check a little. '*Acting* Detective Constable.' They glared at each other, whilst Aisha's innocent face looked from one to the other.

She settled on Diane and continued, 'Acting Detective Constable, I would say that working in the department library through the night was the mark of a scholar. I am sufficiently interested in my subject that I spend long hours of private study diversifying my knowledge and deepening my understanding.'

'Is it not true that you had been spending much time with Hamish Elliott before his death?'

Tears could be seen brimming in Aisha's dark brown eyes, but her facial expression remained controlled. 'Hamish was such a sweet man. We spent some time together, yes, but only well organised events, my father would not allow anything else. And certainly not to the detriment of my studies.'

'So you claim you weren't sleeping with him?'

Aisha looked shocked. 'Of course not. He was very nice, but my father would never allow me to go out with a non-Indian. And we don't believe in sex before marriage.'

'Sorry, "we"? Elliott would bed anyone who didn't run away fast enough.'

Tears now escaped her eyes and trickled slowly down the perfectly smooth skin of Aisha's cheeks. Her voice became tremulous. 'I meant my family.'

'And they decide who you sleep with, do they?'

The DS again glared at his ADC, but Meredith ignored him, remaining focussed on her weeping suspect. The young woman looked to Milburn but, as his face was turned, she answered, with restraint in her voice, 'Family life for Hindus is not the same as for the English. We value the support and guidance of our elders, and understand the importance of these values in building strong communities.'

Tony was itching in his clothes. He wanted this to end. 'Sorry to upset you, Miss Pathan, we are trying to find out what happened to Hamish, and death is never a pleasant subject.' The room was silent. In this case, Tony was the uncomfortable one who broke the silence. 'How did you get home that night? We might be able to spot your car on street CCTV.'

'I don't have a car. I caught a taxi from the market place. It was pretty busy, but you might be able to make me out on the cameras. I would have been there a few minutes after 1am.'

Thursday nights in Durham City are often as busy as Friday and Saturday, so Milburn expected that she would not be easy to find amongst the hordes criss-crossing the market square, moving from pubs to clubs, at that time. He stood up and replied, 'Many thanks for your time, we'll let you know if we need any more information.' Diane was staring intently at Aisha, until Tony touched her shoulder. She looked up at him and smiled.

As they headed back towards the car, which now had the boot closed again, he demanded, 'What was all that about?'

'Sorry, what do you mean?'

'You were a bit rough on her, weren't you?'

'Well, my dear, as soon she opened the door, I knew I was going to have to be the bad cop.'

'There's good cop, bad cop, and there's asking questions of a woman whose boyfriend just died.'

'Who may have murdered her boyfriend you mean.'

'Look, softly, softly, catchy monkey in this game. Good cop, bad cop is good for the interview room, but in detective work if we put their guard up at a first meeting, they may go and destroy evidence.'

Diane stopped walking and put her hand on Tony's arm. He stopped, too, and, as they faced each other, nobody spoke for a long pause. She finally said, 'I'm sorry, Tony. I really do appreciate all you can teach me about CID work. I so want to make it work, this is what I've dreamed about since I joined up.' Tony's closed mouth smiled slightly, and he gave her a little nod.

They got into the car, and Penfold asked how the meeting with Aisha had gone. Milburn handed him his notebook so Penfold could read through the information. Before starting on it though, Penfold looked across to the driver's seat, and reminded Tony that it would be a useful interview to arrange to meet Daniel Ramsbotham in the presence of Pieter Hamilton. They might give something away if forced into weaving a tangled web together. Milburn nodded and started the car. Penfold had skimmed the notes before they even left the cricket club car park. At the point where the detective's scribblings told of Pieter Hamilton suggesting they interview Aisha, he had annotated the little page with the statement 'NOT A CRIME OF RAGE'.

Monday 25th March

Milburn leaned back on his black padded chair and opened the large brown envelope. The crime scene investigators' report about Hamish Elliot's flat had finally arrived. Their office would claim that they rushed it through, as they don't work on weekends. Milburn couldn't believe that they had taken so long to type up just over four pages of notes. The flat had been locked from the inside, but only on the drop latch, so that wouldn't confirm suicide; it was a lock that could be set by a murderer on leaving the premises. No other point of forced entry, although that didn't surprise him, with the flat being on the third floor.

The young bachelor had apparently not been one for much in the way of regularly cleaning, as the place had been littered with DNA – hairs mostly – from many different people. In this situation, the scene examiners concentrated on what could be found near the body in the bedroom.

The forensic evidence confirmed the presence of Jim Harris. 'Well done, lads, how did you work that one out?' Tony mocked out loud, although he was alone in the CID office he normally shared with another detective sergeant.

111

Three hairs had been found in the bed, all from females. One was already on the DNA database: Kate Withenshaw, the blonde from the BMW. Milburn looked her up on his desk computer. She had been reported to the police for cannabis use by Exeter Girls High School. A police caution and an expulsion later, and somehow she still ended up at Durham University. She had already confirmed the occasional overnight stay at Elliott's flat, so this evidence didn't advance the investigations. He wrote on a notepad that he should send Meredith out to collect DNA from all the other females connected to the dead bowler. This triggered a connection in his mind, and he added to the note for her to confirm Kate Withenshaw's alibi with Daniel Ramsbotham. Tony rubbed his chin and mused that he wouldn't trust the alibi's veracity, but all boxes had to be ticked if a case was ever to be successful in court.

The scene examiners' report continued with mention of the only message on Elliott's answering machine. There was a USB memory stick in the report envelope with an audio copy of the message on it. After plugging the stick in and wrestling with his computer's anti-virus messages, he made the message play, suddenly filling the quiet office with a loud, formal voice. The message was from a representative of the National Anti-Doping Panel regarding an appointment on Friday 22nd March at the cricketer's training session.

Tony leaned back in his chair and put his feet up on a low filing cabinet beside his desk, thinking. Had Jim Harris picked up his friend as planned, the dead man would have had to undertake a drugs test. The detective put his hands behind his head and looked at the ceiling, contemplating how this news fitted in with the other aspects of the case. It could potentially have been a motive for suicide. However, Tony reminded himself that, barring the drugs in his system from Thursday night, the toxicology report had confirmed he was drug-free for the previous two months. So, the phone message was unlikely to have contributed to a suicide. But there was no telling the timeline for listening to the message. If he had ever listened to it. Milburn exhaled deeply. He did not seem to be able to get any information that actually confirmed anything.

Acting DC Diane Meredith breezed into the office and closed the door behind her. She looked stunning. She wore a close fitting knee-length dark skirt, and a cream blouse, which was very flatteringly cut around her bosom. Her short, straight hair bobbed around as she moved, whilst her big brown eyes fixed on his. Any man would be taken by the sight, and Tony Milburn was only a man. She smiled at him and, after leaning towards him from the far side of the desk to see what he was reading, she sat in the seat opposite him. Milburn was wrestling with his eyes to stop them looking at her cleavage, and did not speak. She smiled engagingly and, with a little nod towards the report folder asked, 'Anything helpful?'

Tony had to look at the report himself to remember what it was that she was asking about. 'Yes and no,' he summed up. 'Three female hairs. One was Kate Withenshaw – she got a drugs caution at school you know – and the others unidentified. He had an appointment for a sports doping test scheduled for last Friday. And that's as far as I've read so far.'

'OK, we'll have to get DNA samples from all the other females that we know of. I've made a list of supposed conquests.'

'Um, right, let's see what else there is.' He scanned further down the same page. 'Ah. Did I tell you how we found a syringe in the bin in his bedroom? Empty, looked used.'

'Yes. What was in it?'

'Well, no Priapra but definitely Somnulone. But better than that is a partial print on the plunger top. And not from Hamish. Not yet identified, mind, but could be a clincher if we can get a suspect.'

'Anyone who we identify as matching a hair is worth a test.'

'Aye. I guess Kate Withenshaw is the place to start. And we still haven't gotten hold of that boyfriend of hers to check her alibi. What was his name again?'

'Daniel Ramsbotham, although I wouldn't trust much in what the two of them say.'

The two detectives looked at each other, both thinking through points of the investigation. Tony looked briefly down to the report on his desk and then back to Diane's face. 'Penfold reckoned we should check on what Ramsbotham and that South African know of each other. He seems to think there's a connection there.'

Meredith gave a slight sneer. 'Sounds like a shot in the dark to me.'

Tony nodded a little, his grey temple on the right side catching the sunlight coming in the window behind him. 'They were talking in the car park. We don't have anything conclusive at the moment, so we'll need something random to make a connection I reckon.'

'Bit of faith, Tony. Come on, with you and me on the case, the killer doesn't stand a chance.' Her face became a

114

gigantic smile, all perfect white teeth and happiness. She looked like a gleeful child. Tony couldn't help himself but to join in the smiling. 'What do you say we go and collect some DNA samples and alibis right now?'

He didn't answer, and they both stood up together and walked out of the office still beaming. As they passed Sergeant Bainbridge on the front desk of the city's main police station, the smiles persisted. Baz Bainbridge was a huge beast of a copper: six foot four and very close-cut hair. He stared at the two of them as they walked out, light as air and good-humoured. He shook his head, remembering the day he had had to physically carry Tony into the custody suite to keep him from assaulting Meredith.

The house that Kate Withenshaw shared with Daniel Ramsbotham and two other women was a five-minute walk from the police station, but nobody was home. Milburn and Meredith were suddenly lost by this unexpected situation. Tony pulled his phone out, more in the hope that it would inspire him than to actually make a call. In his jacket pocket he also came across the business card Vivender Pathan had given him. It had surprised Milburn that a cricket coach would have a business card at all, but he quickly dialled the mobile phone number on the card. His partner asked what he was doing, but he just held up a forefinger to silence her.

'Mr Pathan, it's DS Milburn here.' He paused as Vivender greeted him. 'We need a sample of Aisha's DNA to eliminate her from our inquiries. Could you bring her to the station in Durham City right now please.' Tony's request was brief and deliberately forceful. The Indian briefly protested that he was on his way to a training session, but Tony quickly quashed this.

115

It was lucky that, in fact, Vivender was in his car with Aisha at the time. The father was keen to show the world that his daughter was not what rumours claimed, so it was easy for him to acquiesce to the detective's request.

During Tony's call, Diane made a radio request back to the station, and as he hung up, she suggested they go to Jilly Jones house. It was two streets over from Kate's house, so would barely increase their return walk time. A blonde with large pearl earrings and a blue padded riding jacket opened the door. She had tight black leggings on and thickly padded suede boots. 'Miss Jones, I'm Detective Sergeant Milburn from Durham Police, and I believe you've met ADC Meredith?'

She turned back into the old house. 'Jilly, it's for you.'

Tony looked to Diane quizzically. She smiled at him. 'They all look the bloody same,' he muttered.

A doppelganger of the first woman came to the door. This one had a blue cashmere sweater and no boots on, but otherwise they could have been the same person. Meredith jumped in from behind her boss, 'Hello again, Jilly. This is my partner, DS Tony Milburn. We've got a bit further with the death of Hamish Elliott, but that means we'd like to ask you for a DNA sample, so we can eliminate you from the enquiries.'

Her blue eyes scanned Tony up and down and then they moved back to Diane. She shrugged and replied, 'OK, what do I need to do?'

Milburn stepped back and to the side so Meredith could come forward and take the lead. She had pulled a cheek swab kit from her jacket pocket. 'Well, if we can come inside, the first thing I need is for you to rinse your mouth with a glass of water.'

They followed Jilly down the long hallway to the tiny kitchen extension at the back of the house. Most student houses in Durham followed a typical format of modernised Victorian terraced house. The original two up two down construction was split into a bedroom and lounge downstairs, and the two upstairs had usually been turned into three bedrooms and a bathroom. And, finally, an extension into the small yard housed the kitchen.

Jilly's was no different to all the others that the police officers had had cause to visit over the years, despite the tenants' seeming high breeding. Diane was loath to put the DNA envelope down anywhere in the dirty kitchen and in the end took a clean plate from the drying rack for it to lie on. 'OK, this is called a Buccal Sample. There are two cotton buds that we need you to swab inside each cheek for about a minute on each side.' Jilly started on this process and the ADC filled in some of the case details on the envelope. Each was sealed in a separate little pouch with a bar code sticker placed across the seal. 'Right, now if you can put your name and date of birth in the places on the stickers there, then sign them both, and then choose one to keep for yourself.'

Whilst she was struggling to write on the sticker, on the cotton bud stick, on the plate, the woman asked, 'What do I need one for?'

Tony replied, 'The law says we have to give you one of the samples. Don't open it, and if you ever need to check, or dispute, the DNA evidence we get from our one, you have your own as a backup. If you break the sticker seal, you won't be able to rely on yours as evidence. The DNA on the swab is guaranteed to survive for 2 years at room temperature, so just keep the sample somewhere safe.'

Jilly frowned at this response. 'I thought you wanted to eliminate me?'

Diane came back into the conversation, 'Yes, of course. We work on the basis that you didn't commit any crime, and this may confirm that.' She held up the swab pouch. 'If it turns out you have done something wrong then, of course, nothing can eliminate you.' The student shrugged and nodded, and they all headed back to the front door.

As Milburn and Meredith walked in through the front door of Durham City Police station, Baz Bainbridge was carefully explaining to Vivender Pathan that they would be with him soon, and he was sorry, but waiting was their only option. The squat Indian, in a navy polo shirt and tracksuit trousers had both hands on the counter top, and was looking high up through the glass shield to the towering sergeant's round face. Tony took over.

'Ah, Mr Pathan, Aisha, so sorry for the delay, please come through. Sergeant Bainbridge, we'll be in Meeting Room 2 if that's free, is it?' Baz just nodded as he watched Meredith's broad smile follow the other three through a door from the reception area. The four sat down around the table in the small room, police on one side, suspects on the other. Vivender was not much taller than his daughter, but she was as petite as he was stocky. Meredith and Milburn by contrast were both taller than both of the Pathans, but much more similarly built. They sat like a Battenberg cake, with each man opposite a lady.

The detectives remained silent, and Pathan began. 'Please, Mr Milburn, what is all this. My daughter was friendly with

Hamish, we have told you this, but that was all. Aisha was not involved with his death.'

'How about you?' Meredith interrupted. Milburn closed his eyes for a moment. When he re-opened them, he found Vivender looking diagonally across at him.

'What is this? You tell me to bring Aisha in for DNA, and then you accuse me, and we've already told you where we were on Thursday. This is the sort of thing I might expect from the Indian police but in England you are supposed to have honour. Where is British justice?'

Tony held up a flat hand and said, 'Yes.' He paused for a moment. 'The investigators searching the crime scene found hairs from some people that we haven't yet identified. We'd like a DNA sample from Aisha to confirm that they are not hers, and this will help towards proving her alibi.'

Aisha turned sharply to look at her father, but he had another bee in his bonnet now. 'How can you believe me but not my daughter? Why don't you want to test my DNA as well? I have been to his flat before, but Aisha never has. You have already decided she is the one.'

Meredith jumped in, 'The hairs were found in his bed, Mr Pathan, did you ever sleep with Mr Elliott?'

He turned back to Diane, incredulous. 'What is this? Do you people hate Indians?'

Again Tony put up his pacification hand. 'Sorry, sir, we are not out to imply anything. What my colleague is trying to get across is that the scientists have already determined that the hairs are all from females. We know Aisha and Hamish were friends, so we must confirm that she was not in his flat in order to move our investigations on to other people.'

119

Silence descended on the room for many seconds, Aisha looking at the side of her father's face throughout, whilst Vivender looked back and forth between the detective sergeant and acting DC. Finally, Diane looked aside to her boss, who nodded. She pulled another Buccal sample kit from her jacket and laid it on the table in front of her.

Tony looked to the daughter, who had shrunk even smaller than normal. 'So, Aisha, will you give us a sample of cheek cells please?' Her face remained pointed to her father, but her eyes flicked to Tony for a moment and then back to Vivender. He was staring at the swab packet on the table and his eyes looked as if they had glazed over. Without turning her head back, Aisha nodded slowly.

As Meredith's smooth fingers manipulated the pouches and cotton buds, explaining the process, the father was completely mesmerised by the movements. He did not speak or look away from the small white envelopes until they were pushed over to his daughter for her signature. At that moment, he got up and left the room. Aisha wrote quickly, picked up one envelope, and chased out after him.

The detectives both stood up and moved around the table to the door. Tony picked up the remaining sample, and they were then face to face at the door. 'I know I said good cop, bad cop in the interview room, but you're still too confrontational. A less civilised suspect would probably have punched you.'

'I can handle myself, Tony, you know that,' she countered smiling. She put her hand on his shoulder and continued, 'Sorry I didn't follow the script you might have been expecting, but we got exactly the outcome we wanted.'

120

He couldn't help but smile back at her, asking rhetorically, 'we did?'

'Of course, the trusted old routine: good cop, bad girl!' At this, she thrust her chest forward slightly so that her cleavage was emphasised, and gave it a little shake. Diane started giggling and after a moment or two Tony joined in.

In the corridor they were met by a young PC with a note for Meredith. She looked at it, and explained to Milburn that she had asked them to find out from the university where Kate Withenshaw could be found that day. Assuming she turned up, Kate was scheduled to have a lecture in the Elvet building directly opposite the police station. Tony quipped that it was lucky she studied English and not science, so they didn't have to walk all of ten minutes to the University science site.

Outside, the sun was shining, and both police officers were smiling quietly as they crossed into the humanities lecture building to find room ER141. They had to wait fifteen minutes before the lecture finished, and each took up a position beside one of the two exits.

Miss Withenshaw's blonde hair was distinct, even before Diane made her out in the crowd of students leaving the lecture theatre. The group of English Literature students were predominantly well-groomed, but Kate's hair only attempted the same well-coiffured look – it did not achieve it. When she spotted Meredith, the young woman attempted to sneak past amongst a crowd of other students.

Diane gave a withering snort to herself, and followed the crowd outside, radioing Milburn to join her. In the sunshine at the bottom of the building's steps, she grabbed Kate by the arm. 'Hello again. We need a bit of a chat, if you wouldn't mind coming across the road with us.' She released her grip on the arm, and indicated the police station with a wave of her hand.

Kate put a hand to her hair, which was partly falling out of the thick band that held it in place. 'Oh, I'd really love to, but I'm desperately late for an appointment. Sorry, I must go. I'll come this afternoon, I'll have more time then.'

'Sorry, Miss Withenshaw, but we need to speak to you now,' Tony countered.

She started to move her skinny legs in small steps away up the street, still looking at Meredith. 'No, look it's not convenient. I must go.' She turned away and increased the length of her strides. Looking at Milburn, Diane put her fingers to her own eyes and pushed them wide open. He nodded, and they quickstepped to catch up with her, walking one on each side.

'Perhaps we can just walk with you a little. What appointment is it, we could let them know you'll be late?'

'Oh, no, I can't miss it. It's a business meeting.'

'Really, I thought you were studying English, do you have a business on the side?' Diane continued the conversation, sounding interested and sincere.

'Oh, yes, I'm going to set up an online fashion store. Daniel's got these great contacts in London to supply big name clothes, and we're going to sell them to Durham students. There's a lot of demand for good fashions here you know. Daniel's going to do all the website stuff and deal with the suppliers, and I'm going to do the advertising and deliver things around Durham. I'm going to start with a fashion show – that's what my meeting is about. Daniel and I are going to sort out all the details.'

'Your meeting is with Daniel Ramsbotham?'

'Yes, he knows all sorts about business. You know he's already set up two companies of his own. I'm going to be the fashion side of things: of course he doesn't know so much about that. We make a great team, and we should be able to make quite a bit of money. Not that Daniel needs money, you know his dad runs a bank in the City. Anyway, I must get off to the meeting, so I'll see you later.'

She tried to increase her pace, but the detectives kept up with her, and Milburn replied, 'Sorry, Kate, but Daniel will have to wait. We need your help now.' This time, he grabbed her by the arm and pulled the group to a stop. She strained at his grip, but only slightly, not expectant of getting away. 'You'll have to come with us now. Don't worry, it'll only take about half an hour.'

She remained silent, looking back and forth between the other two faces. He led them back along the street beside the police station and through the gate into the rear car park, opposite the Court Inn pub. Only when in the car park did Tony release her wrist. He opened the rear door of his black car and indicated her to get in. When the door closed, Meredith looked across the car roof to him with a quizzical look. 'I've got a sneaky idea,' he grinned. 'Just go along with it.' Diane grinned too and shook her head a little, just enough to swish the brown bob of hair back and forth across her small features.

They got in the front seats of the car and turned to look at Kate in the back. 'Now, Kate, this is going to be a bit difficult, but we really need your help. Hamish Elliott had no family within 200 miles, so we need a friend to identify his body. As

123

far as we can tell, you were his best friend, so we're asking you to do it.'

Without a pause, Diane joined in, 'Please help us, Kate. We can't close the investigation unless we have a positive id on the body.' Her eyes were beseeching.

Kate looked slightly stunned. She thought for a second or two. 'Is that up at the hospital?' Meredith nodded solemnly.

'OK, I guess I can do that.' Suddenly the pace of her words increased. 'Just let me call Daniel to tell him, to tell him I won't be at the meeting. I'll just be a second.' She tried to get out of the car, her phone already in her hand, but the rear doors were set to only be opened from the outside. She continued talking at nineteen to the dozen, 'Please let me out to make this call, I'm not going to run off, but obviously this is an important business meeting, so I must make sure that he knows I'll be late. But I'd like a bit of privacy, if that's OK, this business is still a secret. We haven't issued any of our press releases or anything, so I need to keep the details hush hush.' It was now Kate's expression that was imploring Diane.

Meredith turned to Tony, who gave a little nod and said, 'You stay here, we'll step out. That way you won't have the wind disrupting the call.' They both got back out of the car and shut their doors.

Across the roof, Tony indicated to his partner that she should listen to the call as best she could, whilst he himself was going to make a call. He wandered a little way across the sunny car park, speaking to Gerard at the hospital morgue to arrange the unorthodox body identification scenario. It was all a ruse to shake her up – not only had Jim Harris identified the body on day one, but the dead man's photograph was on the cricket club's website. What Tony really wanted was some inside information about Daniel Ramsbotham. As he returned to his car, Diane looked beautiful leaning up against it. She had sunglasses on, and looked for all the world like a model advertising the vehicle.

She pirouetted slowly as he returned to the driver's side until she was facing him, her palms flat on the car roof, elbows out sideways, and a big smile. Barely louder than a whisper, Diane relayed their witness's phone conversation, 'She didn't say much more than that she was going to the hospital with us. But she really emphasised the hospital and told him it was like they had talked about.' Meredith turned her hands upwards to accompany a shrug. They both got in, and Tony drove them all up to the hospital.

Throughout the walk from the car park, through the hospital's main corridor, and down to the basement entrance to the mortuary, Kate was looking carefully around her. She looked at everything, observing keenly, as if there would be a test at the end. However, she did not seem to be learning her surroundings methodically – her blonde head kept turning this way and that. The observations were much more of a scattergun approach than would have made for a coherent survey.

Milburn and Meredith looked at each other every so often, sharing confusion, and silently laughing at the student's childlike interest in all the new sights and sounds. When Miss Withenshaw stepped out of the elevator in front of them, Diane attracted Tony's attention by touching his hand with hers. She mimed snorting cocaine with a questioning look, and they both looked ahead to re-assess her movements in the light of this suggestion.

As they reached the threshold of Pathology Lab 2 and a corpse under a white sheet could be seen through the doorway, the skinny suspect shied away. 'Sorry, I thought I could do this, but I really don't think I can.' Without any further discussion, Kate ran back up the cool, dim corridor. She ran straight into the staircase beside the lift shaft.

ADC Meredith took off after her, but the DS moved the other way through the two pathology labs to the fire escape ladder. As he ascended the metal rungs, Tony realised that not only was the fire escape ludicrous for the disabled, but it was very tricky even for an able-bodied person. The rungs were so thin it was difficult to balance his feet on them, and the opening up to the first floor was so small he could barely get through. He stepped over the black and yellow safety chain and marched in to the corridor right beside the hospital exit.

Seeing no sign of Kate along the corridor, Tony, took a moment to straighten his suit and dust it down, and ran a hand through his short hair. He considered leaning casually against a wall to wait for her to come through the nearest set of double doors and see him there, but decided that wasn't really the Tony Milburn way. The doors in question opened, about 10 yards in front of him, and Meredith came bursting through. She skidded to a halt abruptly, eyes fixed on him.

'Where is she,' Diane demanded.

Tony's brow furrowed. 'What do you mean, you're chasing her?'

'Well, she only just got out of the stairwell ahead of me, how long have you been here?'

'About 30 seconds or a minute maybe. How far ahead was she?'

'No you'd have caught her then.' The exertions of running up the stairs caught up with Diane and she started taking very deep breaths.

The A&E department reception was through a door to his right, so he ran to the desk and told them to call hospital security to find his suspect. Whilst he was on the phone to the security office, they told him they could see her on the CCTV cameras, apparently rampaging along a fourth floor corridor. The staff nurse on the geriatric ward up there had already called them.

The ADC was still standing in the same place in the entrance corridor, hands on hips to settle her breathing again, and watching for Kate Withenshaw. 'She's flipped,' Tony shouted as he grabbed Diane by the wrist to pull her along to the lift. 'Fourth floor, they say she's wrecking the place.'

As they stood, willing the lift doors to open sooner, Diane looked Tony in the eyes and said, 'What the fuck? I know she looked like she might be on something, but a violent rampage?'

'Yeah, dunno.' Tony threw his hands up. 'Let's just catch her, and find out what it's all about later.

By the time they reached the ward, there were several old people in various states of dress and ill health, watching Kate cornered and threatening to throw a fire extinguisher at two nurses who had blocked her in behind a bed. The old woman in the bed was silent and wide-eyed, constantly looking back and forth from the scary young student to the more scary nurses. The woman felt more concern for what the nurses would do to Kate, if they caught her, than for the injury she might suffer if mad blonde threw the fire extinguisher badly. Years of nursing had given the capturers the strength and capabilities of any

127

prison guard. There were two hospital security staff standing in the threshold of the four-bed room, but they also knew that the two nurses would undoubtedly do a better job of ensnaring than they could. As the two detectives found the right place, several more security guards also arrived.

'Ladies, I'm DS Milburn, and this is my prisoner, so if you could step back, we'll take it from here.' The two nurses edged back, not taking their eyes off Kate. Meredith stepped in front of her boss and edged forwards, her hands defensively out in front.

Kate was grinning, the fire extinguisher swaying left and right. 'Prisoner, I thought I was just helping with your investigation?' Her mad grin showed that she didn't actually care what the answer was.

'Yes, that was true, Kate, but you have just trashed several parts of the hospital, so we will be arresting you.'

'If you can catch me, you mean!'

Diane replied impatiently, 'Look around, Kate, the only exit is through the door with all the security guards.' She turned her head wildly to look to the large windows, straggles of blonde hair swinging. Meredith added, 'And this is the fourth floor.'

'And the windows only open three inches,' the more senior nurse added.

'Not if I smash it,' Kate laughed. She took a huge swing with the fire extinguisher and hurled it towards the central windowpane. It was in fact made from reinforced plastic, so the red metal canister glanced off and thudded to the floor. Meredith took her chance and shot round the end of the bed embracing Kate in a smother tackle. She was suddenly calm and placid, staring blankly ahead and smiling to herself. Tony produced his handcuffs and stepped forward to take hold of the bizarre student.

The two police officers took their prisoner down in the lift, with two of the security staff. When they walked out of the lift at the bottom, there was chaos in the corridor, nurses and administrative staff running back and forth, and many members of the public being comforted and guided by hospital staff. One nurse stopped at the security guards. 'There you are, why aren't you answering your phone?'

'We've been on M ward to catch this maniac.' The man jerked a thumb towards Kate.

'The pharmacy has been robbed. A man with a shotgun and a balaclava.'

'What, where is he now?'

'Long gone, I assume. He ran out that door at least five minutes ago.' She pointed at the exit doorway, and Milburn and Meredith stared at each other.

'You did this,' Diane accused the smiling student.

Slowly, Withenshaw looked up into Diane's face, the smile continuing. 'I was upstairs with you the whole time, how could I have done it?'

'You know what I mean. I heard you on the phone to Ramsbotham. Where is he?'

'I just told him I would miss our meeting. By now he'll be in a history lecture anyway, so he can't have done it.'

'Come on, we'll work it all out at the station.' Tony pushed her forward towards the exit. 'Sorry, guys, you'll need to call the police to come and sort this out – we need to get her back and into custody. Don't let any of the witnesses leave till our colleagues get here.' The two security guards looked at each other and then at the milling people who remained highly animated, and then back to each other, and finally back to Milburn. He and Meredith were already shuffling Kate outside.

On arrival at the police station, Kate Withenshaw re-tied her unkempt mane into the broad hairband that had struggled to restrain it thus far. At the point where Sergeant Andrew Singh checked her in to a cell, she produced a business card from her handbag, naming her London-based lawyer. The Sikh custody sergeant was more impressed than Milburn and Meredith who rolled their eyes at each other in response. They left Sergeant Singh to telephone for the solicitor and went upstairs to the CID offices to plan the search for Daniel Ramsbotham.

Tony's officemate was working busily at his computer as they came in so, without a word, Diane spun round and collected a chair from the main, open-plan part of CID. She brought it in and lifted it carefully over to the same side of Tony's desk as his own chair, and sat down beside him to look at his computer screen. The other detective muttered a greeting but did his best to get on with his work without engaging the pair.

Diane picked up the desk telephone and started to dial. Watching her slender fingers, which were neatly manicured, Milburn recognised the phone number of the university's central switchboard. She tucked her chocolate hair behind an ear to put the phone to it, and started asking for some help identifying Ramsbotham.

Whilst she spoke, he got the computer into action to try and search for information on the suspect. Once Diane had a date of birth, they immediately found him on the police database. This gave them an old picture to print out and some interesting background. They did not speak much, but quickly developed a system of pointing at the screen to follow through a chain of information.

Mr Ramsbotham had been at the private Durney College in south London as a schoolboy. He had come to the attention of Surrey police when another boy at the school had been beaten, almost to death, after being smashed on the head with a paving slab. There had been no witnesses, the boy himself had not seen the initial strike with the stone slab, and was then unconscious when beaten. No action was taken against Ramsbotham, and the case remained open.

'Another one who learnt the criminal trade in school. What are they teaching at these private schools?' Tony was absorbed, and Diane looked at him but said nothing.

They did not have enough to gain a search warrant for the student house that he and Withenshaw shared but, with a note of his university timetable, decided to try the house first. After two lectures and a tutorial session timetabled for that afternoon, Daniel Ramsbotham should have been free from 5.15pm. Diane had left her jacket in the DS office and only had the tight white blouse covering her wristwatch. Pulling up the cuff revealed that they were standing in the sunshine on his doorstep at 5.25.

'Can I help you?' A tall, handsome young man spoke down at the two detectives from behind them on the path.

'We're looking for Daniel Ramsbotham,' Milburn replied.

The boy dragged a hand through his drooping fair hair, the smile never leaving. 'And you are?' He stepped in front of them and put a key into the door lock. Tony showed his warrant card and identified both of them. 'Well, I'm Daniel Ramsbotham, but I think you must have made a mistake – there's no reason why the police should have any interest in me.'

'Could we come in and explain, sir?' Diane offered the prettiest smile she had.

'I don't think so, officers. As I said, I'm not your man.'

Milburn took a small step closer to the threshold. 'Mr Ramsbotham, we haven't told you what we are interested in, how do you know you are not a witness, or alibi perhaps, for a crime you are unaware of.'

Daniel's smile broadened and he gave a faint nod. Putting his hands into the front pockets of his dark green jeans, and standing square on the doorstep, he answered, 'You're right, what are you here about?'

Diane tried her sweet look again, requesting, 'We'd really prefer not to talk out in the street, if we could talk inside?'

'No.'

Diane and Tony looked at each other briefly, before Tony turned his head back to Ramsbotham. 'Well, we aren't going to talk in public, so if you won't let us in, we'll have to go to the police station.'

'No thanks. If you're not going to tell me what you want, I'll say goodbye and go inside.' The history student stood still.

There was a pause as the three stared each other out. DS Milburn broke the tension. 'Daniel Ramsbotham, I'm arresting you in connection with the supply of Class A drugs. You do not have to say anything. But it may harm your defence if you do not mention, when questioned, something which you later rely on in court. Anything you do say may be given in evidence. Please lock your door and turn around for the handcuffs.'

Mr Ramsbotham shook his head, still smiling, and then complied with the policeman's request. They all walked the 200 yards back to the rear of the police station in silence. Andrew Singh checked Daniel into a cell, and came back to Tony and Diane with another business card from Arthur Smythe – Kate Withenshaw's London lawyer. Milburn took the card and he and Meredith frowned at it together. Sergeant Singh told them that Mr Smythe had advised him he would arrive in Durham by 8pm that same day.

Alone in Tony's office, Meredith quizzed him about Daniel's arrest. 'Are you sure it was wise to arrest him with so little to go on? I don't get the feeling he's the sort to just spill his guts. Or even to get caught out in interview.'

'I couldn't let the smug bastard get away. He's selling Priapra round the university and I'm sure he held up the hospital pharmacy. And she's in it up to her neck too. She'll give him up, I'm sure of it. Once she starts hanging out, she'll say anything to get out of custody so she can score.'

Diane touched Tony's arm. 'That's what I'm afraid of. If she's that addicted, she'll be shit in court.'

He inhaled deeply and nodded appreciatively. 'I know. What I'm hoping is that she'll give up enough that we can actually get evidence on him. You're right we'll never convict him on her testimony.'

Diane's hand remained on his sleeve. 'Do you think he killed Elliott?'

'God knows. As far as I can tell, it seems equally likely that any of them could have, including Pieter Hamilton, but just as likely that he OD'ed on purpose with that doping test coming up, and equally likely that it was an accident. There's still the Pathans to consider. Father, daughter, both of them together, who knows? We need to find out more about his mind-set on Thursday night, and more about his movements and who was with him. So far, I don't trust any of the alibis we've had.'

She led him to his chair and they sat down beside each other. 'Let's run through everything again, and put together the best timeline we can, and add in the forensic evidence and post-mortem report.' She took the pile of reports from the side of his desk and spread them out in front of them both. Tony reached into his pocket and put his notepad on the table as well. They looked at each other and then back to the various papers before each reached for a random choice to read.

Bright sunny weather tends to reduce the size of the ocean waves in Britain, and Penfold was happy to be surprised at the waist high breakers rolling gently in to the long, flat, sandy beach across the road from his home. Waist high is no Hawaiian death swell, but for Penfold, small could be beautiful. Surfing held a spiritual importance to him, and spending time in the water was his prayers at temple. Indeed, the challenge of riding waves that had barely enough energy to start you moving was often more rewarding to the tanned kiwi. Wading into the water with his board floating beside him, Penfold smiled to himself that this was fortunate, as the waves in Hartlepool are often small.

His preferred spot along the mile of golden-grey sand was at the point where the beach starts to bow gently east into the North Sea, from its long straight north-south stretch. This curvature alters the shape of the seabed so that the waves break from the north to the south, sending a surfer to his left as he looks inshore. Penfold particularly liked the challenge of this, as the majority of the surfbreaks he had grown up on are right-handers. For Penfold's religion, lifelong learning was part of the fun.

Sitting behind the place were the waves started breaking – "out back" – he bobbed up and down in the sunshine and thought through some of the information he had picked up regarding smuggling of Priapra and Somnulone. This threw up a number of potential connections to the suspects that Milburn had identified. He had been surprised that the leg pads he had retrieved at the cricket club had not yielded any positive drugs results. Apart from cocaine, but Penfold reminded himself that everything comes up positive for cocaine. The powder is so fine and so ubiquitous that it permeates every part of the developed world, albeit at a microscopic level. He mused further on this apparent dead-end.

The waves were lowering slightly with every set, and Penfold was not paying attention to them any more. Pieter Hamilton had publicly thrown those pads away, without the foam padding in the front. And they then tested clear for most drugs, particularly the one that Hamilton had been implicated in supplying. So either those suggestions about him were false, or he kept the drugs away from his cricket kit.

As he rose and fell over a wave and watched the Sun glittering off the water, Penfold frowned. Something did not tessellate in this pattern of events, but he could not chase it down. He had a methodology of research behaviour that involved self-distraction. When a problem seemed locked up,

Penfold would look into some separate aspect of the situation deeply, and this would allow his sub-conscious to work over things whilst still touching on the problem and continuously receiving new input. Reconciling this extra information into the jigsaw puzzle tended to highlight where there was a flaw in the picture.

He decided to go inside and research the backgrounds of all the characters involved. Having made this decision, Penfold suffered the Last Wave Paradox. It is bizarre how often a surfer's decided "last wave of the day" will be the best they catch all day. And this then throws up an internal crisis, as the surfer has to decide if they really want to go home when the surfing is so good. He stood in the shallows, board pulled up into his armpit, and watched three more waves come in and push against his thighs. His free hand shook dripping saltwater from his thick golden hair and Penfold turned to walk up the beach.

Back in his office, he wrote Hamish Elliott's name at the centre of a large whiteboard. Scattered around this, he wrote the names of all the other people that Milburn had told him about. With a cup of black coffee in one hand, cupped against his chest, he leaned back and pressed the power button to switch on his computer. As it went through the various warming up stages, he stared at the names and de-focussed his eyes, so the names blurred into a sort of cloud in his mind.

Meredith and Milburn were sitting so close to each other that their shoulders were in constant contact. They had a system of summarizing the evidence, in which Diane wrote on a big sheet of paper in a thick green pen, whilst Tony organized notes and reports into a sequence at the top of the desk. They were often leaning across each other to point and comment on salient items on either's material.

Finishing up the organization of the last page of notes, he put it at the right hand end of all the information laid out; Tony tipped back and put his hands behind his head to survey what they had achieved. Diane moved the big paper centrally in front of them, and as she leaned across to do so, he could smell the coconut fragrance of her hair. Sitting straighter again, she patted his thigh and, with a smile in her voice, said, 'Tony, it's excellent.' She left her hand on his thigh.

'Yeah, doesn't solve it but, you're right, we can definitely use this as a guide for where to go with the investigations. The timeline will make it really easy to cross these people off as we prove alibis that cover the crucial timeslot.' He took his left hand off his head and gave her a hug round the shoulders. She squeezed his thigh gently and they lingered a moment, both looking at their summary flipchart sheet. The DS let his grip loosen and, bringing his arm back over, instructed, 'Right, I reckon that'll be long enough for Mr Smythe to chat to his clients. Who should we interview first?'

They stood up and she turned to face him. 'I say go with Kate. If she's as addicted as she looked, she'll be desperate to talk to us.' Tony smiled and nodded brightly.

When the detectives entered the interview room, Kate and her lawyer were sitting looking up at them. Mr Smythe appeared formal in his charcoal pinstriped suit and red and navy striped tie. Kate looked demure and had tidied herself up considerably since her somewhat dishevelled entry into the police station in handcuffs. She smiled amiably as they sat down opposite.

Once the recording machine had been started, and without any question to prompt her, Kate leapt in. 'Look, I'm really sorry about what happened in the hospital. Seeing poor Hamish's body under that sheet completely freaked me out. I'm really sorry if I frightened anybody, and I'll pay for any damage I did.'

There was silence in the small, dark room as the police assessed this apparently reasonable confession. DS Milburn leant his head back slightly to take in the ceiling for a moment, and then looked at Mr Smythe, who waited patiently with pen in hand. Turning to Kate, Tony retorted, 'Miss Withenshaw, any damages at the hospital are the least of your worries. Quite apart from investigating your part in the armed robbery that took place there at the same time, we have your DNA in the same bed as "poor Hamish's body".'

Mr Smythe interjected, 'You have never received a legitimate DNA sample from my client, so connecting her to the scene of Mr Elliott's demise is speculation at this point. And before you ask, you can't have a sample now unless you have considerably more evidence that she is involved...' Arthur Smythe paused for effect and then sardonically continued, '... in that accidental death.'

'Accidental? Do you have information we don't that you would care to share with us?' Tony also paused for effect. 'In any case, she may not have informed you, but Miss Withenshaw had a DNA sample taken several years ago. She is on the police database along with many other criminals and drug users.'

'Detective, she was fourteen – a child – and the sample was taken without her consent.'

'A child criminal. Cannabis use was still a crime all those years ago.' Tony revelled in the chance to play a solicitor at his own game. At this point, he again wondered if he had missed a better potential career as a lawyer.

'Those allegations were never proven, but it would make no difference – the sample was taken by her school nurse, hardly a forensic science expert. Approximately five minutes in court, depending on the punctuality of the judge, and we would be leaving court again.'

ADC Meredith had been sitting quietly, one finger slowly twirling the side of her bob haircut. Her mouth had been hanging slightly open, as she watched and nobody paid any attention to her. At this point she jumped in. 'Was Hamish or Daniel better in bed?' Everyone looked at Diane.

'What kind of a question is that?' Kate whined.

'Tread carefully, Acting Detective, I have been responsible for the stalled careers of several Metropolitan Police officers who thought that American TV was a good model for interviews.' Mr Smythe's tone was measured, almost apologetic, but he wrote extensively on his notepad after saying this.

Meredith's face remained like stone. 'You told me you and Elliott were lovers, and seeing you in the car with Mr Ramsbotham the other day, I just guessed about you and him. You know how a girl can tell these things.' At this, Diane opened up a knowing smile for Kate. The student blinked, nonplussed, but before she could reply, the solicitor put a hand on her arm.

'Unless you have some specific point, perhaps we could refrain from the salacious questions.' Mr Smythe had addressed this to Meredith, but then looked back to her boss with a meek smile.

Tony responded, 'This is a sordid case. It involves drugs, sex, and a celebrity cricketer, and is looking increasing like it also encompasses drug dealing and armed robbery. So, we will take the questioning into whatever dark corners we need to. Miss Withenshaw, were you and Daniel Ramsbotham lovers? And remember that we will be searching your house whilst you are in custody, so any DNA clues will tell us the truth anyway.'

She looked at her legal advisor who raised his eyebrows and gave a nod. 'Sometimes. We aren't boyfriend and girlfriend, but we live in the same house, so when we get drunk, sometimes things happen.'

Meredith came back in again. 'So it was Mr Ramsbotham in the car with you at the cricket training session on Friday morning?'

'Yes.' She looked at Diane, wondering why Daniel being in the car would be important. 'It's OK though, my dad put him on the insurance.'

The policewoman smiled reassuringly. 'That's good. Why were you two at the cricket ground that morning?'

'Daniel had to go and see Pieter.'

'Yes, we saw Mr Hamilton talking to the two of you in the car park. What was it about?'

'Well,' Kate faltered momentarily, and then brightly continued, 'they're cousins, so they often like to meet and chat.'

There was a long silence in the room as the detectives tried to process this new information without giving away that it was news to them. Diane recovered first. 'OK, but you drove five miles or so out there, and then they spoke for perhaps thirty seconds, before Daniel sped away at the sight of the police, us. What were they chatting about that took such a short time but they had to meet for?' Kate looked blankly at Meredith, caught in a logical trap for which she could not work out an answer.

Arthur Smythe leant across the table ever so slightly, putting himself between his client and her interviewer just enough to break the spell. 'I think that the banal chit-chat between two cousins is probably taking us off the point here. Do you have any questions relating to Mr Elliott's death? And I note that his death has not yet been classified, so you are simply wasting our time anyway.'

Tony pulled the knot of his tie up a little and responded, 'Both Mr Ramsbotham and Mr Hamilton are suspects in this case too, so their interaction is vitally important. Let's not have you taking us off the point here. And you know very well that we have to investigate a mysterious death as murder until we find otherwise.'

Smythe appeared chastened as he sat back and casually asked, 'Mr Hamilton is a suspect now, too?'

Tony looked directly at the solicitor, but re-iterated the question to Kate, 'What did Daniel and Pieter talk about in the car park on Friday?'

Kate looked at Mr Smythe who briefly shook his head. 'I don't remember.'

Diane turned her head towards Kate theatrically, 'You don't remember? It can't have been more than a minute's conversation. You're supposed to be a Durham University student – you must have a better memory than that.'

141

Still leaning back slightly, Smythe chimed in, 'Banal chit-chat, I told you, not even memorable.'

DS Milburn weighed in, 'Please let your client answer, Mr Smythe, I'm sure you wouldn't want to be accused of coercing her to perjury.' Smythe's eyes narrowed but he said nothing further. 'Kate, what was said in the car park?'

'I don't remember.' She gave a conspiratorial smile towards Meredith. 'Those two boys really talk a load of nonsense when they get together.'

Milburn continued, 'Last chance, Kate, what did they talk about?'

'I told you, just boys' talk: cricket and girls and stuff.'

'Right, you had your chance. If you could go back to your cell, we'll see what Mr Ramsbotham has to say for himself.' Milburn got up to show Kate to the door, and the London lawyer went with them to exchange one interviewee for the other. Several minutes later, he returned and showed Daniel to Kate's old seat. Before they spoke, Diane showed Tony a brief note she had made:

Cricket and girls and stuff = cricketing girls & "stuff" ????

And why wasn't she more strung out? She was really in control of herself. Has Smythe given her something??

He nodded, and she then pointed further down the page to a note written smaller:

Kate left a hair on the seat – bagged it for DNA, in view of the videocamera.

He looked at her and nodded again as Meredith turned over the page in her notebook to hide these messages.

Arthur Smythe was the first to speak. 'You said earlier that Mr Ramsbotham is a suspect in the death of Mr Elliott. Could you explain what evidence you have to back up that suspicion please. Of course, if you don't have any then we'll be leaving now.'

Milburn replied, with restraint in his voice, 'Mr Smythe, if we did not have a suitable cause to question him, none of us would be here, as we would be wasting our time, which would be better spent finding evidence. So, rest assured, we have good reason to be questioning Mr Ramsbotham.'

'Her Majesty's prisons are full of innocent people for whom that was the story the police told themselves. Moreover though, it makes no odds, if you think you have good reason, we are entitled to hear it. Otherwise I shall have a writ of habeas corpus with Judge McDaid within the hour.'

The detective sergeant paused at the sound of this southerner naming a local purple judge as if they worked the same courtrooms regularly. However, Tony knew he had to offer something here, so he tried to keep it as brief as possible. 'Hamish Elliott died as the result of an overdose of the Class A drug Priapra. Mr Ramsbotham has been named several times in our enquiries as a supplier of this drug, and indeed is the only known dealer of this particular drug in the city.'

'Alleged dealer.'

'If you say so.'

143

'In actuality, I say it is fabrication and that Mr Ramsbotham is a law-abiding citizen.'

'Right, well let's find out shall we?' Smythe sat silently watching Milburn. 'Mr Ramsbotham, where were you on Thursday night from, let's say, 11pm until 2am Friday morning.'

Mr Smythe interrupted, 'Do you mean Thursday 21st March?'

Tony exhaled in a show of exasperation, 'Yes, last Thursday, when Hamish Elliott died.'

The young man was sitting patiently, happy not to get involved. His solicitor waved a hand to him, indicating permission to answer the question. Daniel pulled his right hand through his mop of hair, and looked across at each of the detectives. Addressing Milburn, he said, 'I was at my flat on the Bailey, with Kate, for all of that time period.'

'I thought you lived at the house on Hallgarth Street where we arrested you,' Diane took her chance to jump in to the interrogation.

'That's Kate's house. I have a room there, but I also own a flat on the Bailey.'

This was news to the police, as the university's police liaison secretary had told them Ramsbotham's address as being the same as Withenshaw's on Hallgarth Street. It surprised Milburn less than it annoyed him. The silver spoon upbringing of these two students got his back up. The two residences referred to could not be more than 300 yards apart, so having both was utterly unnecessary. Worse though, as the Bailey ran past the east end of the cathedral, within the World Heritage

Site, a flat there could not cost less than ten years salary for a detective sergeant.

Meredith returned, 'But Kate's alibi is that she was at home all that time. And she claims she was with you.'

'She often calls my flat home.'

'Are you and Miss Withenshaw lovers?' Diane continued.

Daniel shrugged. 'Sometimes.'

'She's your girlfriend?'

He shook his head slightly and curled his lip up. 'No. We've known each other for years, we share the same houses, she's an easy shag when she's drunk. It happens every so often. And yes, we slept together on Thursday night.'

'Was Kate drunk on Thursday night, then?'

'Enough. She was certainly very horny.' The boy gave Diane a knowing smile, which infuriated her.

The DS saw her hand clench into a fist under the table and so he stepped into the conversation. 'Does Kate take drugs other than alcohol?'

'She smokes a fair bit.'

'Do you mean tobacco, or other drugs?'

'Oh, sorry,' he replied obsequiously, 'cigarettes.'

The verbal dance continued back and forth between the four of them for another fifteen minutes. Milburn became increasingly frustrated at the choreography – Smythe obviously had his charge prepared well to offer the idea that he and Kate had numerous vices, but were not criminals. This framework extended to the discussion of Pieter Hamilton, who was confirmed as Daniel's cousin. Pieter's father and Daniel's mother had taken half the grandfather's fortune each and set themselves up in business, one in South Africa with his Afrikaans wife, and the other in London.

Mrs Ramsbotham had magnified her inheritance, and married a very wealthy banker; to the extent that she could now afford a top level London lawyer who would drop everything to travel the length of England to assist her son against the police. Every expansion of Tony's knowledge of the pair increased his dislike for them, and convinced him further that they must be criminals, even if not actually Hamish Elliott's murderers. Although he maintained hope that he could find one of them guilty of that too.

After forty minutes in the interview room with Daniel and Mr Smythe though, they had little more to go on than at the start. Neither of the interviews had given them enough evidence to gain a search warrant for their house, or his flat, despite Milburn's earlier bluff to Kate. With some considerable argument from Smythe, and a little exaggeration in their representations to Andrew Singh, the custody sergeant, Milburn and Meredith kept both suspects in the cells overnight, pending further investigations the following day.

Tony made it home just before 11pm. Kathy was waiting up for him and hugged him as he came through the door. 'Fancy some cheese on toast,' she asked with a tired-looking smile. Before he had a chance to answer, she took him by the hand and led him through to the kitchen, pushing him down to a seat at the kitchen table. She started readying ingredients and said, 'So, I want to hear all about the developments today.'

Tony looked up at her and blinked. He wasn't quite sure where to start or what depth to go in to. 'Um, right, well, we arrested both Kate Withenshaw and Daniel Ramsbotham. Kate went apeshit up at the hospital – threw a fire extinguisher at Diane.'

'I hope it hit her?' Kathy's tone made her statement into a question, but she did not turn away from pushing the grill pan into the oven.

Tony smiled slightly and continued. 'Well, whilst everyone in the hospital was trying to subdue her, the hospital pharmacy was held up. And she'd phoned Ramsbotham just before we took her up there. We're convinced he did the robbery whilst she was distracting everyone.'

'We?'

Tony frowned slightly. 'Me and Diane. Meredith,' he half corrected himself. 'Anyway, they both had the same smarmy lawyer. You'll never believe this: he flew up from London for the interviews!'

At this Kathy did turn round and pulled her head back with wide eyes. 'No way,' she chuckled.

Leaning on the table, Tony nodded back and continued, 'Diane is convinced that he gave Withenshaw some drugs, coz she went from behaving quite strangely to perfectly normal and demure in the space of his visit. And then he had them both coached to offer perfectly matching stories that give us nothing. We've had them kept in overnight, but we've got no search warrant and we can't really see how to get any further with them. I reckon they'll get out tomorrow afternoon and we'll be back to square one. Or further now they know we've got them in the frame.'

'I take it things are going well with the Crazy Cow? You've mentioned her five times now.'

147

Tony looked quickly down at the floor and ran the conversation back through his mind. 'You know we're working this case together. She's been nothing but professional, and very competent.' He didn't sound convinced himself.

Kathy put the plate of cheesy toast in front of him and left the room. From the bottom of the stairs she called back, 'I'm going to bed.'

Milburn sat staring at his food and played the day's events back through his mind. He spent over twenty minutes slowly working through the cheese on toast and washing up the plate. When he entered their bedroom, Kathy was in bed and the room was dark. He knew she wasn't asleep but neither of them spoke. He undressed and slipped under the covers quickly, without even brushing his teeth. He didn't dare reach out to touch Kathy.

Tony's mind was a whirl of memories of the events of the day, and he tried to distract himself from thinking about Diane by running through all that he knew of the drugs cases and the death of Elliott. Every salient point though just reminded him of her writing it onto their summary timeline poster. The more he tried to focus on the forensic elements of the day, the more his mind threw in images of Diane's smile, or dancing hair, or worse: her cleavage, tight skirt or flawless skin.

Tony suffered insomnia occasionally during difficult or complex investigations where thinking about them filled his consciousness with activity. This was one of those nights, and all the periods of sleep that he did manage were fitful and troubled by vivid and bizarre dreams. Kathy often talked of cheese giving people nightmares. As Tony rubbed his closed eyes at a little after four in the morning he knew that this was nothing to do with his cheese supper.

Tuesday 26th March

Although DCI Hardwick was always in his office long before 8am, Milburn knew that he would get a much better reception if he let Harry settle in and finish his morning pot of tea. Harry had to be onside that morning. However, Tony could wait no longer when, from the CID office window, he saw Meredith parking her car. He almost ran up the stairs, but then did his best to breeze casually into Hardwick's office.

'Tony,' Harry's gruff greeting was accompanied by a quizzical eyeing up.

'Morning, H.' His response was as breezy as his entrance.

'So, where are we at with that cricketer, then?'

'He's coming along, but we've got a real problem.'

'Hmm,' Milburn's boss grumbled.

Tony proceeded to explain to Harry that the investigation was progressing, and told him most of the salient elements of it. However, Milburn took great pains to skew their activities of the previous twenty-four hours into a honey trap organised by Meredith. The way Tony told it, she was focussing only on him and effectively disrupting the investigation as a consequence.

Milburn related all the times when she had physically touched him, and explained how she had dressed very

150

inappropriately. He minimised her useful input, and implied that they still had little to conclude about the death of Hamish Elliott, as a direct result of her focus on Tony, as opposed to police work. At the end of this, Hardwick leant his stout frame back in the black leather chair and eyed his detective sergeant without speaking. Milburn was not fazed. He knew that he had spoken enough, and that Harry would pronounce shortly.

'OK, Tony, let's say everything you've just told me is a correct and unbiased version of events.' Milburn's blue eyes could not look Harry in the face. 'Even if so, why are you telling me?'

'Well, you know how it all went to shit before. And you're my boss. You're her boss.'

'Of course, but what do you want me to do? Why are you here?'

'Well, it's obvious isn't it? I can't work with her any more. You need to re-assign her.' Tony's words came out quickly, and afterwards there was silence again. They looked at each other until Hardwick turned his head so that his good eye was staring up at a corner of the ceiling tiles.

'You can't work the case on your own.'

Tony hadn't worked out the answer to this. Other detectives flashed into his mind, but in each case, he knew that they were busy beyond the hours available in a day. There weren't any obviously sensible re-assignments. He put a hand to his chin and quietly, attempting thoughtfully, suggested Penfold as an assistant. When DCI Hardwick rolled his eye, whilst the other remained frozen, it was disconcerting at best. Milburn was looking at the carpet though.

'You know he can't do interviews with you, which effectively means it's a waste of time letting him help. Especially in this case, where we have a lot of suspects and little evidence. This one is going to come out from interviews.'

He appealed. 'Look, H, I can't work with Diane, she's harassing me. You're the boss, you will have to work out what to do. Another day like yesterday and I'll be off on the sick with Barnes.'

Tony knew that whilst he may have exaggerated the situation, he was in danger of getting sucked in again, exactly like the previous time. This time he had Kathy to lose from the start, and he knew Kathy would not brook any bullshit from him. Milburn thought of Kathy and Meredith facing off, and he felt helpless, lost.

'Hmm, I'm not happy about this, Tony. Not happy at all.'

'You think you're unhappy? Try having a crazy woman fixated on you.'

'Yes, yes. Look, for now, continue the investigation on your own. I'll assign you a partner when I can. If you must talk to Penfold about it, keep him out of the station, and don't tell me about it. And if you can send Meredith to me, and I'll find her something else to do.'

'If you weren't the boss, H, I'd kiss you.' Tony beamed.

'Don't stuff this up, Milburn. Everybody needs to come out of this a winner, not just you.' Milburn was out of his seat but, at this, he paused and frowned slightly. He had no idea quite what Hardwick meant. No further explanation was coming though, so he walked slowly out of the office and back down the stairs. En route, he sent Kathy a text message explaining that he had engineered Meredith's removal.

It was quite cold in the detective sergeants' office, but Diane's jacket was on the back of a chair already stationed next to Tony's, and she was in the main office, in a smart pinstripe skirt and cream blouse, photocopying. Meredith smiled over to him as he walked back in, putting his phone away. 'Morning,' she called. Although there were four other detectives at work at various places around the office, for both Tony and Diane, it was as if they were alone. 'How's things?'

'OK. Harry wants to see you.'

'Really, what for?'

Milburn shrugged. 'How should I know? See how your first couple of days in CID went? Dunno. In his office now, though.' Diane scowled, and handed him the sheets she had copied as she passed to collect her jacket. He stood still, and let her come back again. Their eyes met as she passed, and he was startled to see their normal brown hue appeared closer to black.

Whilst she was gone, he filed the transcripts of Sunday's interviews in the case file, and placed the copies into the evidence-supported timeline that they had constructed to determine the direction to follow. He also moved the extra chair back out to the open plan CID space, and put her handbag on it out there.

Milburn closed the office door and went back to his desk. His next action was to send Penfold a text message, inviting him to lunch later so they could go over the case and his friend could start helping. The message also relayed the information of Meredith's re-assignment. Text messaging had worked its way under Penfold's skin, the minimalist styles it induced were a challenge he relished. Haiku was his most common approach, but he would also often attempt the six-word-story format, after

Hemingway's famous favourite. He replied in this case with, 'Fatal attraction displaced. Rome burns; lunch.' This made little sense to Tony, but he knew that Penfold would be chuckling away to himself at some clever cultural reference or word play.

Milburn got a cup of coffee, loosened his tie, and sat down to look again at the various sheets relating to Elliott's death, to see if he could fathom any other angle, or route, that might help him and Penfold to solve it. After twenty minutes of paper shuffling and re-shuffling, his phone rang. It was Hardwick, telling Tony to return to the DCI's office.

As he entered the room, Tony's heart sank. Diane was sitting next to William Santara. Uniform Sergeant Santara was the Police Federation Rep who had represented her, or at least acted as her Federation support, throughout the previous troubles. If he was present, it was to be a formal meeting.

'Sit down, Tony.' Hardwick pointed to a chair that had been placed half-facing Diane and her rep.

'What's going on, boss?' Tony asked quietly, not really expecting anyone to believe that he was in the dark.

The DCI continued, 'ADC Meredith is moving to CID. As you know, she should have started with us this morning, and we asked her to help you out over the weekend. So, on her actual start date, this morning, I asked Diane to move from partnering you to assisting Jonjon and Dave with the spate of house burglaries up Sherburn Road. They've got something like a dozen that all seem connected, and so I want as many bodies as possible dealing with it. However, Diane believes that this is some sort of slight and that I am not assigning her as I would anybody else and, despite not actually having started in CID yet, that I am holding her career back by taking her from a suspicious death to burglaries.'

'I....' Hardwick held up a hand to interrupt Milburn.

'As her Federation Rep, Will is in agreement with ADC Meredith, and they are formally requesting that I assign her back to assisting you. Otherwise, she has threatened to invoke a formal grievance procedure against me. I have reminded both of them of the circumstances under which you and she struggled eleven months ago, but Diane insists that this has nothing to do with today's events. Do you have anything you could add to our considerations?'

Tony was shell-shocked. However, he had been through formal meetings exactly like this before and knew how to play the game. 'As this is a formal meeting, I will need to make sure that whatever I say is properly considered, before I say it.' William was taking notes. 'Give me a minute or two to work out what contribution I think would help progress things here.'

Milburn took out his notebook and pen, and made a show of thinking carefully and making some notes for his own reference. Everyone waited in silence.

'OK. I am certain that the systems we had in place previously, in which Meredith and I worked apart were the best for everyone, based on the events of the past.' Diane was glowering at Tony. 'The case that I am working on is struggling to go anywhere, and, to be honest, I think more than one person on it is a waste of manpower. Personpower.' The DS looked up from his notes.

'That's nonsense, Tony,' she retorted. 'You need all the help you can get on it, if we're going to solve the murder. And the two days we've spent on it together have been thoroughly professional and successful. How can you deny that?'

Again, Milburn paused, and made a couple of notes in his book. 'I can't point to anything specific that has been a problem over the last 48 hours, but I really do think it's best for everyone if I work alone on this one.'

At this, the chief inspector frowned. But he followed up with: 'My understanding is that this is not yet certain as a murder and, as such, I can't waste resources. Let's go with a compromise here. Until we know it is murder, Tony works it alone. If it does come up as murder, then Meredith re-joins him to investigate.'

She was glaring at Hardwick now. Santara leaned over to speak quietly to her. Everyone could hear him though. 'Diane, I do think we're a bit previous to be going over the top just yet. The DCI's being reasonable here. I'd recommend we go with this, and we'll just make sure you always get a fair crack of the whip on assignments.'

Now her dagger eyes were boring into William. She spoke to Hardwick, 'This had better not be the sort of glass ceiling I can expect from you as a boss. If you hold me back, you'll be sorry.' Harry's face was inscrutable. Meredith stood and smoothed out her skirt. She scowled at Hardwick again, and turned to give Tony the same. He was looking out of the window to avoid her. She left the room. Will Santara stood and gave an apologetic shrug, before following her out.

Harry and Tony looked at each other. Hardwick's face remained impossible to read and Milburn simply said, 'Thank you.'

'All I can say is, find our murderer, before we find out it's murder!'

Tony nodded, stood and left, stalling on the threshold briefly to ensure that Diane was not waiting for him outside. He went to the canteen and ordered a cup of tea. He was hoping that a bit of space and a few minutes break would give him the chance to figure out how to work in the CID offices with her there as well. Milburn was further hoping that his two colleagues would take her out of the building as part of their investigations.

A phone call to Dave at his desk was answered by Diane, so Tony hung up without speaking and decided he would just have to deal with it. A brisk walk straight through to shut himself in his office was the plan he came up with. It went to plan, but there was a tension in the whole place as he walked through the CID open plan. It was silent, which was unheard of. Closing his door behind him, Milburn hoped that he hadn't also alienated the rest of the detectives by making them work with Meredith.

Fortunately, distraction came in the form of a phone call from Elliott's sister. She told Milburn that her brother's funeral was that morning at 10am. Tony already knew this, but she then proceeded to invite him to the wake. As all of his family lived far away, few could make it to the funeral, and she was worried that there would only be a couple of people in attendance. He thought that a cricket club of people should probably be enough, but didn't want to upset the woman by arguing with her. So, he asked if Penfold could attend too.

'Yes, of course, is he another detective?'

'Of sorts. What are the details of time and place?'

'It's going to be at his flat. I picked up the keys with his...' she paused and Milburn could just make out quiet sobs. She must have been muffling the mouthpiece with her hand.

'OK, straight after the service I assume, so something like 11am?' There was no immediate reply, and he suddenly had a shock realisation. 'Um, has anybody been to clean the place?'

'What? No.' Harriet Elliott sounded confused. 'I was told the police work was finished, and we'd be OK to go in. That is right isn't it? We've told everyone now.' The distress in her voice was evident.

'Yes, that's fine, but ... um, the place was a real mess.'

'Oh, no, there won't be any time. I've got to pick up the buffet from the supermarket on my way to the funeral home. What needs cleaning?' She was now very worked up.

'Look, don't worry about it at all. I'll meet you at the funeral home and get the keys from you and then Penfold and I will clean the place up before anybody arrives. In fact, if we take the food from you then, we can lay that out for you, and save you any trouble.'

'What? Are you sure, that seems very generous. Don't you have things to do yourself?'

'Don't worry about it at all, Miss Elliott. I'll leave now and meet you there.'

'Right, OK. Thank you so much.'

Tony raced out of his office and through the open plan, with his mobile phone to his ear as it rang through to Penfold. Descending the stairs and out to his car was time enough to explain to Penfold to meet him at Elliott's flat, and to bring all the cleaning products that Penfold could find. It was going to be a perfect opportunity to get out of the police station, and also to find out a bit more background. He hoped that more relatives than just the sister were going to show up.

Harriet Elliott was considerably shorter and more fulsome than her brother had been, but she had the same red hair and pale freckled skin. There were plenty of people already waiting for the funeral. The ones Milburn recognised were mostly from the cricket club. He didn't waste time asking any questions of Harriet, and her extensive thanks became quite difficult for him to break away from.

By the time Milburn and Penfold were in the flat with all the food, drink and cleaning products, they had less than half an hour to clean the place up. Given the amount of blood on the bedroom floor, and that it had been tracked through to the lounge carpet, they knew they were facing an impossible task.

'Even if we had time, those stains will not shift.' Penfold was pointing at Jim Harris's trail of bloody footprints on the sky blue carpet of the lounge.

'No,' Milburn muttered. 'Shit, shit! What are we going to do? Those footprints look like insensitive police at best. At worst a psycho murderer went running around in the blood. And now I've said we'll clean it, it's our fault if it's still dirty. Shit!'

There was quiet as they both stared at the bloody carpet. 'I've got a couple of ideas. You start unpacking the food and I'll do what I can with this lot.'

Milburn looked at his friend, trying to make sense of the crow's feet around the eyes of the tanned face. There passed a silent moment of agreement, and they jumped into their tasks. The kitchen counter, combined with the breakfast bar, made for enough space to lay out the pre-packaged buffet trays, with space for drinks at the very end beyond the cooking hob.

159

Milburn filled the kettle and set it to boil, before returning to assist Penfold. He was disappointed to see little progress had been made. The floppy blond hair was bobbing slightly as Penfold's powerful arms scrubbed at the polished wood floor of the hallway. It looked well scrubbed – at least the floor was wet right through to the front door – but Tony could see that Penfold had started on the easy job.

'What about in here? There'll never be time to get this lot off.' Milburn was scraping his shoe on a red footprint stain on the carpet as he spoke.

'No, there never was enough time. And the congealed blood in the bed is starting to stink a bit. I'm thinking we put a sign on the bedroom door that says "No Entry" or something like that, and then if we move the furniture in the lounge around a bit, we should be able to hide most of it. What do you think?' Penfold stopped scrubbing and looked up at Tony.

He looked around the room at the available furniture and the stains to be hidden, and shrugged. 'No better plan, I guess.' By the time Penfold had finished the hallway, Milburn had shuffled the sofa, footstool and TV unit so that some of the blood trail was no longer visible. 'You finished down there? There's a big rug in the bedroom, which I think avoided getting bloody.' Penfold laid the rug in the lounge entrance, where Harris's biggest collection of footprints had surrounded the telephone table, and the detective sergeant produced a fairly neat looking No Entry sign.

'Well, the organization in this room now looks ridiculous; let's hope no one speaks ill of the dead about it.'

'Trouble is there's that spot there, and I can't fathom a way to hide it.' Tony's forefinger was aimed at a blotch of purple looking stain about eight inches by twelve inches. 'Do you think we'd get away with a sort of comedy red wine spillage early on?'

'I think that would attract people's attention to looking at the floor too closely. You can still see everything, if you get down low and look under the edges of these things. Here's a plan though: I'll stand on it all the time. If you occasionally bring me bits and pieces of food and drinks, then I can just hold my ground until everyone leaves.' Tony frowned. 'Needs must, Milburn. Actually, don't bring me too many drinks or I'll need the toilet.' Milburn made a face that said, "I can't really believe I'm going along with this, but OK."

A few minutes later, the closest relatives arrived, and Tony showed them where everything was. He claimed that the bedroom must stay out of bounds for forensic reasons, but that he had decided the little sign would be kinder on everyone than blue and white police tape. He then proceeded to take on the job of doorman, so that he could monitor that nobody strayed into the bedroom. He also made sure the hall light remained off, so that any failings in Penfold's scrubbing would hopefully be lost in shadows.

The flat's small lounge was quickly filled, by the time more than thirty staff and players from the county cricket club had arrived. In addition to Harriet Elliott, Hamish's parents were there, and a grandmother. DS Milburn discovered that the role of doorman also allowed him to ask everybody how they were connected to the deceased. Outside his family and work colleagues, and Aisha Pathan, there were no other mourners. Elliott appeared to have led a highly focussed existence. Or he had no friends. None of the girlfriends had appeared, although Kate Withenshaw was still in custody.

After the cricket lesson he had received two days previously, Penfold managed to catch Vivender Pathan into conversation. He maintained that it was surprising that the police should think that anyone would want to harm Elliott. Penfold inquired after Aisha and how she was coping with the grief. Her father offered little more than a polite positive rejoinder. Aisha was standing with the two men, but remained silent throughout.

Milburn was trying to draw some background information from the family members. Hamish's sister was the most forthcoming, and seemed to know him better than the rest of the family. She knew of nothing in his life that could lead to a grudge, although she did not seem to be describing the same lifestyle that Jim Harris had related. Harriet knew that her brother was very committed to his cricket, and that he had been increasingly successful. She commented that he had been concerned that his thin frame – "scrawny" was the word she used – would never allow him to bowl with enough pace. He was "deadly accurate" but just not powerful enough, and this had been a regular moan when they had spoken on the telephone. The family all still lived in the Scottish port of Oban, and he had not visited much since moving up after Bristol University, despite the relatively shorter distance from Durham.

Penfold moved his conversation on to cricketing matters. 'I understand Hamish was quite an important member of the team? He'll be sorely missed this season, I expect?'

Aisha nodded, and a tear escaped past the big lashes of one eye. Her father concurred also, 'Yes, he was never what the

162

pundits refer to as an "enforcer", but he was very consistent. He could keep the ball difficult to play for many overs at a time, even if he didn't take wickets. Keeping the batsmen to low scoring can make them frustrated and cause them to make mistakes.'

Penfold nodded to show he was carefully taking this on board. 'So what will you do without him? Who are the other good bowlers waiting in the wings?'

Coach Pathan looked into his whiskey glass, and watched as the honey-coloured liquid washed back and forth over the surface of two ice cubes. Penfold was a good foot taller than the Indian, and Vivender's head looked up at nearly a 45-degree angle to meet the surfer's blue eyes.

'There are plenty who would like to be there – we have maybe twenty really good junior bowlers in the County Academy. But who would be good enough to play in the first team regularly? I'm not sure yet; this will be a very difficult time for selection. There will always be a big psychological problem for anybody we select to take the place of a dead man. It is just not normal sports stuff, the players don't have experience at dealing with that kind of thing.'

'No, very true. There will always be a self doubt about whether you live up to the standards of the man who should be there,' Penfold agreed. Aisha was, silently, crying in full flow. She was listening to the conversation and watching both men, but her face was now sodden with tears. 'But you are going to have to play matches very soon, who are the most likely people you'll try it out with?'

Pathan nodded. 'We have a pre-season friendly match against Durham Uni in two weeks time. At this moment, I have just no idea who I will put out to play in that game.'

'Well, who is there to choose from?' Penfold shifted his weight back and forth to relieve his leg muscles, which were aching a little from being rooted to the spot.

'I think Pieter Hamilton is probably top of the list. I'm sure he is not going to be worried about filling Elliott's shoes.'

'He's a brute.' Aisha had muttered this to her orange juice, but it was loud enough that both men looked at her. He scowled, and she quickly averted her gaze back to her glass.

'I don't know what you get so worked up about, girl. These cricketers are all the same. They are in a world of celebrity and have forgotten what the game is about. Elliott was no different, he took his big money and threw it away on drink and girls. You know this is true, why do you cry?' Aisha did not look up. Her feet stuck in place, but she was visibly shaking.

Without moving his body, Penfold's eyes flitted around the room to see if anybody had heard Pathan's remarks, inappropriate at best at the man's funeral. When she looked back up at her father, the tears had left Aisha's eyeballs. Penfold saw that she was shaking with anger. She did not speak and after a couple of seconds, her father turned back to him. 'I told her many times not to be friends with any of these men. They do not know what it means to be a gentleman.' Still silent, not disturbing the quiet murmur of the wake, Aisha straightened her arms down by her sides, rotated on the balls of her feet and walked stiffly out to the hallway.

Nobody else in the room appeared to notice any of this. The father took a couple of small steps and strained to look

164

.through the crowd, trying to see his daughter in the hall. A gap was emerging between Penfold and the coach, and socially he should have followed a pace or two to keep a constant space between them. But Penfold could not let his feet leave the bloodstain that they were hiding. He quickly tried to steer Vivender back to the question of replacement bowlers and draw him back towards the same spot in the room. 'Yes? As you know, I don't know much about cricket, but Hamilton did look good at your training session the other day. I saw him hit the stumps anyway.' Having leant forward slightly as Aisha left, Penfold now bent himself backwards reeling the other man in.

'He thinks he is better than he is. He is good, but he doesn't have a perfect head for when things don't go his way. Jim Harris is similar, but he has the opposite mind problem. He is better than he believes of himself.'

Quietly, Penfold added, 'And, of course, he was very good friends with Hamish. And was first to find him dead, so he could be really out of kilter psychologically.'

The shorter man nodded again. 'I have a feeling that I may be best to choose a third option. Gary Short is probably next in line. It would be a surprise selection, but he's been down the list all the time so far, so wasn't as close to Hamish as the others.'

'It might be best to go with a surprise choice when circumstances are so extreme.' Penfold offered positive support.

Penfold held the coffee shop door open for an old man to leave, gratefully putting his hat on, as his hands were now free. The Daily Espresso was a favourite hangout for the kiwi surfer, and

Detective Sergeant Milburn enjoyed the chance to order coffee volubly emphasising that he'd like it with milk and sugar.

They had left Hamish Elliott's family to deal with the remaining cleaning after the funeral wake, which was a job you wouldn't wish on anybody. Lunch, though, was a good opportunity for the two to debrief each other about what they had gleaned from conversations with the other mourners.

Penfold explained how Vivender Pathan had put forward three names as potential successors to Elliott in the cricket club's first eleven. Leaning back and trying to redirect some of his blond locks into a less windswept look, the de facto detective ventured that Gary Short could be discounted in terms of motive for murdering Hamish. His selection as a replacement had been described by the coach as what would be a surprise to all, and thus he could not have anticipated gaining by killing the dead man. That left Pieter Hamilton and Jim Harris with a direct potential motive. Milburn posited that this was not news, and Penfold managed to nod with his coffee cup held to his mouth.

The detective had little new information either. Harriet Elliott had confirmed that her brother was enthusiastic and committed to his cricket, whilst being quite concerned that his physical slightness, in comparison to his competition, would limit his ultimate achievements. She had said that he had mentioned it on most occasions she had talked to him in the last eight or ten months. Tony concluded, 'So, we're still at square one. Could be murder, suicide or accident, and our list of suspects is no narrower.'

'The Pathans were an interesting pair to talk to.'

'Interesting, how?'

'I learnt as much about them as they he told me about the other cricketing suspects,' the kiwi pondered staring at the surface of the drink, held close to his face in both hands.

'Well, both Vivender and Aisha potentially have a motive – over protective father, and jealous lover.'

'Sorry, which is which?' Penfold smiled as Tony snorted into his coffee.

'So, which one killed him?' Tony batted the ball back to his friend.

The New Zealander returned to a serious consideration. 'Hmm. In Aisha there was genuine grief. But even if she killed him in a fit of passion, she'd still be grief stricken. He was the man she loved.'

'I'm not sure I feel more sorry for her that her loved one is dead, or that she was in love with him in the first place.'

Penfold raised his eyebrows knowingly, and moved on to the father. 'The coach also had bottled-up emotions about the whole thing, and is clearly stuck in a cross-cultural and cross-generational abyss. There'll be tears before bedtime with such a bright and beautiful daughter.'

'Do you want to throw any more suspects into the ring?'

'Actually, did you see my entry in your notebook the other day?'

'Oh, yeah, what makes you think it wasn't a crime of passion?'

'Crime of passion, maybe; but not a crime committed in a fit of rage. The methodology is all wrong. Not only would the murderer have to research the drugs in question, and source them, but to administer them with no signs of a struggle? That is no sudden loss of temper.'

'He clearly had a motive for injecting Somnulone, his sister reckoned he was obsessive about being undersized. Which brings us back to suicide or accident.' The detective leant his cheek against his hand and swirled the final inch of coffee around in the tall white mug.

'Oh, it's murder.'

Milburn's phone rang and he frowned, looking at the police station's phone number on the screen. He fully expected Meredith to be calling. He pictured her acting bright and bubbly, as if nothing had happened that morning. 'DS Milburn.' It was Andrew Singh calling to tell Tony that Kate and Daniel were both being released from custody. No more evidence had been passed to Sergeant Singh, so he couldn't argue with, or stall, Mr Smythe any longer. It was almost 24 hours they had been in custody anyway. Sitting in the back corner of The Daily Espresso, Tony knew he had nothing with which to argue against this. 'Right, thanks for telling me.' He hung up, said nothing further, and went back to staring into his drink.

'Bad news, Milburn?'

Without looking up, Tony replied, 'I don't know. Kate Withenshaw and Daniel Ramsbotham are being released from custody. There's at least two other cases slipping away from us. And one of them could be Elliott's killer too.' His voice was tired and monotone.

Penfold was upbeat. 'Well, given that you've not got enough evidence on them, maybe it's best that they're out and about, so they can get into bother and give you the evidence you need. Maybe they'll go running to Hamilton, and between the three of them somebody will slip up.'

Milburn and Penfold stood for 20 minutes, silently watching the Durham County Cricket squad practising. Penfold was intrigued with the fielding practice that had a dozen of them engaged in, what appeared to be, a sort of synchronised dance where they occasionally threw a cricket ball around. Although not as perfectly timed as a military marching band, they seemed to run in and out of each other without communicating, and always stop ready to catch the ball as it was thrown to them. There was little in the exercise that Penfold could relate to the activities of an actual cricket match.

Tony was much more interested in watching the remainder of the players who were in a nets practice again. When the pavilion clock reached exactly 3pm, Vivender Pathan, standing in the midst of the fielding practice blew three times on his whistle. Those practising on the grass swapped with those queuing up to bowl. The batsmen in the nets stayed where they were, taking a few moments to adjust their padding, or lift their helmet to wipe sweat from the brow.

When the training restarted, those on the pitch were engaged in a totally new fielding exercise. The specialist fielding coach, a short, stocky man with a shaven head, would whack a ball away towards the boundary, and a pair of players would chase after it. As the lead man caught up with the ball, he would dive and slide after it and, whilst sliding, flick it up and back for his colleague to catch at an easy height and throw back at the stumps, where a wicket-keeper was ready to catch it and pretend to flay the stumps. Penfold knew how cricket worked, but this was detailed stuff. He made a mental note to return and watch again, once the case was finished and he could concentrate on the technical details.

169

Pieter Hamilton had just joined the fielding practice, whilst Australian Gary Short had moved to the bowling lines. Jim Harris was nowhere to be seen, although he had been at the funeral four hours previously.

Milburn and Penfold chatted briefly about how they were going to conduct these interviews. The detective had to do all the talking, and they agreed that they would not waste time with Mr Short. Penfold reckoned that they should speak to each man separately, but with Coach Pathan present. This would beef up any witnessing that might be needed, and they could watch his body language at the same time. And it assumed that Jim Harris was somewhere nearby.

Penfold finished their planning by adding, 'Also, we shouldn't forget that there may have been some other motive entirely that we haven't thought of. We should confirm with Pathan that there are no other suspects we should be looking into.'

Milburn nodded with resignation. He was quite pale in the cold March air, and this made him look positively ill. The last thing Tony wanted to do was to increase the size of the suspect pool. As usual, Penfold was wearing baggy shorts. They were in quite a staid, stone colour, but nonetheless it had perturbed Tony that his friend had considered them suitable for a funeral. Let alone suitable for the weather. They had decided to wait until the current fielding practice was complete before accosting the suspects. Leaning as casually as possible against the corner of a grandstand wall, Tony pushed both hands down in the pockets of his dark trousers, and tried to take a light-hearted approach. 'Are shorts normal attire for a funeral in New Zealand?'

170

Penfold also had his hands in his baggy pockets, and turned to look at the detective. Unhurriedly, a smile played about his lips and he responded, 'Probably not. I've never been to a funeral in New Zealand. Are they suitable for a funeral in England?'

Tony looked confused and stood up straighter, without the aid of the wall. 'I'm sure you told me your father died several years ago?'

Penfold did not alter his body position at all, but the smile left his face. 'You asked about funerals in New Zealand, and I told you: I have no experience of them.'

'He must have had a funeral though, surely?'

'Milburn, I only deal in facts, you know this. When I say I've never been to a kiwi funeral, what part of that don't you understand?' Penfold was staring straight into Tony's eyes with a ferocious intensity.

Tony was rattled by this response from his easy-going friend, and decided it would be prudent not to pursue it. 'Well, they aren't the done thing for a funeral here. I can't imagine what the Elliotts must have thought of you. Strange non-policeman standing in exactly the same place throughout their son's funeral, in shorts.' Milburn shook his head. When he looked up at Penfold, the olive skinned face was intently watching the action on the cricket field, but there was a touch of a smile again.

Coach Pathan blew his whistle three times again, and the cricketers stopped the exercises they were engaged in. DS Milburn waved to Vivender Pathan and once he had explained the need for further inquiries, the little Indian called the South

171

African over. He also explained that Harris was at the university sports ground coaching their women's team.

'For God's sake, people, I've told you all I know, isn't it.' Hamilton started aggressively.

'I'm sorry to disrupt your training again, Mr Hamilton. Just a few more questions.' Milburn knew he had to take the moral high ground so that Pathan would continue to support their questioning at the club. 'We know you were rivals with Mr Elliott for selection to the first team here. Were you also friends?'

'Look, I'm new to the club, I hardly knew him. And I didn't really want him as a friend. He was weak, you know. So, you see, I didn't know him. I didn't know anything about him, I can't help you.' Pieter turned to walk up to the nets.

Penfold quietly chimed in, his kiwi accent sounding strongly. 'You know nobody else is being confrontational about helping us. Even those who didn't really know the guy are doing their best to help find out what happened to him.'

Hamilton stopped and turned back to face them. After a pause, he smiled. 'Go on, then. What great questions do you have that you think I can answer?' He ran his hand across his sweaty scalp.

Detective Sergeant Milburn turned a page in his notebook, looked back up and continued. 'Who do you think would stand to gain most by Hamish Elliott's death? I mean here at the club.'

'Man, I have no idea. I intend to be a permanent selection for the first team, but that would have happened anyway, even if Elliott were still alive. He was no match for me.'

172

'Mr Pathan doesn't seem to think that that is quite such a given as you do.'

'Look, I'm new to the club, isn't it. The coach hasn't had a chance to see me enough to know what I'm capable of. But he will.' Vivender was silent and Tony looked at him to gauge whether the coach considered Hamilton's argument plausible. His round, dark face was impossible to read. Pathan's eyes were darting all over Hamilton's face.

Penfold rebutted, 'You played for Durham University for three years, so your abilities should be well known here. And your bowling figures with them don't point to an extraordinary talent.'

Hamilton stormed back the half dozen paces he had left between them. He had a cricket ball in his hand and waved it in Penfold's face, as if he were shaking his fist. 'What would you know about it? I've seen you in the nets here. You don't know the first thing about cricket.' Penfold did not reply, and moved back a step.

Milburn jumped in. 'So you don't reckon that anybody would stand to gain from his death?'

'He was a waste of space – I reckon everybody's better off!' There was a clear grin that passed fleetingly over Pieter's face. 'Look man, are we gonna stand here talking all day, or are we gonna play some cricket. I need to show Coach Pathan what I can do, so how about one of you guys bat for a bit, and I'll show you that I'm good enough for the first team.' He held up the cricket ball towards Milburn and then Penfold, offering it up.

The New Zealander replied first, 'Oh no, thanks. As you saw when I was in the nets the other day, I'm really no good. I prefer tennis.' The tall bowler turned, sweeping the outstretched cricket ball under the detective's nose.

Tony looked Hamilton in the face, ignoring the waving ball. He calmly stated, 'I'd love to.' They all walked up to the long, netted alleys, and Pieter opened his kit bag and started passing Tony items of padding to put on. The first item any batsman puts on is always the genital protector, and DS Milburn was quick to notice when Hamilton failed to hand him one. 'Sorry, I'll need a box.'

Hamilton smiled knowingly, implying that this omission had been a deliberate joke. He passed over the hard white plastic cup, which Milburn struggled to seat securely in his boxer shorts. Strapping the remainder of the legs pads on allowed him to support it well enough for what he knew would only be a few balls practice. 'These leg pads seem thinner than I remember is normal?'

'They're a new development with interchangeable padding inserts. Thinner if I'm doing a light practice, or if the match situation means I need to do a lot of running; thicker if we're up against some real fast bowling.'

As he joined the Velcro that held the gloves in place and tested the feeling of the bat handle, Tony casually said, 'Daniel Ramsbotham tells me you two are cousins.' Hamilton did not reply, but glared. The detective continued, having to look up through the grille on the helmet to observe the seething face under short blond hair, 'Yes, and it's pretty clear that you two are in business together. Kate pretty much told as much about his visit here the other day.'

Pieter bent over and put his face right to the bars on the helmet. Milburn could feel strong heat from the other's face.

His voice was breathy and the volume clipped. 'You don't want to go messing in my business. In South Africa we have some very nasty ways of showing policemen exactly what they need to be investigating and what they don't.' Penfold and Pathan had stopped a short distance away to watch Milburn's batting attempts and, although they could see a clear confrontation taking place, nobody else could hear what was being said. The coach moved to intervene, but Penfold held his arm to indicate that he should not. Milburn turned and walked into the net, positioning himself in front of the practice wicket at the far end.

There were three bowlers and Hamilton taking turns to bowl at him. The first two lobbed up very slow and easy balls which Tony hit with a modicum of success. He smiled as the second one shot back towards the bowler in a nice defensive stroke. Then Pieter hurled one in which bounced up and smashed into Milburn's rib cage. He was immediately winded, struggling for air, and had to stand, hanging on to the side netting, for a good two minutes before he was able to continue. The practice continued, and occasionally Vivender would make some brief comment about how DS Milburn could improve. Every ball from Hamilton, however, hit Tony's body somewhere. He even took one on the helmet, which, fortunately, did its job well.

Penfold was observing all around the practice area. He made no movement or comment to anyone, but saw Daniel Ramsbotham pull up in his girlfriend's BMW and take a parcel to the main reception desk of the cricket club. Ramsbotham did not wait, or even look out at the practising players. He handed in the large cardboard box and left.

THE CRICKETER'S CORPSE

When the South African finally succeeded in hitting Milburn in the ill-fitting box, Vivender Pathan called a halt to it.

'Remember what I told you, policeman,' Pieter called to him, as Tony leant on his bat, trying to regain the capability to walk out of the practice area. Hamilton pointed his finger at Tony, and turned to go into the all-glass building. He met Penfold coming out. Pushing past Penfold, Hamilton continued his threats. 'You better keep him out of my affairs.' He jerked a thumb over his shoulder back at Milburn, and disappeared inside.

They drove back to Durham to pay a visit to the practice session of the university women's team. Penfold explained that his chat with the receptionist at the cricket club had revealed that Hamilton had had a box of spare inserts for his leg pads delivered.

DS Milburn wasn't surprised by this news. 'Yes, he told me his sponsor is developing a new system with variable thickness pads that are interchangeable.'

Penfold nodded. 'Sounds like a most innovative idea. They were delivered to the club's reception desk by a lad about the same height as me, and with floppy blond hair...'

Tony couldn't help but interrupt flippantly, 'Why did you deliver them?!'

'Ha ha,' Penfold responded deadpan. 'The delivery boy drove a green BMW with this number plate. In his large, brown hand, Penfold held up a notepad with a car registration written in the middle of the page.

To look at the paper, Milburn took his foot off the accelerator and the car coasted along the dual carriageway.

'Fuck me, Daniel Ramsbotham. Why would he be delivering Hamilton's gear?'

'Didn't you say they're cousins?' Penfold looked sidelong at his friend's greying temples. It had started to rain, and beyond Tony's face, the side window had streaked raindrops pursuing a wiggly path towards the back of the car. Penfold's gaze was attracted to these, and he continued holding out the notepad unnecessarily.

Tony put his foot down again, and above the revving of the engine countered, 'Yes, but that's no reason for Ramsbotham to deliver them. Why doesn't his sponsor just post them?'

Penfold paused for a while, his eyes now unfocussed although still aimed at the driver's window. His thoughts came back when Tony pushed his hand away. 'Maybe he has a stack of them and needed some more.'

'Wouldn't you keep them at your own house? Shit, check that folder on the back seat – they don't live at the same address do they? How could we have missed that?'

Penfold rifled through the manila folder that held the summary of all information that Milburn had managed to put together thus far. 'Hmm, no, Hamilton has a Chester-le-Street address.'

'God knows. This case, or cases, seem to make less and less sense the more we find out.' As they parked in front of the university's brand new sports centre, Tony held up both hands and exhaled loudly. 'At least the new nets facility here is indoor.'

The two men wandered in to the sports hall which, was sectioned off into several cricket practice lanes. There were several groups of female cricketers. Beside one line up of bowlers stood Jim Harris, talking to the group whilst simultaneously demonstrating a straight arm circling action, to show them some finer point of bowling technique. DS Milburn interrupted this and took Harris to an empty far corner of the hall to chat.

In the meantime, Penfold charmed the ladies with his nonchalant good looks, and the continued implication that he knew next to nothing about the game of cricket. Ten minutes later, Tony walked back ahead of the powerful bowler to extract Penfold from half a dozen women explaining to him all the details of leather and willow. Harris paused several yards away, with his back to the remainder of the people. Penfold towered over them and to him it appeared from behind as if the guest coach was wiping his eyes. The impressionable young women cooed farewells as Milburn metaphorically dragged his friend back outside.

The sports centre cafe had some outside seating, all of which was empty. A big red umbrella in the centre of each table was closed up for the day. Rainclouds had blown through and two men sat in the chilly sunshine, which was growing rapidly colder as the sun approached the horizon. In this instance, the horizon was the top of a steep, wooded hill the other side of the main cricket field from their table. The disappearing sun silhouetted the trees on the hill so that the wood, looking down from 50 yards above, appeared dark and menacing. Its shadow was already nearer than the most recently cut wicket on the field.

Tony thought he spotted Penfold shiver, but it was so fleeting that he could not be sure he hadn't imagined the

178

movement. They compared notes from their interviews. Milburn rested his cheek against a fist, the arm of which was resting on the table at the elbow. He looked bored, reading from his policeman's notebook. Harris had been suitably upset, having been to a friend's funeral earlier in the day. And he had not seemed particularly interested in the future bowling selections of Vivender Pathan. Tony reckoned that the man had seemed quite detached from the idea of playing a professional game of cricket at all. Moreover, Harris had suggested that he fully expected the club to recruit a replacement player, and thus the competition for a place in the first team was likely still as difficult for him as ever.

Tony's conclusion, mainly based on copper's gut instinct, rather than the man's actual statements, was that Jim Harris did not kill his friend for a chance at greater professional success. The detective sergeant was careful to confirm, more to himself than to Penfold, that there could have been other motivations for it, but not to win a place in the first team's bowling line up.

Tony flipped the notebook closed, and became aware of how cold his fingers were. The sun had now disappeared behind what the rugby players referred to as Hill 45, as they knew its 45-degree angle from having to run up it during training. Penfold waved towards the car, and the two got up to head back to it. As they walked, he passed on what had been gleaned from the female cricketers he had spoken to.

'The general feeling was that they don't like Harris much personally. He's a good cricketer and they recognise that as being useful to help improve their own game, bowling in particular. But the consensus was that he was more there to show off to them than through a genuine interest in coaching for its own sake.'

'Doesn't surprise me, my guess is that that is the case for most of the coaches from the county club.'

Penfold nodded, 'Well, yes, probably. I did ask about drugs, and that brought more condemnation. They think female sport is sufficiently low on the totem pole that there is no point in drug induced performance enhancement, so they were utterly underwhelmed when Harris boasted of being able to supply them with a guaranteed no-trace steroid.'

'Really? That's not what I expected.' Tony turned his head to look at his friend as they walked.

'Did you think our lady cricketers were like East German shot-putters from the Soviet era then?'

Milburn smiled as he clicked the car's remote central locking open. 'I meant I didn't expect Harris to be the drugs supplier, out of our group of suspects. Mind you, he does have the sort of physique that steroids could bring, and I bet not being in the first team reduces the drug testing regime you're subjected to.'

They sat in the front seats of Tony's unmarked police car. Penfold added in agreement, 'And even if he were to get banned, he's lost little, but could still practise as much until the return from any ban.'

'It's not right though. I'm sure he's too … I don't know, his character's just wrong for it.' Again, the detective turned to take in Penfold's body language.

'I know what you mean, he's not really alpha male material. Indeed, the girls all grimaced when they recalled how he had asked most of them out at one time or another.'

'Mind you, most of the drug dealing scrotes I have dealt with in the past make him look like a Greek god.'

Penfold frowned. 'But he just doesn't have the aggression you'd associate with steroids. Not even a strut.'

As Milburn drove them the few minutes back to the police station to pick up Penfold's car, they sat in silence, speculative as to what, if anything, they had found out.

It was 6pm when Penfold and Milburn parked up in convoy outside Penfold's seaside home. The rain was falling again, albeit only lightly, but a cold offshore wind made the March night very cold.

Inside, Mantoro immediately supplied both men with the obligatory cup of black tar, which passes for coffee at Casa de Penfold. Mantoro himself had no drink, but held a saucer of cashew nuts, which he munched on methodically. The three men moved to Penfold's study, where he had promised Milburn a summary of the research he had undertaken regarding the drugs involved in the case. This was highly magnanimous, as Milburn would later comment ironically, because Trident and Mantoro had actually done the bulk of the work.

Penfold's computer screen suddenly filled with the cartoonized version of Trident. 'Yo Bro!'

'Must you be so?' her brother chastised.

'Whadup?'

'Your end is coming soon – you will burn in a bonfire of the vernaculars.' Penfold and his sister's avatar were both smiling. They liked to keep a playful check on each other's sensibilities. 'Milburn is here.'

Trident turned to try and look sideways out of the screen, and at this prompt, Tony moved closer to Penfold so he was likely to be in the view of the webcam which was wall-mounted behind the desk at which Penfold sat. 'Tonester!' Trident cried excitedly.

'Enough frippery, you loon: tell us what you've found out.' The seated kiwi pointed a finger straight at cartoon Trident and she pulled a mockingly straight face, lips sealed for a moment.

Her face then brightened to a natural glow, like her brother's normal appearance. Milburn was surprised that the computer software could deliver such an aura, which, in Penfold, could not be isolated as any particular physical manifestation. 'Well, firstly, none of your suspects have any drug records from anywhere in the world, except Kate Withenshaw's cannabis caution, but I believe you already know about that.'

'Yeah,' Tony sounded non-committal.

Trident smiled out of the screen and continued, 'But, of course, steroids are not illegal in many parts of the world.'

'Uh, huh,' Penfold waved his hand in a circling motion to encourage Trident to get to the meat of her information.

'Now, the Priapra/Somnulone drug combination is principally used as a means of secret export from the Indian Subcontinent – mostly Pakistan, but also significant amounts from India – and Southern Africa, there mostly the RSA.' Tony moved his hand towards his friend's shoulder, with a quizzical look on his face, but Trident spotted him and clarified, 'Republic of South Africa.' The detective nodded. 'Both have suitably large chemical industries for the equipment and

182

technical skills to be readily available. And they're also sufficiently corrupt for such an industrial carry-on. Indeed, there is some, as yet uncorroborated, evidence that the same Asian criminal gang is responsible for the whole lot, with separate set-ups in the three countries.'

Mantoro joined in. 'These days, there's no real need though for any level of developed economy in order for drug gangs to do their work. The labs can be set up anywhere: they have access to Antonov planes and Chinooks, and can just transport the whole lot to a jungle or a desert area that they control.' He drawled without looking up from his cashews.

'Jungle generally preferred, as it's harder to see from the air,' Trident was nodding. 'However, there are plenty of chemical factories in these countries where these things could just carry on without really any questions being asked. Especially if you're producing something like life jackets. Even the employees don't realise what they're working with is illegal.'

'Life jackets … or cricketing leg pads,' Penfold chimed in. His sister just shrugged.

Mantoro though answered what hadn't actually been a question, 'Yes, possibly, but there wasn't enough in those outer covers you brought to make any conclusions. Because you need to separate the two chemicals first and then test, I wasn't able to find anything for certain.'

'Um, what is he talking about?' DS Milburn asked slowly.

'Let's go downstairs and I'll show you.' Penfold fairly leapt out of his chair, put his hands on Tony's shoulders and physically turned him towards the door.

'Later, loser,' Trident crowed and then disappeared.

183

As they descended the stone staircase into a gloomy and thoroughly Victorian basement, Milburn thought that the whole place had the look of a grainy old Frankenstein movie. There were even cobwebs. He was unprepared, though for the continuance of this mad scientist lair that affronted him when he turned back from the bottom of the stairs into the main underground room.

There was a giant wooden table, perhaps 15 feet square, covered in the interconnected glassware of a giant chemical experiment. There was a Bunsen burner flickering away at the far end of the table, not actually heating any part of the experiment. The nearest flask was shaped like a pear and contained a milky white liquid. From the top of this, a glass tube travelled vertically upwards, before curving 90 degrees to enter another flask, which held a black metallic powder, and had three other tubes coming off it. Milburn's gaze followed the one that descended at a diagonal angle down towards the table top and was encased in a separate helical tube through which water ran continuously, supplied from somewhere out of sight under the staircase.

He had stopped at the sight of the giant chemistry set, but Penfold and Mantoro had moved to different points at the table, and were fiddling with bits and pieces of the glassware, turning glass taps, adjusting and moving the Bunsen burner, removing beakers and replacing them.

Tony looked towards the surfer playing chemist and barely managed to articulate, 'What the fuck…?'

In reply, he was greeted with the beaming, tanned smile that Penfold wore when he was showing off. 'We've set this up to split up the Somnulone/Priapra mixture, so that if we find anything that might be it in smuggling form, we can test if that's what it is. It'll be far quicker than waiting for the police labs – they've only ever previously done this test down in London.'

'Don't overheat that acid,' Mantoro said urgently, pointing across the table to where Penfold was playing the Bunsen burner's hottest flame setting onto a round-bottomed flask containing a transparent liquid.

Penfold looked quickly down at what he was doing, and placed the burner aside. 'Oops. No harm done, though, we haven't started the test. Well, the demonstration test. Mantoro has already established that we need more test substance to make any conclusions.'

Milburn wore a baffled look. 'What test substance? What exactly are you doing here?'

'South Africa is one of the likely sources of these drugs, right?'

'Ok.'

'So, when Hamilton threw away some leg pads the other day, I took them back out of the bin and brought them to test.'

Mantoro interrupted, 'But we need the actual padding, the outer covers aren't going to be the drugs and not enough of the padding will come off in them to separate and then test.'

Penfold scowled at the little Latino. 'Yes, it turns out he only threw away the outer parts – the inner padding was missing. When we get some more to sample, we can use this experiment to prove it's the source of these drugs in the North-east.'

'More?'

'Yes, we need to get hold of some of the padding from inside his leg pads.'

185

'Eh, why?'

'Because that's how he's smuggling the stuff into the country. Spare leg padding from his South African "sponsors", half of which are real pads, and half are these drugs.'

The detective sergeant was concerned that his sometimes conceited friend was fixated on one particular outcome. Moreover though, Tony felt like his associate was taking over and when he got his teeth into an investigative bone, it was very difficult to get him to give it up. 'Well, hang on. India. Cricket leg pads. What about Pathan?'

The flaxen mop of hair shook, and Penfold stated blankly, 'You're mixing your motives. The enraged father who is also a drug dealer to his team? Pathan's not the one.'

Milburn was not going to let Penfold run the show. Whether he turned out to be right or not, they had to investigate all options. 'Well, the India connection is enough to warrant interviewing the coach again. Besides, we still need to interview him and his family together to see how the alibis hang together. It's Sunday evening, they should all be at home now, I'm going to go and see what they have to say for themselves.'

Penfold shrugged, 'Suit yourself.'

Tony's awkwardness at this was doubled when he stepped towards the stairs to leave the dingy basement and the New Zealander's strong frame remained rooted to the spot aside the large table. 'Are you gonna come along?'

'Do you want me to?'

The notion that he was having to accommodate a spoilt child flitted through Tony's mind, but he was glad to have an opportunity to take the moral high ground and remain utterly professional. 'Of course, come and do your human observation

186

thing, and then debrief me as to why neither Aisha or her father are the culprit.' He knew that this challenge, although undoubtedly a transparent ploy to Penfold, would do the trick. Penfold invariably proved, and liked to be seen to prove, that he had been right all along. Tony had, however, seen enough occasions where, one surf later, the man had been intelligent enough to overcome his pride and revamp a theory in a different direction in light of new evidence. More importantly though, even if Penfold was right all along, this would be Tony's investigation. Leads followed, suspects interviewed, and evidence gathered, all following his direction.

The black car DS Milburn was using pulled up in the Pathan's driveway at around 8pm. The evening was dark and crisp, but the new street was well lit with the orange glow of urban night.

Vivender Pathan invited them inside and showed them to the same room that Milburn had been in previously. The best room for visitors, with its cream and red colour scheme, and much gold braid, gave a very Indian look. Aisha entered the room as the two investigators sat down. Vivender shuffled awkwardly around one of the sofas, and excused himself to go and get Mrs Pathan. Aisha approached and stopped in front of Milburn, who looked vaguely ginger in the light entering behind him from the street. She stood with her head down, black hair tied behind in a ponytail, and a lone tear trickling down her cheek.

Watching from the other sofa, the scene appeared to Penfold like a good little girl unfortunate to be standing in front of her headmaster for some reason. Aisha spoke so quietly that he could not make out the words that cut at Tony's heart. She was either an incredibly good, evil, actress, or was genuinely heartbroken.

'You will catch them, won't you?' she barely croaked the sentence out. Milburn's hands fidgeted with his notebook, and his mouth moved silently a couple of times, like a fish. Before he could compose himself to produce a bureaucratic, non-committal response, she continued, a little louder and with more composure – enough so Penfold could also now hear. 'This was no accident, he was murdered. I don't know why. I loved him.'

As the policeman sat nonplussed, gazing at her, and the surfer deliberated over whether she meant she didn't know why he was murdered, or she didn't know why she loved him, Aisha went to sit on the single armchair that completed the triangle with their sofas.

Mr and Mrs Pathan came into the room and took up standing positions on either side of Aisha's armchair so the family lined up united against their interrogators. The parents looked very much like each other, both in stocky build with chubby limbs, and in facial appearance. Each had a round, brown visage, framed by short-cut dark hair, and mottled skin like walnut shell. Mrs Pathan could be distinguished from her husband by a full bosom and a pair of small, round spectacles. She also wore a sari that matched the colour scheme of the room, whereas the father wore a white shirt and business style grey trousers. The formality of their dress was somewhat lessened though as neither parent wore shoes. Aisha was also without shoes, but she wore her normal blue jeans and white blouse, so the black socks on her feet were in keeping.

'Many thanks for seeing us on a Sunday evening,' Milburn began formally, but in a friendly tone.

'You are always welcome in our home.' Mrs Pathan's response was equally formal and sounded insincere – a keeping-up-appearances type of answer.

'Thank you, madam, we are here for two different reasons, so I'll start with the straightforward part.' Milburn addressed Vivender, 'I'd like your support to ask your cricketers to complete an anonymised questionnaire about the use of drugs within professional cricket. It will not be used against them or the club, and will cover medications, recreational and performance-enhancing drugs. I really need to know what the background to this case is, and particularly to find out if we're looking in the wrong place by seeking a drugs connection to Mr Elliott's death. Would that be OK, Mr Pathan?'

The coach stood silently for some time, thinking through the question and working out what his answer would be. Everyone waited for the pronouncement. Quietly, and hesitantly, he finally answered, 'I don't think I can see any problem with that. I'll have to clear it with the director and the players' union rep, but let's assume yes. Everybody is keen to help in your investigations. We have a pre-practice meeting tomorrow morning at 9am, if you would like to come to the ground then. I'm assuming it will only take a few minutes of our time?'

Tony nodded and made a brief note in his little book. 'OK, secondly then, we'd like you to tell us more about Aisha's relationship with Hamish Elliott, in detail, from the first time they met until the last time she saw him. Including Aisha's whereabouts on the night he died, and I'd like to hear it first from Mrs Pathan, please.' As Milburn spoke, his eyes had moved backwards and forwards along the family line-up. Penfold smiled wryly to himself, noting that his detective pal was deliberately trying to antagonise without saying anything at all confrontational.

Vivender Pathan jumped straight in, 'Now, just a minute Detective Sergeant, we have already explained those facts to you previously, and submitted to DNA testing, to prove Aisha had nothing to do with the man. He worked for me and she is my daughter, so their paths will have crossed, but that is the limit of their relationship. There was no relationship.'

Penfold uncrossed his bare legs – cargo shorts and sports sandals again – and sat up to interrupt proceedings, 'Coach Pathan, do you have any cricket equipment?' Everyone else in the room turned, in bewildered confusion, to look at the tanned surfer, who wore a happy expression of childlike innocence.

The Indian stuttered, 'I… um… I… what?'

'I know you're no longer a player, but do you have any kit? Gloves or pads, or maybe a bat?'

'I still have my wicket-keeping stuff, but I haven't used it since I came here. Like you said, I'm the coach.'

'Would you mind showing it to me?'

The coach looked questioningly back to Milburn, who still wore a befuddled expression himself, but slowly said, 'Yes, please, Mr Pathan, if you could.' Tony also slowly waved his hand towards the door to indicate that they should go.

Vivender looked at his wife and daughter, appeared to try to say something, and then seemed to lose track of what he was going to say, and shuffled off towards the doorway muttering, 'My kitbag is in the garage.' Penfold leapt up and followed.

Milburn turned back to the females, and repeated, 'Mrs Pathan, tell me of Aisha's time with Hamish.'

Aisha's mother looked at her daughter who was looking up sadly. She then proceeded, albeit falteringly, to tell a similar story to that which DS Milburn had already heard from the daughter herself. It was a low-key friendship, which slowly moved to include coffee or the occasional dinner together. She was insistent that they were not boyfriend and girlfriend, and became quite upset when Milburn pursued questioning about any sexual liaisons. At this point, Aisha held up her hand to hold her mother's. They remained supporting each other like this as Mrs Pathan repeatedly insisted that Aisha was not that sort of girl, and they had never given her the opportunity in any case. He concluded by confirming the details of Aisha's non-alibi for the previous Thursday night. Her mother's version of events tallied well with the way it had previously been told to him and to Meredith.

Penfold followed the diminutive old cricketer along the hallway and, from the bright kitchen, a door entered the attached garage. It also lit up brightly when he switched on the tube on the ceiling, and the space was a mass of cardboard boxes and old suitcases, which gave the impression that they were all full.

On the floor, by the middle of the back wall, Vivender showed him a large, green canvas kitbag. He opened it and stood back offering Penfold the kit to rummage through. This was done silently, and in a rather arbitrary manner, occasionally holding a leg pad to his own long limbs, or a small glove to his large hands. In every case, it was obvious that the equipment would never fit him, especially as wicket keeping leg pads were

191

shorter than normal ones. Vivender wondered what was going through the man's mind.

Finally, Penfold retained the newest-looking pair of leg pads, and asked if he might borrow them, especially as Pathan no longer ever used them. He was so confused by this whole scene, that Vivender didn't even try to ask what Penfold might want them for, or argue that they were not his size. He simply shrugged and said, 'I suppose so.'

When the two re-entered the front room, where Milburn was eyeing up the two ladies holding hands for mutual support, Penfold held up the leg pads, like a boy who had just been given a new toy from a favourite uncle. Pathan wandered over to take up his position on the other side of Aisha to her mother. He wore a look of resignation.

The detective proceeded to goad him again, 'Mrs Pathan was just telling me about how you cannot account for Aisha's whereabouts on the night of Mr Elliott's death; or, indeed, on many nights when she met up with him.' Aisha scowled, as that was patently not what her mother had just outlined, but the two women both remained silent.

Vivender's submissive body language immediately left him, and he noticeably increased in stature as his blood boiled. 'How many times do I have to tell you that my daughter had nothing to do with his death? She had nothing to do with Hamish at all.'

'Now, that's not really true, is it?' The DS paused for a moment to let his question be open for any of the family members, before continuing, 'Aisha, you and Hamish had a very close relationship did you not?'

Another single tear slid from the Aisha's left eye, and her head turned slightly upwards towards her father. He did not look down, but took a small step towards the policeman. There was a coffee table between them, but the bottled anger was plain.

Through gritted teeth, the aggrieved man hissed, 'Detective, we will ask my daughter one last time, and this time you will listen to her answer and take it on board. Then you will leave my house, and you will leave us alone. Hamish Elliott was told in no uncertain terms that my daughter was completely off limits to him, and all the men in the cricket club. Now….' The dark man turn to his lighter skinned, beautiful daughter and said very slowly, 'Aisha, tell the detective, so he is completely clear, that you and Mr Elliott had no more contact than the occasional conversation at the cricket club. Tell him you never saw the man socially, and that you have never had a boyfriend at all, let alone that man.'

Aisha had two thin streams of tears lining her face and her gaze was locked on Tony. After her father had completed his question, there was a disturbing silence for a long time. The distressed young woman started to shake slightly, a barely perceptible and silent vibration, but Milburn noticed it. Her father breathed in deeply, inflating his chest. His fingers clenched slightly, not into fists but turning his hands more into claws. Breathing out slowly, he repeated, 'Daughter.'

She was breathing through a slightly open mouth, laboured breaths, and slowly turned her head from staring at Tony to look up to her father. She said nothing, staring questioningly at him, with slightly widened and red eyes. The two continued to look at each other without speaking.

193

Mrs Pathan let go of her daughter's hand and took a step forward, so that she was physically between both Penfold and Milburn and her family. 'Gentlemen, I think you have all the answers we can give you. If you don't mind.' She held her hand up to the doorway.

There was a slight further pause, as Milburn eyed her up, and then the two men looked at each other with a slight nod, and got up to leave. They were the only ones to move – the Indian family appeared to have been turned to stone.

As they let themselves out of the front door, the DS called back, 'See you tomorrow, then.' Sitting in the car in the driveway, they could see a tremendous argument through the bay window. Mrs Pathan quickly drew the curtains until just her round face was left peeping out, with an aura of light encircling it.

'She looks like an eclipse,' Penfold mused.

Wednesday 27th March

Tony had been in the CID office since just before 7am. He was producing the drugs questionnaire to be given to the Durham County Cricketers at their training session, and had to get it completed and copied before the morning briefing at 8am.

Whilst standing at the rumbling photocopier, Tony absent-mindedly watched the people coming and going in the car park behind the police station. He was simultaneously fiddling with his hair, stroking the greying temples, and then backwards and down behind his ears. Normally, he got his hair cut at the end of the month, but had missed it the previous week as his barber of 12 years had been away skiing. Tony was loath to let anyone else cut his hair, not because the straight hair being cut short, back and sides, required hairdressing talent, but because he had always found the negotiations with an unknown hairdresser surprisingly stressful. Alan knew how he liked it, and they had no need to discuss his hair when he went for a haircut. That simplicity appealed to Milburn; and Alan was cheap. Nearly a week late for his monthly cut then meant that Tony's hair was bigger than he really ever liked it to be. Probably only noticeably bigger in his own mind, rather than perceptibly to

195

everybody else, but this caused him to groom it a lot more than normal, to make sure nothing untoward was happening up there.

He stopped suddenly, hand in hair, and leant forward, as a thin figure scurried between cars to the rear entrance almost directly below the CID office windows. He was sure that he had just seen Godolphin Barnes coming in to work. This was unusual in itself as his immediate boss was absent with various ailments as often as he was working. However, DI Barnes had particularly emphasised on Friday night that he would be working this week, but at County HQ on a training course. The course was scheduled to last all week, and this was only Wednesday morning.

The dozen or so officers began gathering around the room just as the photocopier was coming to the end of the print run. Last to arrive were Diane Meredith, immaculately turned out as always, and DCI Harry Hardwick, vaguely dishevelled as always. Barnes had not appeared in CID.

Hardwick closed the door to the big office behind himself, and coughed gruffly to begin the meeting. He presented a number of investigations, new and on-going, outlining any updates since the day before, and any changes to assignments. Hamish Elliott's death didn't feature at all, although Tony hadn't expected it to – not conclusively a murder, and he hadn't reported any updates to his boss.

Once he had dismissed the staff and detectives present, the DCI took Meredith and Milburn into Milburn's office and shut the door behind them. There was a large safety window in the wooden door and a couple of their colleagues gawped through it as they moved around the main office. Hardwick positioned his large back in front of it. Neither of the others spoke, and Diane had her arms folded across her chest, whilst looking back and forth between the two men. Tony stood in front of his desk, and leant slightly so that his left hand was resting on it.

The boss handed him a sheet of paper: it was a standard form from the Coroner's office, a follow up to a post-mortem, making conclusions from that and any other forensic evidence. This one identified Elliott's death as murder. Tony slumped back so that he was almost sitting on the edge of his desk. He tried to read the various sections of the one page document, but his mind would not focus on any given item in it for long enough to take it in. With Meredith ushered in by the DCI, this could only mean that she was to re-join him in investigating.

In the end, Tony gave up trying to read, waved the paper a little towards Hardwick and asked, 'Sorry, how is it murder now? There's no more evidence than before.'

'Read the cause of death section.' Harry's voice sounded particularly stentorian booming around the small closed office.

Diane stood up straighter, but her arms remained folded, and she interjected, 'Overdose by injection, and not his print on the only syringe they found. Ergo somebody else injected him; i.e. murder.'

'Best case situation is manslaughter, but I still want them caught. Now, you and ADC Meredith go and find out who it was please.'

Tony's brain was still whirling clouds. He knew something didn't add up. Weren't they only supposed to be put back to work together if it was murder? How had Gerard only just come up with this conclusion? And why wasn't Barnes re-joining him instead of Meredith? 'I just saw DI Barnes arrive in the building. I don't know why he hasn't come up here yet, but shouldn't he be taking charge of this? I can bring him up to speed, and then we can interview some more cricketers.'

'I got him an appointment with the Occupational Health. He'll be back at Ayckley Heads for his course before they start at nine.' As Tony's mind continued to struggle through the funk of emotional confusion, Hardwick turned and left the room.

Diane stepped closer to Tony, and put her hands behind her back. This had the effect of propelling her chest forward, but Milburn did not notice her until she spoke. 'We've fingerprinted all the girls, and none of them match, so let's see what we can do getting fingerprints off the men in this case. I've already called Visas and Immigration, and they're going to email me the prints for Hamilton and Pathan from their work visa applications. So we also need Jim Harris and Ramsbotham. Ooh, Ramsbotham will have had his done in custody on Monday. I'll have a look on the computer now. Have you got the forensics report so I can compare them?' She sounded as if she had never been off the case. Tony remained catatonic. Having sat herself down in front of Milburn's computer, Diane leaned across the desk and gave his arm a gentle shake. 'Tony.'

He recoiled as if he'd been stung. Mumbling as he backed towards the office door, the DS pointed to a pile of folders. 'Nnthere.' When his back touched the door, the detective put his hand behind to grab the handle, and, without his eyes leaving her, he exited quickly.

Again, the Gents toilet became his sanctuary to try and work out what to do. After some water splashing in the face, and a lot of deep breathing, he calmed down enough to think clearly. 'Get a grip on yourself, Tony, man.' A minute's further pause and self-study in the mirror gave him the strength to stand straight up and adjust his suit jacket: more an act of self-confidence building than causing any improvement in the presentation of his attire. 'Right, just professional. H has obviously had his hand forced, so no whining to him. Just gonna have to deal with her. She can't get away with anything unprofessional, so just play it all straight and focus on the case.' He inhaled and exhaled once, slowly and deeply, looked himself in the eyes, and strode out of the toilets.

When he re-entered the office, ADC Meredith's boss looked like the boss. He stood large at the desk and picked up the pile of drug questionnaires he had produced. 'Right, I'm going to the cricket ground in Chester-le-Street. You carry on with checking those fingerprint matches.' He turned to leave quickly.

'All done. That fingerprint still doesn't match any suspect. No match for Pathan, Hamilton or Ramsbotham. So, it's Jim Harris – he's the only one we don't have a fingerprint for.'

'It's not him. I met him at the bodyfind – it's not him. I don't think it's murder.' In Tony's heart, he was convinced that foul play was behind Elliott's death, but he was doing his best to keep pushing Meredith away. However, she had jumped from her seat and put her suit jacket on in one movement, and was at his side as they exited the small office. CID eyes followed them across the room without subtlety.

In the cricket club car park, Penfold was leaning against his car. An original VW Beetle from the early 70s, it was tangerine, with white trim inside, and shiny chrome bumpers and hubcaps to complement externally. Tony had on occasion described it as "gruesome". This had always tickled the kiwi, as the last thing that the colour scheme engendered was the grisly or macabre. He could understand if his suit-wearing friend considered it ugly, or even shocking, but it was definitively hippy in its outlook. The simplest reference to it had been Kathy's smiling first impressions: a pause, followed by, 'That's bright.'

As Tony and Diane stepped out of the 40 years younger police VW, Penfold's face crinkled in just a touch of a frown. 'Morning,' he commented in a non-committal tone.

'What's he doing here?' Meredith demanded of Tony.

'Nice to see you, too,' Penfold replied, still deadpan.

'I organised this meeting last night, with Penfold coming along to help me out.'

'Well, I'm assisting Tony now, Mr Penfold, so you can go home and play with your surfboards.' She put particular emphasis on the word "Mister".

'I'd like Penfold to join us as an observer. He can watch body language, and see if anybody gives anything away.'

'I can observe body language just as well as he can. In fact, you and I have been trained in it. Has he?'

Milburn waved for Penfold to walk in with them, and countered, 'We'll all look out for suspicious body language.' Penfold paused at the entrance door, and waited for Diane to enter in front of him. She strutted through, almost with her nose in the air. The two men followed, Penfold's face straight and unblinking, Tony's in a grimace.

A middle-aged blond man with a warm smile and a tablet computer, on which he was constantly writing notes, met them in the club foyer. Jeremy Barnstaple was the cricket club's PR and media relations man. He was anxious to ensure that the police did not "take away any idea that Durham County Cricket Club fosters an atmosphere in which drug taking is acceptable".

Detective Sergeant Milburn, expecting Penfold to jump in with a cynical comment, quickly responded that the investigations were to try and establish background about the player who had died, and not the club. Moreover, Milburn claimed, none of the details of the investigation would become public as that could affect the outcome of a trial. He had to meet PR with PR, or the club would most likely veto this whole line of inquiry. Tony knew he had only teed it up with the coach, and a big business like this sports club would probably have a policy and procedure to follow to authorise a questionnaire like this, which would be a quagmire of red tape. Mr Barnstaple never stopped writing on his iPad.

By the time the three were ushered into the cricket ground's modern and luxurious conference room, the players were all seated around the large central meeting table, chatting. Vivender Pathan, dressed in his blue club tracksuit, stood fidgeting at the front.

He made a show of tapping his watch, and asked them to be as quick as possible as they were already disrupting preparations for the first pre-season match. The county club were to take on Durham MCC University's 1st XI the next day. Despite the university technically being an amateur side, this was rarely the case in reality, as most players had professional county contracts to play for most of the summer, after the uni term finished. This made for a sometimes close contest in the annual pre-season showcase match, especially on the occasions that the professional club chose to blood some of its younger recruits. Indeed, these newcomers gaining a try-out to impress the coaches were often alumni of the opposition team, and very keen to put one over on their old colleagues. Sometimes the combination of pressures on them was too much and caused poor play.

Diane passed around the table giving out the one-page questionnaires. Having scanned the room once, Penfold asked Coach Pathan where the nearest toilet was, and left, having received the directions. As his assistant moved around the room, DS Milburn explained to the group that the questionnaires could be anonymous if people did not wish for any follow-up, but he implored them to be as open and honest as possible, as he was trying to establish the background behind Hamish Elliott's death.

One pale young cricketer with long, dark and greasy hair asked how Elliott had died, and Milburn had to fob him off with an excuse about not wanting to influence their responses to the questions in front of them. He asked them all to save questions until after everyone had finished. He was hoping that either they would forget to ask again, or the coaches would be anxious to get them back to training with as little as possible to disturb their thoughts.

After a few minutes, most of the players were either finished or finishing up. ADC Meredith smoothed out her skirt and went round again to hand each player a blank manila envelope to seal his answers in. She then explained that this would ensure they remained anonymous, as they would not open them or look at any responses before arriving back at the police station. She walked around the table, waiting for each man to seal his envelope and hand it to her. Coach Pathan then hurried them all out for training, just as Tony had hoped. He thanked the blond PR man, who gushed a little, before also rushing off and leaving the two detectives alone.

'What's with the envelopes?' the DS asked across the conference table, which he had carefully ensured was between the two of them. She was holding the stack slightly fanned out and writing something in the top corner of each envelope.

'You don't believe in maintaining the witnesses' anonymity?' she counter-questioned with a grin and a flick of her shiny brown hair.

'No, and neither do you.' He was smiling. 'Tell me.'

Meredith came around the table holding up her notebook. There was the tiniest swagger in her steps. The page showed a rectangle with names around the outside and positions numbered in the rectangle beside each name. She then showed the numbers she had written on the envelopes. 'Each person has sealed their fingerprints in their own envelope. She pulled out envelope number four: 'And this is Jim Harris's – the only missing fingerprint.'

Tony laughed, 'Crime Scene's gonna love you. You know how they hate getting fingerprints off paper.'

Grinning, she mimicked an American accent, saying, 'They can kiss my lily white ass.' At the same time, Diane turned and stuck her bottom out towards Tony, and pointedly pointed at it.

He was also grinning now. 'If you tell them that, they might well hurry up with the fingerprints.' He looked down again at her presented bum. The dark skirt hugged her precisely, showing the slight fissure – a perfect peach shape. He had a brief memory, a vision of her naked, creamy buttocks and then snapped out of it with a start. Tony turned and rushed around to the other side of the conference table. The room was on the first floor up, and had a full-length window filling one wall and overlooking the cricket pitch. He put his hands up to the glass and stared out at the players acting out cricket in their training session. His breathing was short and fast. After a moment, he leaned his forehead against the glass and stood motionless.

'What is it? Is something happening out there?' Diane had spotted Tony's blue eyes transfixed by her pose, but had missed the colour drain from his face a moment later, and assumed he had seen something occurring on the field below.

The gods were smiling on DS Milburn. As his subordinate siren approached the glass beside him, Pieter Hamilton and Vivender Pathan outside were engaging in a full-blown argument. It was silent through the thick glass, but their body movements showed clearly what was going on. Contrary to expectations though, it was the Indian who appeared to have completely lost his temper: shouting the loudest, and waving his arms the most.

After several seconds of finger waving by Hamilton, Vivender whose fists had been opening and closing throughout, put both hands to the South African's chest and pushed him backwards. The coach stormed back towards the building and out of view underneath the detectives. Hamilton was unmoved by the smaller, weaker man, but remained stationary, shoulders hunched forwards, watching his coach depart. At the sound of a crash below them, the detectives leapt for the exit, and then paused at the top of the stairs down, craning through gaps around the chrome and glass stairway to try and see or hear Pathan. There was no further activity beneath, so they descended slowly, and saw no further sign of him. A silent shrug from Tony was the cue for them to leave and head back to the car.

Penfold was leaning against the side of his Beetle, closed eyes towards the Sun. His elbows were tucked back to lean on the car's bright orange roof. As the two detectives approached, Penfold commented without moving or opening his eyes, 'I assume you heard all that between Pathan and Hamilton?'

They stopped walking a few feet from the New Zealander, and towards the front of his car. Tony replied, 'We saw it from the conference window, but the glass was too thick to hear anything.'

'Ha, we're like the three monkeys.' Penfold opened his eyes, stood up, and turned to converse with his friend. 'You hear no evil, I see no evil, and they shout a lot of evil. It didn't sound coherent though. And not really about cricket either. Both men essentially telling the other to keep out of his business. The coach had totally lost it though, cursing in every Hindu way possible. I doubt, though, if Hamilton will be particularly concerned that the Curse of Krishna has been called down upon him.'

Stepping forward to point into the rear passenger window of the Beetle, Meredith demanded, 'What are you doing with cricket pads?'

The kiwi looked down at her brown bob haircut and accusing air. He answered calmly, 'I took them from Hamilton's kit bag whilst you were all upstairs.'

Tony's head bobbed in a double-take, and he leaned forward to see into the vehicle's back seat. A bright white pair of pads gleamed back at him. 'What the hell, Penfold. Do you know how much trouble you could get us into? What are you doing?'

'I'm going to follow up on a theory – need to test it out at home with these. I'll let you know if it incriminates Hamilton.'

Diane stepped slightly closer to Tony, and censured Penfold, 'You know anything you find won't be admissible as evidence and will bugger our whole investigation?'

'I'll keep quiet about it if you will. I'll tell you what I find and, if you play it right, you'll be able to follow up on my findings legitimately.' He turned and got into the car.

Diane turned to face Tony and they were very close. 'Are you going to let him do this?' she urged. He looked at Penfold's profile as the surfer pulled forward to drive away from them, and then back to her pretty, outraged face. When he did nothing further, her features softened slightly and she put a hand on one hip. Milburn stepped around her crooked elbow and walked to his car.

In Detective Sergeant Milburn's office, the other DS he shared it with was staring at his own computer screen, with a cup of tea held to his lips. He was concentrating on some text on display and appeared to have frozen in that position. The ingress of Tony and ADC Meredith snapped him out of it, and he put the tea down. The officer muttered a greeting to them, but didn't turn around to engage them any further. Tony pointedly placed a chair for Diane on the opposite side of his desk to his own chair. Having sat down facing her, he held out his hands for the envelopes she carried. Their return from the cricket ground had consisted of very little conversation and she continued this by instructing her boss with a single word: 'Gloves.'

'Our prints are already on many of them anyway.'

'I know, but you might smudge or cover some.' He hadn't really intended to protest her suggestion, and was already in the process of retrieving a box of latex gloves from the top drawer of his desk.

The two of them carried on working without speaking, as they read through half of the questionnaires each. Each summarised what they found on a sheet of paper, and then when they had completed them all, swapped papers and perused the overall outcomes.

The clearest thing that came through was that Durham County Cricket Club is not a haven of sporting drug cheats, at least not on the strength of this survey. Whilst drug use was admitted in some instances, there was a particularly notable absence of anything approaching a pattern. Three of them mentioned Somnulone, two named nandrolone, various suggested various recreational drugs, most commonly cocaine or marijuana. Sometimes the references were personal experiences, sometimes the claim was that another (always unnamed) team member had used the drug, and on some forms the assertion was historical, along the lines of "when I was younger", or "before I joined this club".

Arms lying on the armrests of his big chair, Milburn pressed himself back into the hugging black padding, and exhaled long and loud. He was looking at Diane, who was looking straight back at him with a similar resigned expression. She stuck out her bottom lip in a silent question. He nodded slightly, and was about to comment as to how they had really learnt nothing of note from the morning's inquiries, when his phone vibrated on the desk and sounded off. It was a little jazz riff on a piano, which indicated a text message received from Penfold. This interruption said,

'Spring surfing is swell,

Rendezvous at mine one hour

For drugs and much more.'

It titillated Penfold when he could send Milburn messages that could get him into hot water if anybody else read them. In this case, the drugs reference cried, 'delete this message' at the DS. Tony duly deleted the message, and explained to Diane that he had to head to Hartlepool to have Penfold's theory explained to him. She wanted to go with him, but he sent her off to deliver the questionnaires to the forensics team, to try and get a fingerprint matching with the one on the hypodermic found in Elliott's rubbish bin. They put most of the forms in one evidence packet, and separated Jim Harris's into a separate bag, so that ADC Meredith could get an answer on that one while she waited at the lab. She was frowning throughout, but said nothing, and Tony jumped up and left her to finish off packaging them all. He knew it wouldn't take an hour to drive to Penfold's, but it was a perfect excuse to get away from the Crazy Cow; and he chuckled to himself, walking across the open plan CID space.

From Hartlepool's town, the barren beach road led about two miles before it reached the outpost of houses and shops that included Penfold's big whitewashed, old house. Along the first straight stretch of sand and surf, Tony could see three or four surfers bobbing up and down behind the breaking waves.

As he strained to pick out Penfold amongst the group, it was difficult to maintain a straight course along the road whilst looking out of the side window at the same time. The road wasn't very busy, but there was an element of avoiding oncoming cars, and not crashing into the back of those in front. It was long and open, but vehicles had a habit of slowing right down to turn off into one of the car parks that fronted on to the wide promenade.

He stopped looking at the waves and carried on to park up outside the Norton Hotel, just beside Penfold's place. On stepping out of the car, the sea breeze tousled Tony's hair, reminding him again that it remained uncut and annoying. One hand brushed it down, as he saw the unmissable figure of his kiwi friend standing on the lip of a wave curling away to the right as Milburn looked at him. The policeman went to wave his other hand and stopped short, realising that the surfer was concentrating on his ride and would not notice anything onshore.

The waves weren't huge; the figure standing on the board was roughly the same height as a bottom to top measurement of the bulging water. Milburn remembered a conversation he had once had with Penfold about the way surfers describe wave heights. Apparently, the Hawaiian system of measuring from the back of the wave was a little contrary to the more intuitive frontside method, meaning that surfers could easily get confused when travelling to breaks in different parts of the world. The best solution had generally been accepted as being to compare the wave size with a person riding the wave. He decided to ask Penfold when he came out of the water whether "head-high" would be the correct description of these surfing conditions.

As the black rubber figure surged along the wavefront, slipping slightly down and then pushing back up to the lip, a second breaking curl came towards him from the direction he was heading. Just as the two bits of white water met at Penfold, he shot up the face of the wave and high into the air, sending the cream coloured surfboard to the right as he dived behind and to the left. Milburn instinctively went up on his tiptoes to try and see what happened, but could no longer see either man or board.

He walked across the road and by the time he reached the railing that overlooked the sandy beach, Penfold was sitting astride his board far out, facing the horizon. It took ten minutes to attract his friend's attention in the water, and Tony was getting cold. He was just at the point of deciding to sit in the car to wait, when Penfold waved a long arm in a big slow arc, and set off paddling towards the beach. Tony pulled his charcoal mackintosh coat closer around himself, and meandered down the wide stone staircase to the sand to meet the dripping New Zealander.

'Milburn, good to see you.'

'Aren't you cold?'

'On the contrary, I'm boiling.'

Tony shook his head, incredulous. Penfold did, however, walk very briskly the 50 yards to his front door. Leaving the surfboard propped up against the front wall of the house, he proceeded inside leaving a trail of water everywhere he stepped. Tony followed gingerly, to avoid exacerbating the mess being generated by the seawater cascades.

Penfold sent Mantoro and Milburn down to the basement, with a promise to join them in two minutes. They had been standing at the giant chemistry set for closer to just 60 seconds when Penfold bounded into the dingy cellar. Now wearing his uniform of black boardshorts and a long-sleeved, red T-shirt, he moved behind Milburn to the side of the table furthest from the staircase. There were three small glass dishes, two containing a white granular substance that looked rather like the detritus left on a page after using a pencil eraser. A third dish was empty, and the still wet surfer picked up a plastic bag from a shelf against the far wall. It was clear, and although the lighting was not very bright, Tony could see it contained a lump of white foam about the size of a smartphone. By the way the bag waved around, it was clear that the little block was very light.

Tony sounded more jaded than he had intended when he spoke to ignite Penfold's explanation, 'So, what exactly have you got there?'

'Right then, you see these two dishes?' Penfold pointed at the two that already contained white powder. 'These are shavings from the leg pads I took from Hamilton's kit bag, and the ones that Coach Pathan gave me.'

With a big bronzed hand, Penfold slid the two dishes forwards slightly to reveal stickers underneath labelled "Hamilton" and "Pathan". 'And this third one is the control. Mantoro secured us this little block of Somnulone/Priapra mix as used in smuggling.'

Tony turned to look at Mantoro. He was grinning and nodding, whilst chomping on cashew nuts from a saucer on the table beside the Bunsen burner. The big dark hairstyle left Mantoro's face mostly in shadow, which made his blank nodding grin seem sinister, if not downright lunatic. When he turned back to look at Penfold, a cheese grater had appeared in his hand and was grinding additional powder off the drugs block into the third petri dish.

Milburn leaned his hands against the edge of the table, and tried to take it in. He wasn't sure if he was shocked or not. That Mantoro could seemingly pick up any required drug at the drop of a hat should have outraged him. That his cerebral surfer friend should then build an unlicensed lab in his basement to experiment on the drugs should have stunned him. But, somehow, none of it seemed out of place. Tony wondered if he should pinch himself.

'I can't wait to try and write this up in the report of my investigation,' he finally said. Penfold smiled, sealed the remainder of the white foam block back in its bag, and tipped the drugs particles from their dish through a funnel into a pear-shaped glass flask, which he then secured at the bottom of the experimental glassware. Taking the flaming burner, Mantoro then heated a separate round flask, containing a clear liquid. 'You been demoted from heating the acid after yesterday?' Tony teased.

Penfold smiled and placed a large beaker of water around the flask containing the drug powder. Slowly, liquid condensed in it and produced a white solution. After some ten minutes of this, Penfold removed the beaker of water and took the Bunsen burner from Mantoro, to place under that same pear-shaped flask. Mantoro switched on the water supply to the helical condenser tube. This eventually caused a clear liquid to appear in the condenser and drip into a beaker on the far side of the table. Another five minutes passed, and they all silently watched little else happening.

When Penfold switched off the gas supply to the burner and moved it away, a white sludge residue was left in the pear-shaped flask. He pointed at this and commented, 'Priapra: form into pills and dry out. We can confirm what it is with a separate test – I shan't bore you with the details.' Pointing across the table at the dripping clear fluid, he continued, 'Somnulone. Dilute tenfold and inject. Again, there's a conclusive test, which takes another ten minutes or so.'

'OK, so have you got clean flasks and we can test these bits of leg padding then?' Milburn was willing to incorporate whatever contribution this chemical testing might make, even if it was never going to make it to court as evidence. They were far enough along the road that it would be stupid to ignore the findings from the dingy cellar.

'Just a bit of theatre, my man. Mantoro has already tested them both. Over to you my Latino Lavoisier.' Penfold stepped back from the table and looked across to Mantoro.

The short Mexican grinned again, popped a cashew into his mouth, and stepped more into the light, closer to Milburn. He first confused the detective by scratching at his pockmarked cheek and saying, 'More Le Chatelier, I reckon.' Penfold didn't respond but vaguely raised his eyebrows. 'Well, Tony, the pads from the Indian were standard polyurethane foam: normal cricket padding material. Nothing unusual, but I had to keep the ventilation on in here for hours. That is one nasty reaction.'

'OK, and Hamilton's?'

'Yessirree, no question about it – they were the classic Somnulone/Priapra foam mixture.' He turned to a shelf running along the side of the staircase, and picked two beakers up. He held the first one up containing a blue liquid. 'Blue is positive for Priapra.' The other one Mantoro shoved up to Tony's nose, and he got a shocking whiff of vomit odour. He recoiled sharply with a hand immediately up to cover nose and mouth. 'And butyric acid smell confirms Somnulone.' The short man was smiling widely, watching Milburn's horror at the smell.

Milburn spoke from behind his hand, 'Sorry, is that rancid smell a good enough confirmation of a particular chemical? Isn't there a more definite system? Don't you need the mass spectrometer to identify it exactly?'

Penfold answered, 'Probably a defence lawyer would insist on mass spectrometry. Certainly the anti-doping agencies use it for any athlete ban; but from the chemicals that we've put into this set-up, the only thing that could be made to produce that smell is butyric acid, and the only way that could be produced is if Somnulone is present.' He stepped towards Tony and pushed him gently towards the stairs. 'Let's leave Mantoro to clean up his toys; I could do with a cup of coffee – it's a bit chilly down here.'

The two men leant against kitchen counters, each contemplating a mug of black coffee. Penfold dragged his hand through his hair several times. It was drying in salty clumps, which gave something of a lumpy bouffant appearance. His hand combing smoothed out some of the unevenness but worsened the fluffy look. 'So, definitely South African sourcing via Pieter Hamilton, what are you going to do with him?'

Tony frowned slightly. 'Yeah, not quite sure. I don't imagine I'll have much difficulty getting a sample of his padding for the police labs to test, but this still doesn't really get me an answer on Hamish Elliott's death. Did he pinch some of this and accidentally overdose himself? Or did Hamilton use it to kill him? And if so, why?'

Mantoro appeared at the threshold of one of the kitchen's two doors. 'Bit of chemistry needed to get that padding into an injectable solution. Would Elliott have had the skill and equipment to do that?' Tony looked up from his coffee, surprised as usual by the man's thick US accent. But as quick as he had appeared, Mantoro had disappeared.

Milburn frowned again, and Penfold raised his cup in a silent toast to confusion.

Thursday 28th March

Kathy punched Tony in the upper arm. He rocked back laughing, and looked at her beautiful smile. He revelled at how her blue eyes seemed to gleam in the sunshine. It was mid-March, and the sky was totally blue. The temperature was not as high as would be expected for such a glorious day in the summer but, basking in the sun, they did not feel cold. He leaned back and put his arm around her, and she leaned into his shoulder slightly. They were seated about half way up the rows of the North Terrace at Durham County Cricket Club's Riverside Ground. It was a good vantage point to see the match, being located close to the sightscreens at the top end of the ground. The bowler's line would be very clear from these seats. It also gave a good view for Milburn back to the main stand and players' areas so that he could watch proceedings.

The players from both teams were gathering on either side of the wicket for the match. There was to be a minute's silence as a memorial to Hamish Elliott, and his team had chosen to wear their black uniforms that were normally for use in the Sunday matches, or Twenty20 competitions. The opposition for the first pre-season friendly, Durham University, lined up in normal cricket whites, with black armbands.

Being a Thursday, and a friendly match, the stands were fairly empty. The DS had decided he should watch this match to see the various cricket club suspects interacting. He was particularly interested in seeing which bowlers the coach would select, and how they would react to it.

At the suggestion that he would be attending with ADC Meredith, Kathy had insisted that she would join him to keep her eyes on the Crazy Cow. Tony had sat quietly for several minutes when Kathy had told him this. There were several aspects he did not like about the idea. Firstly, the implication that he needed to be watched by his girlfriend had raised his hackles with questions of trust. It was also not the done thing to take one's civilian girlfriend along on a police investigation. Especially having had to keep a wide berth from the boss regarding a surfing friend who had been heavily involved in the investigation, too. Tony really didn't know how he could explain this away to Hardwick, and he had known that Meredith would immediately complain to the DCI. He had reconciled the latter point by texting Diane to meet him at the ground, and not attending the police station beforehand.

He looked over to the Don Robson Pavilion and saw ADC Meredith at the front of the upper stand, leaning against the railing and looking down to the most crowded area immediately below her. He followed her line of sight and could see a couple that appeared to be Kate Withenshaw and Daniel Ramsbotham. Checking with a pair of binoculars, he muttered confirmation of these identifications to himself.

Kathy was about to question what he was talking about, but was cut off by the stadium announcer starting the minute's silence. Through the binoculars, Milburn could see Kate talking incessantly throughout the silence period. Ramsbotham did not appear to be listening to her, but she chattered on regardless. She seemed oblivious to everything around her, giggling occasionally. A couple of nearby spectators glared at her, although they said nothing. The minute of reflection was concluded with applause from the crowd. The teams all shook hands, and the university players left the pitch as they were to bat first.

Looking out over the expanse of lush grass, still very green from the winter's rains, Tony hugged Kathy close, and explained some of the details of what was going on as the first few balls were bowled. She continued to punch him playfully each time he deliberately mocked her lack of knowledge of such a fine English tradition. The game progressed steadily, and the university were scoring pretty quickly.

Away to their left, opposite the main stand where most of the spectators were clustered, Jim Harris was fielding on the boundary as the County's most capped bowler steamed in to let the ball fly at a very heavily built university batsman. Striding towards Jim, but outside the boundary rope, Kathy pointed out an athletic frame in an all white tracksuit with curving black stripes around arms, legs and torso. 'Look. A birthday candle!' The sun lit up his blond head a little like a flame. Milburn could see what she meant, but wasn't convinced by the comparison. And, as soon as he realised who was bearing down on Harris, his attention was rapt on what might transpire.

'That's Pieter Hamilton, the South African.'

'Ooooh,' she responded with intrigue.

Cricketers will quite often walk around the field whilst their teammates are at bat, but it is usually a gentle stroll, or a warm-up jog. Hamilton's team were bowling, and he was marching purposefully, eyes fixed on the slightly shorter man who was concentrating on his own fielding.

DS Milburn followed through the binoculars, and there ensued a highly one-sided exchange. Harris was struggling to maintain a conversation and at the same time concentrate on the action behind him that he might suddenly have to participate in.

The umpire called "Over", for a brief break in events. Jim turned and, although they could not be heard at some 50 yards distance, his shrugging, palms up to support his words, told Tony that the man was apologetic. The South African waved a finger and leant slightly to talk directly into Harris's face. Although both men had similarly athletic builds, the body language was very unbalanced. He tried to make a further apology in the process of moving infield to his new fielding position for the next over, and Hamilton gave Harris a dismissive wave, before turning to storm back up the boundary edge.

There was no printed programme for the match, but the BBC Sports app on Tony's phone gave him the team information. Hamilton had not been selected. He looked up again to watch the man continuing around the boundary to where the rest of the squad were seated in the players' area beside the pitch. These were those players not actually selected to play, one of who might act as a substitute, plus the team management, physiotherapists, specialist coaches, and anyone who could wangle a seat.

THE CRICKETER'S CORPSE

None of Hamilton's colleagues were paying attention to him. All, including head coach Pathan, who stood at the edge of the grass beside blond and ruddy Barnstaple, the PR man, were focussed on the on-field action. They were diverted towards him slightly when Pieter violently kicked a drinks bottle before taking his seat. It was a brief distraction, though, and everyone turned back to the field with little reaction to this eruption. Pathan, with his arms folded across his chest, continued talking to the man with the conjoined clipboard, whilst both watched the game. The coach seemed to rock slightly left and right, constantly shifting his weight from one foot to the other.

Behind the dugout, lurked a familiar pair, and Tony again lifted the binoculars to check he was not mistaken. At the far end of the same lower stand as Kate and Daniel, stood Penfold and Mantoro, looking for all the world like keen cricket fans. They were on the highest row of the bottom tier, and so standing at their seats did not obstruct anybody's view, but it looked less comfortable than they could be in the sunshine. He had to look several times to be sure that Penfold was carrying a battered cricket scorebook under his arm. 'That had better be part of some dumb undercover disguise,' he muttered to himself.

Pieter Hamilton remained unsettled, moving his belongings around on the floor repeatedly, and appearing to chunter to himself. Milburn could not tell if he was speaking aloud, but his teammates seemingly continued to ignore him. After four overs seated, his restlessness forced him up. Climbing over the handrail separating the path in front of the Don Robson stand and the grass of the playing area, Hamilton went to sit next to his cousin, Ramsbotham, three rows back.

They conversed much more amiably than his interactions with anyone else so far. There was still some hand waving from Pieter, indicating first Vivender Pathan, then Jim Harris, followed by the team area in general. Kate Withenshaw sometimes listened and sometimes spoke, but the two men did not pay any attention to her.

Milburn telephoned Penfold. 'Hey, what are you doing here?'

'The same as you I expect, using this match as a chance to observe all our suspects. And Meredith too. You know she hasn't taken her eyes off you two since the game started?'

Tony held up the binoculars with his other hand, and moved along from Penfold to where the ADC was still leaning against the upper tier railing. She was looking straight at him and he quickly moved the view back down to Daniel, Kate and Pieter. 'Shit, that's scary.'

'Indeed. Did you know, a few years ago, the uni were all out for 18 in their second innings – the lowest first class cricket score anywhere in the world since 1983.'

'Forget about that for a moment though, can you hear Hamilton and Bonnie and Clyde at all? From where you are though, I'm sure they'll recognise you if you get too close.' At just that moment, Tony saw Mantoro, alone, take a seat behind the three suspects. 'What the fuck is he doing?' He wore a pair of very dark aviator style sunglasses, almost as dark as his big hair.

He moved his view over to Penfold who remained standing in the original position, and was studiously perusing the inside of his scorebook. Without looking up, the surfer told him, 'If you hang up, Mantoro's gonna call you and you can listen to them.'

He pressed "End call" on the phone's screen and, a moment later, another call came from a blocked number. The unmistakeable American drawl came through 'Andy, my man, how are you? Yeah, I'm at a cricket match. But I've no idea what's going on! I know, I know, crazy!! Can you tell me a few things about how it's played?' That set up the opportunity for the phone call to continue, without Mantoro needing to speak much, so that the conversation in front could be transmitted to the detective with little disruption. The Mexican threw in the occasional 'Uh-huh' to continue the ruse.

The first thing he overheard was Kate Withenshaw bubbling away. 'We should go away. Why not, Daniel? Come on, we could go to your parents lodge in Courchevel. Yes, a bit of skiing, and just relax, and be away from all the police. Come on, Daniel, why don't we.'

Ramsbotham was engaged in a different conversation and ignored her. 'Look, nobody has anything. We don't need to worry about it. And you'll get in the team, no worries. Look, that Harris is getting hit all over the place. First proper match of the season and they'll pick proper players, you'll see.' Hamilton blew threw his lips like a horse, and leaned back in the seat. At the wicket, the stout university batsman hit Harris's bowling away to the far side and set off running. Ramsbotham pointed and said, 'See. Just bide your time. Take it easy and bide your time.'

Kate jumped into the pause that followed. 'Ooh, or how about the Maldives? You love diving. Lets go for a few weeks. Bit of tropical heat to get rid of this chill. Shall we, Daniel?'

He turned to her. 'Kate, will you please shut up. You know we can't go away at the moment. So shut up asking.' Milburn could see through the binoculars that Kate's mouth continued to move, but she was not speaking. She pulled her brown coat a little more closed at the front, and pulled her left hand through her hair, holding the coat shut with the right hand.

Pieter stood up and wandered back down to the railing, and carefully scissor stepped over it on to the grass.

'Go and get me a drink would you.' Daniel handed Kate a ten-pound note, and waved her away along the row of seats. She said nothing and left. Mantoro hung up, but did not move from the seat behind Ramsbotham.

At the end of the next over, Tony's phone's internal jazz pianist signalled the arrival of a text message from Penfold.

'Hindu father talks

To East Indian princess,

"Danger Will Rob'son" '

Milburn shook his head, muttered "nutjob", and picked up the binoculars again. At the near end of the main spectator stand, Aisha Pathan sat alone on the front row, with a thick book on her lap. She was at the very end, beside the doors to enter the main building and the changing room area. With his back to the field of play, her father stood, barely taller than the level of the handrail, talking to her. The conversation grew a little more animated. She closed the book and put it on the adjacent seat, in order to lean forward so that their conversation was very much face-to-face. Vivender took hold of the handrail with his left hand. With the magnified view, Tony could see that he was gripping extremely tightly. For a man with cocoa-coloured skin to have white knuckles must have taken some real squeezing. Vivender's other hand was waving wildly up and down, and sometimes indicating the doors to the building, sometimes the action behind him, sometimes the sky, and often pointing a finger at his daughter.

Tears were again streaming down Aisha's face, but it did not seem like the argument was voluble enough to attract the attention of any nearby spectators, which Tony found astonishing given the vigorous body language from the coach. The argument seemed to go on for an interminably long time, and DS Milburn was not happy that he could not lip read any of what Aisha was saying. Even when she started to join in the arm waving and pointing in various directions, although never at her father, what she was saying was not fathomable.

Tony was pleased to see that above the argument, and in the same line of sight, Diane Meredith was watching Aisha and Vivender, not him and Kathy. He pulled up her number on his phone, and Kathy grabbed his wrist before he could lift the phone to his ear. 'What are you doing?' she demanded.

'She's watching an argument between Pathan and his daughter, I want to know what they're saying.' Kathy gave him a glare, but let go of his wrist.

As Meredith answered, he watched her through the binoculars. 'Are you watching this?' they asked each other simultaneously when the call connected.

Tony continued, 'What's being said?'

'I don't know. They are surprisingly quiet for such an argument, but the odd bits I've caught are in Hindi. Is that what they speak? Perhaps you should come over here and do some police work,' she added sarcastically. Tony pressed a stubby finger to the "End Call" button on his phone screen.

Aisha stood up, pointedly picked up her textbook, and walked quickly up the concrete staircase in the stands, her back to her father. Halfway up, she turned to continue along the path along the row. Milburn followed her movement through the binoculars, and also saw his ADC wave to him to come and join her and follow the young woman.

Tony looked at Kathy, who appeared restless. She was bored with the cricket, and his attention had been elsewhere for at least 15 minutes. She gave him a wan smile. 'It's almost the lunch break,' he began. 'Do you fancy leaving? I really need to get on with some investigations of these people.' Tony waved a hand towards the field in general, and Kathy looked at him with a blank expression. She gathered her handbag from under her seat, and stood up and turned to walk along the row away from him.

Tony sat watching her back for a couple of seconds, and then stood up and followed. At the first gate to the stadium's outer pathway, Kathy cut out and continued to walk away. Tony paused at the gateway; his route to Aisha and Vivender was only 30 yards around the edge of the pitch, but Kathy had not even said goodbye. He looked back towards her exit, but his girlfriend was already out of sight behind the structure supporting the big replay screen.

Diane Meredith met him as she exited the building behind the players' area – the way down from the upper tier went inside the building. The substitutes and unselected team members, plus the team management, including coach Pathan, were all now seated, watching the university batsmen continue to score easily.

They both looked up at where Aisha had last been seen, but she was not amongst the spectators anywhere in the Don Robson stand. The crowd was sufficiently sparse that this was easy to establish quickly. Milburn's seat scanning finished at the far end, where Penfold and Mantoro stood at the top of the side staircase. The short man was watching the cricket, whilst Penfold looked over the redbrick side wall down to where Milburn knew there was a little square with bars and burger stands.

The surfer looked back at Tony and Diane, and he jerked a thumb over the wall to indicate that they should go that way. It took a good ten seconds to work their way along to the end and turn into the mini food court. The place was virtually empty, and Milburn looked up at his friend's tanned face looking over the high wall.

'Aisha walked out of this courtyard back under that walkway.' Penfold indicated the exit route from the area, which was formed underneath the upper level of the building to the rear of the stand and then continued around to form the rear of the next stand. They rushed past the queue for burgers and out into the large concrete area behind the buildings and stands. It was bounded by high iron railings, 20 yards from them.

Looking all around the open space, Aisha was nowhere to be seen. Tony saw Kathy walking out of a big gate in the fence at the top end of the ground, but her back was to him the whole time.

Tony and Diane turned, without words, and walked back through a small surge of people heading for the toilets and bars. When they reached pitchside, the field was empty, the umpires had called "Lunch". Penfold held his hands palm up and shrugged his shoulders.

Tony's inbox had an email from Penfold, and, somehow, these always came in highlighted in purple. The content of the email described how the proportions of Priapra and Somnulone in the leg pads that Mantoro had analysed were identical to the ratio of the two drugs in Gerard's post-mortem report of Hamish Elliott's blood. He scowled, the cogs of his brain clicking through the possibilities implied by this. Pieter Hamilton must therefore be the prime suspect. The final statement was unequivocal: the drugs that killed Elliott were from Hamilton's leg pad smuggling source.

Meredith also had an important email. Hers was from the Crime Scene Investigation department with the results of the fingerprint check on Jim Harris's questionnaire. It matched the fingerprint on the hypodermic that had been found in the bin in the dead man's bedroom. The match was insufficient to stand up in court, but the message from the scientist testing it stated that she was almost certain it would be him. Meredith came into Tony's office from her computer terminal in the CID open plan area, and presented him with this knowledge.

He looked back to the email from Penfold. 'Hmm. Penfold's chemical analysis has Hamilton in the frame for importing Priapra and Somnulone, and his combination of them being in Elliott's tox' screen. But the evidence he got that from is no good, as he pinched the leg padding.'

'I keep telling you he's a waste of space.'

'Diane, solutions please. He's virtually told us who the killer is, all we have to do is work out how to legitimately bring him in and get another sample that our labs can test to find the same answers.'

She thought momentarily. 'What about turning the screws on Jim Harris? The fingerprint is enough to arrest him, and then we get him to name Hamilton as a supplier. That gives us a search warrant, and we can take leg pads on the grounds that we are experts on the methods people use to smuggle Somnulone.' Milburn leaned back in his chair, which squeaked quietly in response. He stared at Meredith, standing a metre in front of him on the other side of the desk, hands on hips. 'Come on, stop wasting time thinking about it – let's go.' She half turned her body, still looking him in the eyes. Tony pressed the button on the computer screen to switch it off, and pushed himself up to standing.

'Right, let's pick him up. You know, I think this may be the most high profile arrest I've ever done. I don't think we'll actually be live on TV around the world, but pretty close. In fact, I think we should probably clear it with H.'

'Wimp,' she smiled. 'I'll start the car.'

'Did you just make a cricket commentary joke?'

'Eh?'

'Obviously not. Right, I'll see you in the car park in five.'

DCI Harry Hardwick gave Milburn the eye for a good few seconds, before giving him the go-ahead to break up a first-class cricket match, albeit a friendly. 'Tread carefully, Tony, it'll all be on TV.' Tony nodded and headed out of his boss's office and quickly down the stairs.

DS Milburn did not want to be on television arresting Harris, but knew it was inevitable. It would be at least another hour until the teabreak, and they couldn't wait that long if they were to book him in, interrogate him enough to get Hamilton's name, and get a search warrant whilst the day Magistrate was still in the office.

Tony knew though that Diane would love the limelight, so he arranged to liaise with PR man Barnstaple, whilst she organised for Vivender to substitute his man off the field, so she could perform the actual arrest pitchside. The colour visibly drained from Jeremy Barnstaple as he understood that they were going to publicly arrest Harris. After a brief consultation between Barnstaple, his coaching staff, the university team's head coach, and the match referee, they agreed that in these unprecedented circumstances, a playing replacement would be permitted.

Coach Pathan was wringing his hands as he looked at the spare players lounging in the team area, even though there were plenty of suitable substitutes. In the end, he told Pieter Hamilton he was going on instead. The South African's face was a beaming grin, as a somewhat confused Harris came jogging off.

Standing next to the blond PR man and his clipboard, DS Milburn was almost certain that his ADC brandished the handcuffs with a theatrical flourish for the cameras. She was still reeling off the arrest patter as she led him past her boss. The sun shone back off her shiny, dark brown hair and this caused Tony to put his hand to the warmth of the Sun on his own brown hair. He followed, without saying anything further to anyone from the cricket club.

In Durham City's police station, they let Andrew Singh perform his formalities as custody sergeant, before taking Harris straight to an interview room. As they had briefed the interview adviser before leaving, he had already prepared an agenda for them, to try and achieve the aim of getting him to name Hamilton as a drug dealer.

Harris was visibly shaking throughout, even when sitting down across the table from Meredith and Milburn. His expression appeared blank, staring across the room to the wall behind the detectives. He answered that he did not want assistance from a solicitor, although Tony was pretty sure that the man had not comprehended the question properly. Diane spoke gently, almost sweetly, as she explained to him that Hamish Elliott had died from a drugs overdose, and the only drugs paraphernalia found was the syringe with his fingerprint on the plunger.

Following the cliché that is good cop-bad cop, Tony followed up straight away, 'Looks like DI Barnes was absolutely right when he accused you on that first meeting of being a drugs cheat. Liar. Wouldn't surprise me if you and Elliott were lovers too, you denied that as well. Why did you kill him, then? Lovers' tiff?'

Jim Harris, a big strong man, seemed to have lost any aura of strength. His listless hands were lying on the table, and he was opening and closing his mouth like a fish, but was unable to actually speak.

Meredith made a show of putting her hand on Tony's arm to silence him. She then leaned forward, and put her other hand on Harris's to refocus him on her. She smiled and suggested, 'Jim, just tell us what happened. Why is there a syringe with your fingerprint on it?' She let go of his hand and leaned back again, mimicking his pose very closely, to put him more at ease. He looked at her deep, chocolate eyes, looked across at Milburn who beheld him sceptically, and then looked back to the welcoming Diane.

'I … I, he just wanted a bit more strength in his bowling.'

'Sorry, what do you mean by that?' Diane continued trying to tease the story from the suspect.

'He was always going on about being too small and weak to really ping balls down the wicket. He knew there were others who would leapfrog him in selection – he was pretty much stuck as a bowler, not improving really.'

'OK, and how does that relate to his death?'

The man leapt to his own defence, blurting out, 'I don't know how he died, I gave him the stuff a week before.'

'What do you mean "gave him the stuff"? What did you do?' Her emphasis was on the word "did".

'So, he wanted to get stronger, and so I got him some Somnulone, and showed him how to mix it up and inject it. That's the syringe you found. We did that about ten days ago.'

'This is bullshit. I don't believe a word of it, ' Tony raged, maintaining his persona in the interrogation.

'It's the truth,' Harris wailed. 'I sold him the stuff, injected him with it, and he was fine. That was a week before he died. I hadn't been back inside his place again until the morning I found him. You don't need to do Somnulone more than once a week.'

'OK then, Mr Bullshit, where did you get the Somnulone? We'll check the dates with your supplier.'

Harris stopped dead, and looked at the DS. He looked imploringly at Diane, and answered stiffly, 'I can't say.'

Milburn carried on loudly, 'I knew it. You've been lying to me at every turn. Meredith, let's take him back to the cells.

We've got enough for murder, I don't even know why we're wasting our time in here.'

'Wait.' The man continued to look into Meredith's eyes. Then he closed his own. 'I did not kill Hamish. He was my friend. I get Somnulone from Pieter Hamilton. I sell some of it for him, so he won't be able to tell you that the stuff I sold Hamish was the last I got from him and that it was ten days ago, 'cause that wasn't the last. I pick up doses from him fairly often for various people around the city. But if someone killed Hamish with it deliberately, I would guess that it was Hamilton.'

Diane's tone was soothing. 'OK, Jim. Where does Hamilton get it from?'

Harris looked slightly confused, as if the question was irrelevant. 'I don't know. I don't have any idea.'

'And does he supply anything else?'

'No. Um, no. At least not that I know of. Somnulone's about the only thing I know of that can beat the doping tests these days.'

'Ever heard of Priapra, Mr Harris?' the DS came back in with an accusing tone.

'I've heard of it. What does that have to do with this? I've never used it.'

The detectives looked at each other without speaking. A slight nod from Milburn and they got up and Diane said, 'OK, Jim, we'll pick up Hamilton and see what he has to say about it all. You'll have to go back to the cell for now.'

A simple tap with the heavy police battering ram broke the lock open on Pieter Hamilton's flat. The flat was bright and modern, not dissimilar to Hamish Elliott's Durham apartment. It was fancier architecture, with a mezzanine type lounge area above the kitchen-dining area. The view was far less impressive though, looking across Chester-le-Street's marketplace from the third floor.

Hamilton was still engaged on the cricket field. DS Milburn's phone sports app told him that the university were down to their last wicket of their first innings, but that the final pair of batsmen were tenaciously holding on. Play was scheduled to finish by 6pm, with the floodlights on early in the March pre-season. With a shower, and a team meeting, it was unlikely that he would be back to his residence much before 7pm, and that gave the police nearly two hours to find any drugs and/or padding.

His presence would not have been a problem, but Tony could picture the ranting and raving that might go on. He had not taken any of Hamilton's personal intimidation seriously, but this search of his home would be the sort of thing that Milburn presumed would qualify for retribution, in the event that Hamilton was sufficiently unhinged that he might act on his threats. Tony had been in that position before though and, as an occupational hazard, he just filled in the appropriate form and got on with things. The training sergeant in his very first police training unit had cautioned them that an officer would quickly become a nervous wreck if he entertained the threats that would be made to them during their career.

Tony sat at the kitchen table with the copy of the search warrant that they would leave there on their exit. Diane and the two uniformed officers with them rifled efficiently through cupboards and drawers and the large collection of sports bags.

Pieter was obviously unconcerned about people entering his flat and finding his drugs, as they easily found a significant collection of pills in unlabelled bags, and powders in either plastic sealed boxes or small brown wax-paper packages. Milburn photographed each item before noting on the search warrant the items to be removed as evidence, and his estimates of the numbers of pills in each bag.

There were also eight inserts for cricket leg pads, which the four of them duly bagged up and labelled. The unknown pills, alongside Jim Harris's statement, meant that this would now become an arrest scenario, as soon as the Afrikaner got home. Once the search was complete, they sat to await the owner's homecoming. Acting DC Meredith was in the process of glibly making them all a cup of tea when they heard the lift to his floor open in the hallway. A noise like a bull elephant charging along the corridor came ahead of him, banging his big cricket bag through the open door.

'Hey, what's going on?' he shouted, looking around the three seated men and then over to Meredith at the kitchen counter. The men stood up together, like a synchronised standing team. The two uniformed constables moved over to flank the cricketer, whilst Tony explained that Hamilton was under arrest, following the finding of unknown drugs in his flat, which had been the product of a legally executed search warrant. The South African was silent, but scowled at Tony continuously. 'Look, I'm not saying anything till I see an advocate.'

'We've got a solicitor waiting for you back at the station.' Tony had not organised this in advance – he had half-expected Hamilton to also use Smythe from London, but when there was

234

no objection to the duty solicitor, the detective gestured to Meredith, indicating that she should phone for the solicitor straight away.

They sent Mr Hamilton back to the station in the panda car, whilst Milburn and Meredith took the drugs evidence from the search directly to the police labs in order to get them processed as quickly as possible. The technician they handed them over to, a very non-Irish man known to all as Paddy, was grateful at the suggestion of what tests to perform. The biggest nightmare for the technicians was to be presented with a totally unknown substance to determine its identity. Parking in the police station car park, over the wall from a very good Asian fusion restaurant, Meredith pointed out the duty solicitor arriving in his battered old Peugeot. She commented on its probable low value and they both smirked.

Milburn had had many previous dealings with Evans, the duty solicitor, and knew him as a fair and reasonable sort. They took Pieter straight into the interrogation room, and left him to discuss matters with Mr Evans for twenty minutes. Short, with brown hair cut in a dull style, and unfashionable glasses, the solicitor was the physical antithesis of his big, blond, sporting hero client.

Tony and Diane sat in the DS office checking that they had the interview agenda and all the evidence mentally prepared before the interrogation with Hamilton. Paddy had already tested the bagged substances and found significant quantities of both Somnulone and Priapra, plus smaller quantities of Ecstasy, and only enough cocaine to be classified as for personal use. Tony was impressed with Paddy's efficiency. He was unsurprised when the email finished by saying that the lab were still in the process of setting up the experiment to try and separate the leg padding samples to see if they were for smuggling use. He thought of Penfold's basement laboratory, and smiled at the thought of Paddy setting it all up, probably for the first time in his career, and thus probably also from a recipe.

Having prepared a full interview strategy, which they also ran by DCI Hardwick for approval, and organised papers and prompt notes, Tony and Diane stood outside the interview room door looking at each other. Without speaking, he nodded to her, silently asking, 'Ready?' She smiled, leaned forward and gave him the briefest kiss on the lips. In a flash, she had opened the door and walked in.

Tony was completely nonplussed. All of his mental preparation was out of the window, as his mind whirled, watching her sleek movement in towards the table and the suspect and his lawyer. Tony was frozen to the spot, his mouth slightly open. He blinked a couple of times, as the three in the room all looked at him hovering on the threshold.

Seeing the surly look on Hamilton's face brought the detective back to full consciousness, and he stepped in and closed the door. DS Milburn knew that they needed to strike whilst the iron was hot, and knew also that Meredith had deliberately timed her action to catch him in a position where he could not complain or get away from her.

Tony put his folder down on the table, explained to the video camera who was present and why and they began to ask questions of the South African about his knowledge, use and sales of Somnulone.

Arms folded across his chest, Hamilton spent most of the interview leaning back in his chair and responding with a stock

MM HUDSON

answer: 'Look, I'm not going to answer that question, isn't it.'
Sometimes he changed things a bit and replied, 'Nothing to say
to that.' At the mention of Harris and his accusation that he sold
Somnulone on behalf of Hamilton, his immediate response was
scathing. 'That little runt,' he said coldly but, after a look from
Evans, continued, 'No comment.' The remainder of the
interview continued in the stonewall manner he had begun it.
There was nothing to say about the large haul of drugs
discovered in his flat; no comment as to whom he sold Priapra
to, or who sold it for him; silence at the idea that he smuggled
both substances into the UK in the form of plastic foam
disguised as cricket leg padding; and no answers when the
questions moved towards Hamish Elliott and his unfortunate
death from Priapra overdose. After 45 frustrating minutes,
Evans had served his client well. Hamilton's answers, or non-
answers, put the ball firmly in the police's court – they would
have to prove everything they wanted to charge him with,
without any help or support from him.

The lack of co-operation from their prime suspect meant
that, throughout the interview, Tony could think of nothing
other than Diane's kiss. There were no revelations to be
assimilated on the hoof, nor quick thinking needed to steer the
interview towards the conclusions they wanted. Hamilton kept
stum, and so Milburn's mind circled. As they climbed the
staircase back to CID, he managed to bite his tongue until they
were both in his office and alone. The thin office door did little
to maintain any privacy though as Tony exploded, 'What the
hell was that?'

Meredith answered in an even tone, 'Well, we did our best, but he's one of the few criminals who understands the value of silence.'

'You know very well what I mean.' Mild-mannered Milburn was completely red-faced from shouting. They were standing facing each other just inside the office door. She looked askance at him, brows slightly furrowed in a confused look. 'It was totally out of order and you know it. This is exactly why I won't work with you.'

She maintained the incredulous lack of understanding. 'Tony, I did my best. That was my first murder interv…'

'Stop!' Having interrupted her, he paused. Pointing at the door, Tony rejected her, 'Get out. Just get out!'

Diane stepped forward and put her hand on his arm. In a soft, treacly voice, she soothed, 'Tony, it's OK.'

He waved the arm violently to shake off her touch, and moved away towards sanctuary behind the desk. In a restrained and quiet voice, he uttered, 'Get out.'

She gave him a wide-eyed look and lowered her head, turned and slipped out of the office.

He punched the rear wall and then held on to the corner of the window frame looking out into the sunny car park.

About an hour later, there was a light knock at the door and Diane stepped inside, holding her phone up like an offering. 'That wrinkled old nurse has just called me saying that Aisha has been admitted to hospital. She's been beaten quite badly.'

'What?'

'Her family brought her in, and she's seriously hurt. Not in danger of dying, but pretty bad.'

He picked up his office phone and telephoned for his boss. Milburn needed assistance to go and investigate, but was not going to have Meredith involved any further. Hardwick would have to remove her from the case for that kiss. Tony was fully intent on making a formal complaint against her too. There was no answer on the telephone, so he got up and stormed out. She smiled at him and said, 'Tony.'

He did not even look at her, but rushed past and up the stairs to talk to DCI Hardwick in person. However, he was thwarted when he got up to the senior manager's office. It was nearly 8pm and Harry had gone home over an hour previously. Tony shook the locked office door handle in angry frustration. 'Fuck,' he cursed, albeit it at a low volume, only for his own benefit.

He took a deep breath, and re-entered the CID work area. Diane now sat in the open plan area, facing the door he was returning through. She was resting her chin on a hand, elbow on the desk, the other hand fiddling with a sheet of paper. On his entry, her face brightened into a smile and she asked, 'Is everything OK, Tony?'

Standing on the threshold, Milburn's immediate inclination was to retort, 'Are you mental?' Instead, he asked and answered this question in his mind. He thought for a moment and responded, 'I'll get Penfold to meet me at the hospital – he has a good relationship with the coach. You might as well go home for the night.'

She leapt up, grabbed her suit jacket from the chair, and her brown winter coat from the stand beside Tony. 'Not a chance, this is part of the same case, you're not leaving me out of the investigations. And you'll need a female officer to talk to a female in her hospital bed.'

He stared at her, wondering how she could possibly not understand that they could not work together. However, he knew that until Hardwick was apprised of the turn of events outside the interview room, he had no authority to get rid of her, and that doing so would make things more difficult when she got the Police Federation involved. He attempted to sound business-like. 'OK, you take your own car though, so we can just go home after speaking with them.'

Without speaking any further, he led them down the staircase towards the rear exit from the station. She asked several questions about Tony's thoughts on the assault on Aisha Pathan, and his own wellbeing. He did not answer, but shook his head on several occasions, in exasperation rather than reply.

Milburn and Meredith spoke to the ward sister for ten minutes or so about Aisha's injuries. The nurse told them she had extensive bruising all over, three rib fractures which had potentially damaged her lungs, although they could not yet be certain, broken bones in the left cheek, and a broken forearm. The victim had indicated that her father had been responsible, but it was her mother and father together who had brought Aisha into the hospital. They were still by her bedside. One of the hospital security guards was in attendance, whilst the hospital called for the police, but the nurse said that that was the call to Diane.

'What made you think that this was related to our visit the other day with that other woman?' DS Milburn asked.

'Miss Pathan kept moaning the name of Hamish Elliott. When I spoke to Diane the other day, she told me about how you'd taken that fruit loop down to identify his body when she flipped out.' Tony looked to Diane who raised her eyebrows and smiled in acknowledgement. He wondered exactly when the two women had had a chance to discuss the matter when they were there three days previously.

They relieved the security guard, and made sympathetic comments to Aisha and her parents. Mrs Pathan was sitting in an uncomfortable-looking beige hospital armchair, next to the bed, holding her daughter's small hand. Aisha's face was swollen and very red. There were four or five red circles, and about 80% of her face was puffed up. The hand her mother held stuck out of the end of a small plaster cast on the forearm. The only other part of her body visible was her right arm, which appeared uninjured.

Vivender Pathan stood a few feet from the bed, adjacent to the large curtain covering the window at the end of the ward. It was also a light brown colour. It was a different ward, but he stood in almost the corresponding spot where Kate Withenshaw had held the forces of order at bay with a fire extinguisher.

ADC Meredith stepped around to stand opposite Mrs Pathan, beside Aisha. Thus she was directly between the injured daughter and her father. Diane put her hand on the available right hand, and soothed, 'We're so sorry you're hurt, Aisha.' She did not move her body, but her eyes looked into Diane's round white face. 'What can you tell us about how you got your injuries?'

Her mum squeezed Aisha's hand, and her eyes flicked across to the mother's face. There was the slightest movement on the pillow, which Tony interpreted as a shake of the head. In obvious pain, her mouth moved slightly and she whispered.

241

Despite the minimal volume of her voice, all five of them plainly heard her accuse her father of the beating.

'Hush now,' her mother responded calmly and quietly.

'Let me confirm, please. You are telling me that this man, your father, beat you up?' Diane spoke simply and clearly and indicated behind herself towards Vivender. She was actually blocking Aisha's view of her father, but the woman nodded with a wince.

'Hold your tongue, daughter.' Mr Pathan spoke sharply, and took a step to the side so that his daughter could see him pointing his finger at her. At his movement, the detective sergeant stepped forward and put an arm up horizontally in front of the short Indian man.

Mrs Pathan continued, 'Family comes first, remember.'

Their only daughter shook her head again and said, 'He's upset that I went to see Hamish often behind his back. We were in love.'

Shouting, Vivender stepped another half step forward against Tony's arm. 'You cannot love him – you don't know him.'

Aisha's voice was so quiet now that Diane leant forward, but the group had crowded close enough so they could all still hear. 'I told him that Hamish and I had made love many times, and that I'm pregnant. He doesn't understand how life is here, and won't accept that he must change if he wants to live here. His only answer was to punch and kick me until I fell down unconscious.'

'You are my daughter. You must obey me.' Mrs Pathan was nodding at her husband's words. 'You have dishonoured your family.'

His pressure to step through Milburn's arm was now so strong that Tony had to step in and hold him back with both hands. 'Mr Pathan, I think you and I had better go outside, so you can cool down a bit. Your daughter is in good hands here. Come and tell me your side of things.'

Tony was pleased to see Penfold arrive at the ward entrance as he guided Mr Pathan past the other beds towards the vestibule and the nurses' station. The tall blond man was once again attired in cargo shorts, but unusually he sported a purple hoody as well. It espoused the environmental pressure group Surfers Against Sewage, and Milburn wondered if he was wearing it in support of this organisation or because it was actually cold enough that he needed the warmth it offered.

Vivender was wringing his dark brown hands together and pacing beside the small reception desk the nurses used for this ward. He was looking at his feet and muttering. Penfold gesticulated with his head towards a set of four chairs. They were green vinyl and looked as if they had escaped from an old airport departure lounge. Tony smiled to himself at the idea that the new hospital was not even two years old. 'Vivender, perhaps we could sit down, please.' The detective's gentle command was not given with an option, as a question. With a hand on the cricketer's arm, Tony guided him and they sat down next to each other. Penfold remained standing, and took up a casual pose leaning against a doorjamb opposite them. The corridor was wide enough so that he was socially outside the conversation space, but in reality he was close enough to hear anything they said. 'So, can you tell me what happened?'

'Why is she so wilful? Her mother is such a proper Indian woman. I don't understand what happened to Aisha.'

'Mr Pathan; how did we all end up here?' Tony pointed at the floor. 'What happened to Aisha?'

The father continued to look at the floor and squeeze his hands together. 'We watched her. We looked after her. How could she do this to us? She will have to go back to India. Yes, I'll get Anmur to take her in. She has many children, this can just be another one of hers.'

'Mr Pathan. Mr Pathan, look at me.' He slowly raised his face to look at Milburn, but the DS still wasn't sure if he was focussed on the dialogue at hand. 'Please think back, and tell me what exactly happened this evening. How did Aisha get injured?'

'I did that. She wouldn't stop. She was taunting me. On and on about sex stuff. It was disgusting. She's no daughter of mine. It's England that's done this to her. I said she should never come with us in the first place, but Mrs Pathan would not hear of it. She can't have any more children, so Aisha was very important to us. That's over now though. She has disgraced us.' His face displayed tiredness.

Milburn spoke very quietly. 'Mr Pathan, did you kill Hamish Elliott?'

The Indian looked up suddenly. 'What?' He was alert and looked scared, his eyes flicking around Tony's face. He took a quick glance over to Penfold who was looking back placidly. Returning his eyes to Tony's, the fear had gone and Pathan answered, 'No, of course not. I didn't know the truth about him until today. I used to think he was a decent man. If he were still alive now, I might kill him, but I am too late.'

'Tony,' Diane interrupted from the threshold of the ward entrance. 'You need to hear this.' She beckoned him in.

244

Mr Pathan also got up, but Milburn instructed him to stay, and nodded to Penfold to keep the man at the waiting area.

When the police officers reached the bed, they could see Aisha's mother leaning close to speak in her ear. Aisha had her bruised face turned away as much as she could manage, but Tony spotted Mrs Pathan release her grip, and he assumed she had been applying a painful pressure on the broken arm to make her daughter listen.

Diane went around and was then directly in Aisha's view. 'Please tell me again what you just said about your pregnancy.' Diane's eyes moved to her right and Aisha followed so that she knew that DS Milburn was now listening in too.

'I'm not pregnant. I just said that to hurt my father. Hamish and I were in love and we did sleep together, but my father just does not understand. So we were arguing, and I said that and he just flipped out. Next thing I knew I woke up here.'

Tony and Diane looked at each other and, after a moment of silence, stepped away to whisper to each other.

'What do we do with that?' she asked.

Tony exhaled slowly, before replying, 'Well, visiting hours are just about over, so we get the parents out of here for tonight and see if she wants to press charges in the morning. He's most concerned about the family honour, so if she's not actually pregnant then I don't think she'll be in danger of another beating. I'm confident he did just flip out, so I think she'll be safe at home in future.'

'Ever the male chauvinist optimist.' She was smiling slightly.

He shrugged. 'Like I say, if she wants to press charges then she'll need to move out of home. If they reconcile in the morning, then I don't think the family disgrace he's worried about will arise, which I'm sure would be the trigger to violence. He's generally a decent guy as far as I can tell.'

'Hmm. I'm wondering if she is actually pregnant but is following your logic so denying it gets her a reprieve for now.'

'Oh god. I don't think we can second guess that sort of thing. How about if we get the nurses to clear out the visitors and then you can come back to check with her?' Meredith nodded, her bottom lip a little stuck out.

Fifteen minutes later, Milburn, Meredith and Penfold sat around Aisha's bed. Tony and Diane sat on either side in place of her mother and father, whilst Penfold had pulled up a third institutional armchair a little past the end of the bed in front of the light brown curtain. The ADC was stroking the injured woman's shoulder gently. She then ran her fingers through her own shiny brown hair, placing the left side behind her ear. Its short length meant it was barely held and the men separately both wondered how long it would stay in place. 'Aisha, we waited until your parents left so we could talk to you without them being here. We really need to know the truth from you. The truth about everything. Not just about your injuries and how you got them, but we also need to know the full story about you and Hamish.' Meredith's voice was gentle and straightforward. 'Start with this evening and your dad.'

She turned her swollen face to the side so she was roughly facing Diane. Gravity pulled a tear out of her eye and off the side of her face to land on the pillow. Whilst the bed sheets were crisp hospital white, the blanket and pillowcase matched the beige of the other soft furnishings in the ward. Although it was just a single teardrop, the pillowcase was discoloured in a surprisingly large, dark, wet circle. 'It started at the cricket match today. He didn't want me there and was asking why I wanted to be there. When I said it reminded me of happy times with Hamish he got mad. He told me to go home. At first I said no and moved out of his way – he had to stay with the team so I just sat high in the stand. But, after a little while, I realised that arguing with him was making me unhappy and I was not having the happy memories I had wanted. The final straw was when I saw that stupid Kate. I can't believe Hamish ever wanted to be friends with her. So I left and went home.

'When dad came home after the match, we had dinner together and he started going on about it again. I told him that I had left a few minutes after our argument, but he was still hassling me. In the end I lost it and started shouting at him. I said all sorts of things I knew would hurt him, like how I'd been sleeping with Hamish. I even said some things about what we had done in bed. My dad is a very upright conservative man, and I knew that hearing such things from his daughter would really get to him. I love my dad, but I was angry. When I finally said that I was pregnant with Hamish's baby that was a step too far. For my father that would be the ultimate shame. Everything he has would be dishonoured – his family, his daughter, his big career in England. I'm not at all surprised that he went crazy, although I've never seen him be violent before. I'm so sorry, what will happen to him?'

Tony let Diane continue, 'That rather depends on what you want to do. You could insist on a prosecution, but unless either you or your mother are willing to give evidence, then he will not be convicted.'

'Good, I've caused my father enough stress. He doesn't deserve punishment for this.'

Here, Tony did interject, 'Really? Are you sure, Aisha? You could have been killed.'

She did not move, but closed her eyes and said, 'I am sure.'

Diane came back in softly. 'So, what is the truth? Were you sleeping with Hamish? And are you pregnant?'

'We were in love, yes we slept together. But, as far as I know, I'm not pregnant. I did just say that to hurt father.'

'You know he was sleeping with other women?' Tony knew he had to clear up the question of whether Aisha had murdered Elliott, although he could not picture this intelligent and sensitive woman being a killer. Tears were now rolling continuously onto her pillow.

'I know he was a bit of a ladies man before we got together, but he was faithful once we started seeing each other. I even asked him straight out, when I was a bit worried one time. That bloody crack whore had been flirting with him at the ground, and I saw him laughing with her. I was jealous then, but he told me she was just an old girlfriend and that he still bumped into her occasionally, as her new boyfriend is Pieter Hamilton's cousin. I can't believe he's gone. That laugh.' Her body was shaking the blanket with her sobs.

Milburn looked at each of the others in turn, with a silent look of incredulity. He was surprised that she could possibly believe Elliott's claims of fidelity. 'But we found hairs in his bed sheets from other females. I don't expect he washed them that often – you must have known he wasn't being faithful.'

Her crying voice rose louder. 'Stop saying that,' she wailed. 'It's not true.'

'Kate Withenshaw even claims she slept with him on the night he died. Did you find out about this and flip out like your dad?'

She was howling. 'No! That's awful. How could you think that? I love Hamish. I could never hurt him.'

A nurse arrived at the end of the bed. 'Officers please. You're disturbing the entire ward. Can't you see Aisha is distressed, what are you doing?'

Milburn stood up. 'Sorry, Sister. And I'm sorry to you, Aisha, we have to ask these questions. We'll leave now.'

Friday 29th March

A six-word story text arrived from Penfold: 'A murderous band: the cousins Grimm.'

Milburn leaned forward in his office chair and texted back: 'Evidence?'

The reply came straight back: 'Means? Check. Motive? Check. Opportunity…? How could they get into his bedroom and inject him with drugs, naked, and without a struggle?'

Tony was in the middle of typing back, 'That's exactly my point!' when he stopped, raised his eyes to the ceiling and then put his phone back in his jacket pocket.

ADC Diane Meredith was very good at her job. Part of this came from a motivation to impress Tony, whilst the means often came about by arriving at work early. This March Friday, she had been there an hour before her shift officially started, and had transcribed her notes from their conversations in the hospital already.

She came into Tony's office to present them to him. He took a cursory glance, put the papers down on his desk and leaned back. Diane was wearing another smart business suit, in navy blue with gold-coloured buttons, and tailored to her curves. She stood straight up with her hands on her hips.

Milburn shifted in his seat and looked at the wall clock again – when would DCI Hardwick arrive at work?

He looked at her flawless face, and asked, 'So, do you think one of the Pathans killed Elliott?' She scrunched up her nose in consideration. The beauty of her face during this action conflicted Tony, and he missed her answer. He paused for a moment, to realise that she had answered. Shaking his head to clear the distraction, he asked again, 'Sorry, I was miles away, say again.'

'I said I'm not sure. That beating he gave Aisha demonstrates a lost temper and enough intensity of feeling about it so that I could see him doing it. She's a bit more tricky. I think she's cleverer about what she says to us, but I wouldn't be surprised if Elliott's philandering would upset her enough to kill him. And she's her father's daughter.'

'Apple doesn't fall far from the tree, you reckon? I don't see it in her, I got the impression she was blinded by her love for him.'

'Like I said, clever in what she tells us. On balance, I'd pick her over her dad. The whole woman scorned things stems basically from a truth about women.' She gave him a closed-lip smile, and raised her eyebrows.

'And don't forget the behind-the-scenes mother too.' Tony considered the ceiling tiles for a few seconds. When he looked back at Diane, he concluded, 'The major difficulty with them though is we have no evidence of access to drugs.'

'I'd expect Hamish to have had a supply of Priapra in his flat, which the killer could have taken away, along with the syringe they used. And she would know he had it, whilst her parents would not. You've convinced me, it was Aisha.' She was grinning, as they both knew this was mere speculation.

Milburn stood up and grabbed on his brown tweed jacket from the seat back. 'Right, let's go and pick up Kate and Daniel. We'll give them a bit of a shake and see what falls out.' Meredith frowned at him at this sudden turn. He shrugged. 'Aisha's not going anywhere.'

As he walked past her to the door, Diane muttered under her breath, 'Except back to India, maybe.'

There was no one home at Kate's student house on Hallgarth Street. From there to Ramsbotham's flat on the Bailey was barely 200 yards. Tony and Diane walked together across the high pedestrian bridge behind the concrete box students' union building, being watched throughout by the all-seeing eye of the giant Rose Window on the East end of Durham Cathedral. It surveyed them all the way past the cathedral towards the building of the student debating chambers.

Daniel Ramsbotham's plush apartment was decorated like a London gentleman's club, with dark wood panelling, Persian rugs and Chesterfield sofas. Conveniently, they found both Daniel and Kate together in the flat, and made two arrests at once. To save more time, Milburn telephoned Mr Smythe's number there and then, so he could start the journey back up from London. They agreed a 2pm start to the interviews. Tony was annoyed that Smythe, a seemingly highly successful London solicitor, was able to drop everything and leave at once. It was vaguely useful to his investigation, but the influence that these wealthy students had upset him. His indignation was soothed somewhat when Diane also found a bag of pills, which looked very much like Priapra, left casually on the dining table.

As they walked the prisoners back the short distance to the police station, Kate was in much the same mood as she had been at the cricket match. She talked continuously, sometimes to her boyfriend, sometimes to the detectives. It was banal and cheerful, as if she was unaware of the ramifications of being arrested.

The weather was cold and clear blue skies again, and crossing the bridge they all lifted their faces slightly to feel the warmth of the sun. In the flat, Ramsbotham had initially instructed Kate to say nothing, but he did not interrupt her flow of chatter as they promenaded as if they were on a double date.

The custody sergeant, Baz Bainbridge, looked down at the fresh-faced pair. Baz was a gentle giant, who could switch on his hard man persona, whether at work or in the boxing ring. His scary hulking copper act seemed to wash over Daniel Ramsbotham, whilst his occasional girlfriend appeared not to notice the sergeant at all. Baz had a thick Geordie accent, and Milburn wondered, at one point, if the southern students were actually unable to understand him.

After Daniel's details were input into the computer, Milburn escorted him to a cell. Meredith and Sergeant Bainbridge attempted to check in Miss Withenshaw. She still had not paused for breath, and was simultaneously fiddling with her blonde fringe whilst looking in a small mirror. Baz had to shake her a little by the upper arm to attract her attention to answer his questions. Kate was reluctant to give over her handbag, and it took some persuasion to make her understand that she had been arrested. ADC Meredith took her along the opposite corridor to a female cell.

Once both detectives were back at the custody suite's reception desk, Baz showed them the inside of Kate's handbag. There were several brand new white syringes. They were a solid bulky shape, rather like individual cigar cases. The sergeant popped the cap off one of them. The small silvery spike gleamed and, after showing to Milburn and Meredith, he replaced the cap and put all her possessions in a large clear plastic bag with "Withenshaw cell F4" written on it.

Two hours or so later, Baz was on the phone to DS Milburn. 'Tony, I'm gonna call the doc in. Your female is really losing it, I'll see if she can give her something.'

'What? Do you mean Kate Withenshaw?'

'You got others in that you 'a'n't told me about?'

'What's wrong with her?'

'Junkies are all the same. I can often guess how long they'll last before shouting and banging at the door. She gan quicker than I'd have put money on. Lucky it's only me down here, so I lost me bet to me. Had a look at 'er and she needs the doc, even if she just says. "screw her, she can't have nowt." Gotta follow the procedure.'

'Right, OK. Give me a call when the doc's in with her.'

Another 30 minutes later, Milburn and Meredith returned to the custody suite to talk with the custody doctor-on-call, to find out about Kate. The doctor was a short woman with designer glasses, and wore a white coat over dark brown trousers and a white shirt. The doctor spoke to Sergeant Bainbridge, but the two detectives stood close. 'What can I tell you? She's addicted to crack cocaine, and she wants something for the withdrawals that she's currently suffering. I'd say that's pretty much the sum of it.'

254

'Are you going to give her anything?' Baz wondered.

The doctor shrugged. 'I'm not going to give her cocaine. And other than that I don't really have anything suitable.' There was a pause. 'Sorry, I should emphasise that I don't have any cocaine. I could give her a valium or similar, but I don't really think it'd be medically beneficial. Given that she's in here, I think it'd be better for her health to have water and a good meal. She may be distracted if you need to interview her.'

DS Milburn scratched his head. 'I take it her fitness for interview will just get worse?'

'Certainly. If she's severely addicted, then she may have to be sedated and possibly hospitalised. Depends how long you plan on keeping her.'

Baz was not looking forward to the remainder of his shift involving a junkie howling at the Moon. He pulled out the bag of her possessions, and showed the doctor the syringes in Kate's handbag. 'I assume we're not allowed to let her have some of her own stash?'

'Definitely not. But in any case, those are diabetic insulin autoinjectors. She will need a dose, but she didn't look bad on that just yet. That meal I mentioned will help her no end.'

He nodded. 'Not a problem, I'm pretty sure lunch will be available in about 20 minutes.' Baz was about to close the handbag to put back in the custody locker under his desk, when he stopped and looked closer, and then tipped the contents out on his desk. Baz had been handling Kate's belongings with latex gloves on, and he picked up one of the syringes. It was fatter than the others and had a recessed hole at the end and no cap. 'What's this one?' He held it up to the doctor.

'It's called a "clipper". It's a safe store for used sharps: each time she uses one of the autoinjectors, she'll clip off the exposed needle, and every month or so this is full and you dispose of it in a sharps bin, perhaps at the pharmacy where she gets the insulin. The rest of the autoinjector is recycled, also at the pharmacy.' Sergeant Bainbridge nodded, learning something new every shift.

Tony jumped in, 'Do you mean that this contains all the needles she's used recently?'

The doctor looked at him, thinking sardonically that that was what she had just said. Out loud, she confirmed, 'Yes, it's likely to be habitual. Pop the autoinjector cap, spike your thigh, clip the needle, both back in your handbag, off you go.'

Tony looked at Diane, and pointed at the clipper. She raised her eyebrows and nodded eagerly. He continued, 'Baz, bag up the clipper and send it for testing. I want to know the chemicals present on every needle in it, and especially whether any have Hamish Elliot's DNA on them.'

The sergeant mimicked a slave from the American Deep South, 'Yez Bozz,' and pulled open a drawer to find a padded envelope for evidence.

Ten minutes later, ADC Meredith was leading an interview with Kate Withenshaw. She looked feral: wide-eyed and straggly haired, nothing like the posh beauty that she had first encountered six days earlier. Her eyes were flicking back and forth across Diane's facial features, and she pressed her fingers on the table in a concert pianist pose. Occasionally, she rocked back a little with increased pressure on the fingers. 'Miss Withenshaw, the police doctor has examined you, and told us that we are permitted to give you something to make you feel better.'

'So let me have it,' Kate opined.

'First, we want something from you. But, we have to check whether or not you are happy to proceed without your lawyer being present. Are we OK to continue?'

'Yes, yes, come on, get on with it.' She looked across at Milburn briefly. He sat slightly back from the table and away to the side so that the conversation was very much woman to woman.

Meredith continued, 'We know that Priapra is a common drug in use by students in the university, but we need to be sure we're looking in the right place for the main supplier. Do you know who that might be?'

Kate looked from face to face again, and then down at the table. She murmured, 'No, I don't.'

'I told you she was a waste of time,' Milburn stated and stood up. He made for the door, and Meredith stood up too.

Kate shouted, 'No, stop!'

'What can you tell us, Kate?' Diane probed.

There was a long pause before Withenshaw replied, barely louder than a whisper, 'No, nothing.'

Diane sat down again, and looked Kate in the eyes with a small smile. 'Kate, we already know the answer. It's just the technicalities of the law mean somebody else has to say so too. You won't be betraying anyone – we already know.'

'Really?'

'Really.'

In a small voice, she said, 'Pieter Hamilton. He brings Priapra in from South Africa.'

257

'We know that. That's not what I asked. Who is the main supplier to the students? Hamilton doesn't sell directly. It's that middleman we need to hear about.'

Kate shifted in her seat and moved her hands into her lap. She looked across the table to Diane. Her mouth moved but no sound came out. The ADC slid forward in her seat, and leaned over the table. She cupped a hand to her ear, pushing back the silky brown hair. Kate mouthed again, but this time the word was audible: 'Daniel.'

'Do you mean Daniel Ramsbotham, who was arrested with you?'

She nodded slightly.

'Well done, Kate. I promise you that you have helped yourself out here.'

The wild eyes stilled to become imploring. 'Can I have my stuff now?' she asked. As Meredith stepped towards the door, Tony opened it and called to Sergeant Bainbridge. He arrived almost immediately with a tray holding a plastic cup of water and a plastic plate of sausages with mashed potatoes. DS Milburn told her, 'This is what the doctor recommended we give you.' Kate looked stunned and did not say anything as she watched the tray lower onto the table. The three police left the room and locked her in.

After two further hours, Smythe was in the police station, and ready to sit with his clients in interviews. They started with another meeting with Kate Withenshaw. She had eaten her meal, earlier, in the relative comfort of the interview room, before being transferred back to her cell. When Bainbridge and Smythe went to collect her, she was sitting on the floor in a corner of the small, single-occupancy cell, F4. Her solicitor smartened her up a little, and asked about her treatment. Kate's demeanour was demure, and she complimented the sergeant on the accommodation. In the interview room, she was still clearly suffering withdrawal symptoms, but was more controlled than they expected. Tony made a mental note to try the canteen sausages himself. They didn't want much more from her, but there needed to be some confirmation of various steps in the investigation, if it were to lead to any convictions in the future.

DS Milburn threw what he hoped would be a curve ball to unsettle smarmy Smythe. 'Miss Withenshaw, when you take your crack cocaine, you smoke it, don't you?'

She was definitely thrown by the question, and looked to her solicitor for guidance. He scowled at Milburn, scrabbling internally to work out where the questioning was aimed to lead. 'DS Milburn, the charge sheet states, rather preposterously, that you have arrested my client for murder. There is no evidence to suggest that she is a drug user, so your question seems absurd at best, downright rude at worst. Can we have questions about the charges you have put forward please?'

'Actually, the on-call doctor is convinced that she is an addict, but you're right, let me ask about something else.' Diane was silent, leaning back in her chair, arms folded across her chest, and watching Tony closely. 'We found a number of syringes in your handbag.'

Without waiting for her lawyer, Kate leapt in, convinced that she could easily deflect the question. 'Oh, yes, I'm a diabetic. They're for my insulin.'

'Oh, ok,' Tony replied as if she had helped him to understand things better. 'And there's a slightly fatter one that doesn't seem to have a needle on it, just a bit of a hole.'

'Yes, that's where you keep the needle after using each of the injections. They have to be disposed off safely in case you have any blood diseases. Not that I do, but that's what you have to do with them.'

Smythe scowled again, but said nothing. The DS finished the questions. 'So the one in your handbag contains all the needles you've used recently, and nobody else's?'

Before the solicitor could stop her, his client blurted out, smiling conclusively, 'Yes, that's right.'

'Don't say anything more, Kate,' Smythe interjected.

'Not a problem, Mr Smythe, that is all we wanted to ask for now.'

Smythe requested half an hour to talk to Ramsbotham before his interview. That gave the detectives time to liaise with their interview advisor, and for Milburn to telephone Penfold and discuss the latest aspects of the investigation. Mostly Tony wanted to let off some steam about Diane kissing him, and how he was forced to continue working with her, as the DCI had gone to a meeting in Leeds for the day and could not be reached. He was not confident about taking his complaints about Meredith to any of the other bosses in the building, as only Hardwick knew all the ins and outs, and how he had worked the system to find a workable solution in the past.

The phone call helped to settle and focus Milburn. However, just before they entered the interview room to put Kate's accusation of drug dealing to Ramsbotham, Penfold threw a spanner in the interview preparations. He sent a text message: 'Headline: Crack addict cracks a dick.' Tony couldn't work out if this was mere commentary, or was supposed to be a six-word story. Penfold seemed to have concluded that Kate murdered Hamish Elliott. As far as DS Milburn was concerned, the evidence was somewhere between incomplete and inconclusive, but he knew that Penfold was consistently and unnervingly correct in his conclusions. It was as if Penfold already knew of a positive result from the lab tests of Miss Withenshaw's needle collection. That would seal it, but Tony wondered where they would be if they came back negative. He shook his head to try and clear the distractions to focus on the interview agenda they had drawn up.

Daniel Ramsbotham was slouched slightly in the white plastic chair. Mr Smythe was standing and putting some papers into his briefcase. He then put it on the floor, sat down and adjusted his glasses to take in the two interrogators. They performed the preamble for the video camera. Then Milburn started. 'Mr Ramsbotham, we need to talk to you about a number of matters.'

Arthur Smythe shook his dark drown head. 'As you well know, Detective Sergeant, we will only be discussing matters related to the murder you have listed on the arrest form.'

Diane interjected, 'As you well know, we can also interview in relation to matters that come to light during investigations whilst suspects are in custody. In this case, Mr Ramsbotham has been implicated in high level Class A drug dealing within the city.'

The London lawyer was cool, and nothing seemed to faze him. 'Well, others may have implicated my clients in order to distract you from their crimes but, until you actually provide any evidence, there is little excuse to continue to hold either Mr Ramsbotham or Miss Withenshaw.'

Meredith sneered – she did not like anything about the students' solicitor – and responded slightly off their planned track, 'This arrogant so-and-so has been specifically named by a witness as the main supplier in Durham of the illegal drug Priapra; and we have pills recovered from his home which when tested will undoubtedly prove to be Priapra. We also have a man murdered by an overdose of Priapra, that was administered by somebody else.'

'Not me,' Daniel stated loudly without shifting in his seat.

'Indeed, and, until there is any evidence to suggest that he was involved, you should prepare the paperwork for my client to leave please.'

'OK.' DS Milburn held his hands up in a placatory gesture, and paused. 'As you can imagine, we are more interested in prosecuting the murder than the drugs offences. We'd like to offer Daniel a deal.' Diane turned to Tony with a look of confusion.

Smythe also shook his head, with an expression of disbelief. 'Detective Sergeant Milburn, I warned you once before about the failings of police officers who watch too much American television. You and I both know perfectly well that the Crown Prosecution Service is not empowered to do "deals".'

Tony replied immediately, 'And as a top-rated criminal lawyer, Mr Smythe, you also know that there are a whole host of means by which those ends can be achieved.'

'Do you hear yourself, detective? You are on camera you know?'

'We're not suggesting anything illegal. You know only too well that a conversation between barristers at court, on our recommendations, can sway what is prosecuted in order that justice can be served. And, in the end, that is what we all want, is it not? For justice to be served.'

Smythe continued to shake his head, and was about to respond, when his client interrupted, 'What is it?'

'The deal you mean?' Milburn clarified, and Ramsbotham's floppy hair nodded in confirmation.

The solicitor leaned over to whisper to Daniel, but all in the room could hear him complain, 'Your father was adamant – no deals.'

The young man waved Mr Smythe away, and repeated, 'The deal?'

'No prison time for these drug charges, providing you can give evidence that will secure a conviction for Hamish Elliott's murder.'

'Done.' Daniel was quick to take the deal and ignored his lawyer's continued protestations. His statement started with the information that the victim had slept with Kate many times. From her, Hamish Elliott had learnt of the money to be made dealing Priapra and had decided to get a piece of the action himself. He had thought that he would have an inside track to Pieter Hamilton, and also to the university women's cricket team. Hamilton had informed his cousin of this competition. At this point, Smythe was literally shaking his client by the arm. Daniel Ramsbotham was eager to quiet the man. He pushed his hand away, and said, 'Get off, I've got a deal.'

'You must listen to me, Daniel.'

'I'm sorry, can you get Mr Smythe out of here.' Daniel looked back and forth to the two detectives, but wouldn't turn to face his solicitor.

'I'm sorry, Mr Smythe, you know the drill.' Meredith was almost gleeful as she pointed to the door.

'I can't help you, Daniel, if you won't let me.' The student sat statuesque, looking at the wall behind Milburn. Making a slow show of packing his papers away, Arthur Smythe's last entreaty was, 'Your father will not be happy with this.'

When only the three of them remained, the Acting DC asked, 'I heard you were the main source of Priapra for the university?'

'I am the source, and Kate suggested that we could get rid of him easily as she was sharing his bed.'

Diane continued, 'So it was Kate's idea to murder Elliott?'

'Yup.'

'And you'll swear to that in court?'

'Yup.'

'So, you gave her an extra large amount of Priapra so she could inject him with it?'

'Yup. Although we had to get him to agree to be injected, so I got some Somnulone off Pieter too. Kate said that he'd used it before and would probably want another injection. She reckoned he was always moaning how skinny he was.'

Diane had been taking notes and turned the page to Ramsbotham. 'We'll have to type it up and get you to sign that as well but, for now, check that what I've written here is accurate and sign the bottom, please.'

He read carefully, and then paused with the pen hovering ready to sign. 'Can you confirm for the camera that signing this gives me immunity from all the drug charges?'

Detective Sergeant Milburn explained, 'Well, the deal was no prison time. As we mentioned with your solicitor, the CPS will still have to go through the motions of prosecuting you, but we'll get the barristers to discuss appropriate sentencing for them.' Tony gave Ramsbotham a conspiratorial wink. The younger man smiled and signed the paper.

They told Daniel to wait for a few minutes, and went to ask Sergeant Bainbridge to bring Kate Withenshaw to a separate room for interview. The woman was struggling with her drugs withdrawal, and was quick to agree to talk without her lawyer, if they would ask the doctor to come and see her again.

Before they went into the interview room, Meredith grabbed Tony's hand and stopped him. He pulled his hand away, stepped back two steps and folded his arms, hugging the case file to his chest. She took a step towards him and said quietly, 'I'm not sure we'll get away with this. That deal business with Ramsbotham was sketchy enough, but she's definitely not fit to be interviewed. It'll get thrown out long before they even get her to court.'

'I'm not after Kate: she's just a puppet. Ramsbotham's the real murderer here, even if he didn't actually do it himself. She never came up with this scheme herself. And I wouldn't be surprised if Hamilton was stirring the pot too. It's those cousins we need to get into jail. She needs rehab more than anything else.'

Kate Withenshaw was leaning against the wall at the end of the table, rocking sideways slightly, so that her head repeatedly bumped gently against it. It took two greetings to engage her attention. Her gaze moved quickly all around the room, sometimes looking at the officers, but mostly in random directions. Tony ignored her, and spoke for the video camera about who was present and the date and time.

Diane put her hand across the table onto Kate's. This focussed the addict. 'We've been speaking to Daniel about what you did to Hamish.' The blue eyes widened and her other hand tugged at her hair. 'He told us that you injected him with Somnulone and Priapra mixed together, and so much that it killed him.'

'Why would he tell you?' she moaned.

Meredith ignored the question. 'He says it was your idea to murder Hamish, and that he gave you the drugs to do it.'

'Noooo,' Kate wailed adamantly. 'He wouldn't tell you that, you're lying.'

'Here's his statement. Look, he's signed it at the bottom. Do you recognise his signature?'

Tears were flowing down Kate's cheeks as she read the paper. She shook her head and screamed, 'No. No. No.' Still loudly, but no longer screaming, she continued, 'It was all his idea.' Her eyes flitted back and forth between Milburn and Meredith. 'He said I could easily do it because Hamish trusted me. I didn't want to do it, but Daniel just kept on at me. He always gets what he wants.'

DS Milburn came into the conversation. 'Will you say so in court?'

'Against Daniel?' She looked distressed at the idea.

Diane squeezed Kate's hand, which she still held, and pointed at the statement with her other hand. 'He's happy to send you to prison for it.'

She looked down at the paper and back at Meredith. Kate then closed her own eyes and nodded. Diane took only a few minutes to tease out the woman's statement, whilst Tony wrote it all down. The details were very similar to Ramsbotham's version but, in Kate's version, it was all his idea in order to stifle competition in the Priapra trade. She emphasised that she had been unwilling to participate. However, he had withheld her crack cocaine one day, until she agreed to the plan. Her angle on that part of the story was more about what a persuasive man Daniel could be, rather than the fact that her addiction would make her do anything he wanted.

Daniel Ramsbotham had been on his own for less than 30 minutes, when they returned with Arthur Smythe and Kate's statement. DS Milburn checked, 'Do you want Mr Smythe in with us now, or not?'

The man leaned back in his chair with his hands clasped behind his head. 'Whatever, I don't mind either way.'

Milburn nodded his head to Smythe to enter with them. The solicitor was shaking his head at his client. Ramsbotham just smiled.

'Mr Ramsbotham, we have checked out your story with Kate Withenshaw.' Daniel shrugged and nodded. 'Great.'

'And she tells it very much like you did, but with one significant conflicting claim. She says it was all your idea.'

Ramsbotham smiled again. 'Well, of course she would. But who are you going to believe? She's a junkie whore, whilst I'm a hard-working student, the son of the owner of a private bank.'

'A self-confessed drug dealer,' Meredith jumped in.

Milburn held his hand up near her to interrupt. 'Well, Mr Ramsbotham, I'm sure your solicitor can apprise you of the details but, in the end, it doesn't matter whose idea it was. You

267

both agree that together you planned the murder. In legal terms, we call that "conspiracy to commit murder". Rest assured, we'll be asking for life imprisonment.'

'Hold on, we had a deal.'

'We will honour our deal. It was "no jail time for your drug offences". Conspiracy to murder is not covered by that.'

Ramsbotham sat staring at the table, and the detectives got up to leave. As Smythe followed them he gave a parting shot to Daniel. 'I told you to shut up.'

They gave Smythe an office to write up his notes, and went upstairs to CID. It was empty as Diane led them in and put the paperwork down on the nearest desk. She turned suddenly, threw her arms around Tony and kissed him full on the lips. He squirmed, but her grip was tight, and she continued the kiss. Finally, he wrestled free and jumped back. 'I love you, Tony Milburn.' Her eyes were bright and she was smiling a perfect smile. Tony looked at her beautiful face. As he looked, he watched his own fist punch her on the jawbone. Meredith's left foot stepped back, but the force was such that she slipped and fell back and sideways. Her left temple hit the ground with a thud. Still a spectator to his own actions, Tony then saw himself step forward and kick her hard in the stomach.

He was about to kick again when he was pulled backwards, and Harry Hardwick stepped around between them. 'Tony, stop! Enough.'

Diane staggered to her feet, holding the side of her head. 'You bastard,' she shouted. 'Harry, he raped me. He assaulted and raped me. Right here in this office. Thank God you've come in. Call Bainbridge up here to arrest him.' She was pointing an accusing finger at Milburn. He lunged forward to attack her again.

Despite his senior years, Hardwick held his detective back with significant strength. 'I said, stop!' His voice was gruff and loud, just short of a shout. 'Tony, get in your office!' The DCI swivelled them both around and pushed Tony backwards to go into his little room. The chief inspector then turned and did not speak. He gave Meredith his Evil Eye look for more than ten seconds. She said nothing, entranced by the eye. Finally, she spun round and ran out.

Monday 1st April

The dark brown wood panelling of the Daily Espresso gave it a dingy atmosphere, even on the brightest days. It had a huge front window, but was so long and narrow that the light level quickly dropped past the coffee service bar. Penfold and Kathy were giggling together on a sofa in the front window, when Tony set down a tray of three large coffee cups on the low table. He had the armchair opposite and flopped into it.

Penfold commented, 'Well, a highly unusual murder solved in a week. That's much quicker than the 37 days, five hours, and approximately 20 minutes average police time taken for unravelling a murder by a stranger. Cheers.' He proffered his white cup, holding pure black coffee, to the other two, and they picked up theirs to join the salutation.

After a brief taste of the froth on his cappuccino, Tony replied, 'Not really a stranger murder, but not your normal domestic killing either, so I think we can count it as solved quickly. An unusual case needs an unusual approach; would have taken at least 37 days if Detective Inspector Barnes had been involved. Thanks for your help with the investigation, Penfold.' Without articulating any reply, Penfold gave a deferential nod.

'Yes, thanks from me too. It's always good to know you're watching out for Tony,' Kathy added.

Penfold put his cup down, looked straight across to Milburn and inquired, 'I trust that the various "non-standard" procedures we employed won't bugger up the prosecutions at all?'

Milburn shook his head with the coffee to his lips. 'No, all the various bits and pieces which could cause problems aren't needed to make the case. And in some instances, like your theft of Hamilton's leg pads, they don't appear in the reports. The real beauty is that, in the end, they confessed, so much of the investigation background is not needed, and the more delicately balanced procedure points won't be scrutinised. Withenshaw's needle store came back with one positively matching the toxicology, including Hamish Elliott's DNA, so we don't even need to rely on her unreliable confession. And, as the drugs come from Hamilton, and we nailed him on a sound search warrant, Ramsbotham's confession is fully backed up too.'

Kathy's face became serious. 'And what happened in your meeting with Harry this morning?' She half turned to Penfold and added, 'They had to work out how to deal with the Crazy Cow.'

'Well, and how to deal with me too, I did give her quite a kicking. In a police station, as well. It's lucky she cried rape and Harry had been watching through the door. He saw her grab and kiss me. I can't believe that was only three days ago, it seems like a different world. Anyway, this morning was pretty tricky. She was there with her Federation rep, and me and Harry. Basically, it was a stalemate: her sexual harassment of me, and my assault on her. Mine was worse, but hers was the cause. Of course, she was pressuring the rep to support her on all sorts of wild claims about me leading her on and stuff. Harry told me beforehand that she would probably win overall if all the cases went the full distance. However, he pointed out to her in the meeting that if all cases were pursued, she would never work for the police again, and that was the clincher. And, somehow, he managed to convince her that not only should everybody drop all claims, but that she should go and work at Bishop Auckland station.'

Kathy leaned back and ran her hands through her golden hair. 'She should be in an institution. And I don't mean the police!'

Penfold asked if Tony had any update on Aisha's condition. She had been released to go home over the weekend, and the only information Tony had been able to garner was from the hospital nurse. She had told him of tension amongst the family as they discharged her, but it seemed like it was muted enough that the family would get through it. In Milburn's estimation, Vivender Pathan had been guilty of domineering his daughter, but Tony didn't believe that Aisha was still in any danger.

'I wonder how that might have turned out if Elliott hadn't been killed,' Kathy mused. Both Penfold and Milburn nodded, inwardly considering the progression possibilities of Aisha and Hamish's relationship, and the Indian father's potential responses.

Penfold crossed his legs and asked, 'Presumably Jim Harris and Pathan really were having dinner as Elliott was being poisoned?'

Milburn shrugged. 'I assume so, too. Harris is likely to get off with a High Level Community Order sentence for his minimal supplying of Somnulone.'

'Finished in cricket, though,' Penfold pointed out. 'Who is there left to bowl for Durham this season?'

Tony smirked. 'I bet that Australian apprentice can't believe his luck.'

Printed in Poland
by Amazon Fulfillment
Poland Sp. z o.o., Wrocław

65788318R00157